SHORTS

STORIES & MORE FROM MEMBERS OF BEACH AUTHOR NETWORK

© 2015, GARY LUCAS
(ON BEHALF OF SUBMITTING AUTHORS)

All rights reserved. No part of this compilation may be reproduced in any form without written permission from each author who contributed to this book. Exception limited to reviews and brief passages selected to be included in such reviews through all media including newspapers, magazines, blogs, social media or transmitted through email.

The following includes works of fiction. Names, characters, places, and incidents either are the product of the author's imagination or are used factiously, and any resemblance to actual persons, living or dead, business establishments, events, or locales is entirely coincidental.

DEDICATION

It is with gratitude and pleasure we dedicate SHORTS to the organizer and leader of Beach Author Network, Mary Anne Benedetto. You gave unselfishly of your time, talents and resources to mold this group of writers, bonded by their writing and situations created by the profession, into a supportive 'family.' We love you and wish you the best in plans for the future.

TABLE OF CONTENTS

Title	Page
Forgiveness	1
Mattress Man	7
The Wild Rose	13
Society's Gift (and more)	21
Mountain Girl	35
The Power of Faith, Family and Friends	49
Preserved Reflections	55
The Girl Who Beat the Band	69
Trail's End	87
A Special Dinner	99
The Battle of Bear Creek Bridge	105
Three Knocks	109
Flight From Fright	129
Freddie's Frozen	137
For Your Amusement	145
Ghost Waltz	171
Popcorn Madness	179
Blame	195
Gathering of Warriors	213
Kangaroo Man	229

Forgiveness
By Maureen O'Brien

The, not so gentle, cerebral suggestion awakened Kathleen from a sound sleep. Like a howling hurricane wind, there was no ignoring it. It over-powered her. Am I having a God attack, she wondered.

Except for the occasional wedding and the all too frequent funerals, Kathleen hadn't stepped foot in a church in over 30 years. What motivated her to attend church today was a mystery to her. Maybe it had something to do with that disturbing dream last week? But why would dreaming about my wicked witch mother inspire me to go to church? Makes no sense, she decided.

There had been a time when she never missed Sunday Mass and even a time when she attended daily Mass. Memories of her son, Michael, an altar boy, from sixth grade through high school came flooding back. Although a solemn child, he had an amazing knack for making her collapse in laughter. She began to giggle. "Ite Missa Est. Deo Gratias. Best part of the Mass," Michael would say, after imitating Father Dolan. "Go, the Mass is ended. Thanks be to God." Oh Michael, why did you have to go and die on me? I miss you so much. I am so sorry.

Now which church? Her Google search showed 20 churches within a 15-mile radius. "That's the South for you," she mused. A recovering Catholic, she deleted St. Joseph's and printed out her findings. With eyes closed, she pointed her finger and recited Eeny,

Meeny, Miny, Moe.

"Well, there you have it, Shammy. I'm off to The Chapel by the Sea. I can say Amen with the best of them." Her redheaded toy poodle cocked her head in agreement. "Besides, I'll be at the beach. You can't beat that." She liked to run her decisions by Shammy. She had no family and having lived the life of a recluse, very few friends.

She poured herself a steaming hot cup of coffee and sat down in her recliner to cuddle with Shamrock. "Shammy, we have an anniversary coming up. Remember, I adopted you on St. Paddy's Day. We'll have to figure out a way to celebrate. Maybe a trip to the bark park for you and a glass of Chardonnay for me. Yeah sure. In my dreams." That reminded her that she had a meeting tomorrow.

A gentle drizzle started. The raindrops clicking on her enclosed courtyard served to relax the tension in her body. "That must be holy water, Shammy. Just in time, don't you think?"

Once in the car, she programmed her navigation system. One last look in the mirror to check her makeup and she realized she had forgotten her scarf. Kathleen seldom dressed up but to go without a scarf was tantamount to not wearing under pants. I can't go without my Linus blanket. I better get it just in case the roof of this church caves in.

She arrived just five minutes before the service and was surprised to see so few cars in the parking lot. Thank God, a small congregation for my debut. A canopy of live oaks, draped with Spanish moss embraced the white stucco chapel, making it look warm and inviting. Pansies of all different colors lined the sidewalk, leading to a heavy oak door. Such happy, smiling flowers. I wish I felt that happy.

An elderly, silver haired man greeted her in the vestibule and indicated the Guest Book. After signing in, she entered the small, intimate chapel and realized there were only about twelve people sitting in the pews. They sat all spread out throughout the chapel. She stifled a giggle. Have they misbehaved and been put into a time-out?

The service began with a recorded hymn for which the congregants stood. The refrain, "Praise the Lord, He is with us" echoed throughout the chapel. Sitting in the rear pew so she could determine the right moves, Kathleen stood with them.

A handsome, young man with streaked blonde hair and a surfer tan walked up the center aisle. "How exciting. We have a guest with us today. Welcome to you, way back there near the door. Thank you for coming to be with the Lord. So glad you came to worship with us."

"Thank you, I'm happy to be here." Under her breath, she muttered, "I think."

The man moved down to her side and placed his hand on her shoulder. "My name is Pastor Thomas. But please call me Tommy. Would you like to introduce yourself?"

She stepped a few feet from the Pastor. "My name is Kathleen O'Grady and I am a fallen away Catholic." Good God, where did that come from? Dear God, is it an AA meeting?

"Well, that's just fine. We accept any person who has fallen from grace. Are you ready to receive grace again?" He didn't wait for an answer. Turning back to the congregation, he raised his arms. "Do I hear an Amen?" Amens reverberated from each corner of the chapel. On cue, the congregants left their positions, moved to the front of the chapel and joined in a hymn *Coming Together for Jesus*. They stood together in a circle, holding hands.

Kathleen remained seated. Why do I feel so trapped? White knuckled and gripping the pew in front of her, she fought the urge to leave. A few more beautiful hymns followed and a succinct sermon, so easy to listen to, given Pastor Tommy's mesmerizing voice. "Today's message is about forgiveness. The Lord forgives all sinners. If you remember just one thing from today's sermon, please remember this. In order to forgive others, you must *first* forgive yourself."

Those were the last words Kathleen heard. The room began to spin. Darkness fell.

A blur of colors appeared before her, different shades of blues and yellows. Must be the pansies, she thought. Then faces came into view. Two women flanked Pastor Tommy. One hovered over Kathleen, offering a paper cup of water, the other wiped her brow with a cool handkerchief. "What a pretty scarf," Kathleen said to the lady dressed in blue. Is it a Hermes?"

The woman turned to Pastor Tommy. "Would you listen to this lady. She just fainted and the first thing she wants to know about is my scarf."

Kathleen squirmed in the pew. "Scarves are my thing. I never go without one."

"Well, a scarf can hide a multitude of sins. But who is Michael? You were asking for him right before you came to. Do you want me to call him?" Pastor Tommy asked.

"No, no, thank you. I'm just fine, just a little woozy. Michael is my son. He's been gone for thirty years."

Kathleen's legs trembled when she attempted to stand up. She sat back down in the pew. Her face was a mask of anguish. She untied her scarf and covered her blistering, tear-filled eyes. "Help me up. I have to get out of here. I hate God. He took Michael away from me. Not once, but twice. I never should have come here."

Pastor Tommy sat down next to her. "Miss Kathleen, please stay. I am so sorry to hear about your son. But Michael is up in heaven with the Lord and heaven is a peaceful, beautiful place. Surely, after all these years you don't hate God for bringing him home."

As gentle and consoling as Pastor Tommy's words were, Kathleen became more enraged. "You don't get it. You can't get it. Michael was only 22 years old the last time I saw him. He came for dinner that night and announced that he was entering the seminary the very next day. He was my only child. I begged him to change his mind. I wanted marriage for him. I wanted grandchildren. I screamed, I cried, I implored. His last words were, "Mom, this is about me. I have to do this for me." He left the house in tears. Thirty minutes later, I received a phone call from the Yonkers Police Department. A car accident, they said. By the time I got to the hospital, he was dead. God took him away from me twice. First, to employ him as a priest and then to kill him on the road. How is that for a loving God? If he hadn't been crying…if he hadn't been so upset when he left, he wouldn't have driven off the road."

Pastor Tommy took her hands in his. "You just said, *if Michael hadn't been crying*. It sounds like you blame yourself for the accident. I could be way off here but I'm wondering if you need to forgive yourself."

The congregants filed out of the chapel. "How about we just sit here and chat, Kathleen. Tell me more about Michael and that horrible night. Tell me more about you and your life. I'm here to listen.

"I've never talked to anyone about the accident," Kathleen said. "I've just been so angry. I've never thought about it before but… maybe, I don't know. Maybe I do blame myself."

Two hours later, Pastor Tommy and Kathleen walked out of the chapel, his arm over her shoulder. She picked two pansies from the garden and handed them to him. "Thank you so much, Pastor Tommy.

I've got some work to do, no question about it. Maybe there will be a time when I can be as happy as these pansies."

Contact info: Email address is: mobrienauthor@aol.com and maureenobrien.net.

Previously published:

Who's Got The Ball? And Other Nagging Questions About Team Life, published by Jossey Bass in 1995.

Waggin' Tales: Bogey's Memoir, published in 2014.

A Prayer for Newtown, published in "The Shine Journal.", 2014

Books are available at amazon.com and Barnes & Noble.com

Mattress Man
By Dee Senchak

Harold Beeson took the folder the woman held out to him, shook his head and said, "I hope this isn't another loser. Lunch time can't come soon enough."

"Going to the book store again today?"

"Yes, I need that mid-day escape time."

"Aw Howard," she smiled at him, "You know you enjoy the challenges these job seekers present."

Through the glass dividing panel, Beeson surveyed the crowded waiting room. He watched a lanky young man in baggy jeans and a rumpled, plaid shirt rise from his seat and wink at the girl on his left.

"Well, unless this guy is an ace, which I doubt from the look of him, I'm going to follow up this interview with a tall latte and a splash of murder mysteries."

As the young man approached his desk, Beeson looked down at the thick folder on his desk and said, "Have a seat, Mr. O'Bryan."

"Just Brian."

Beeson raised his eyes without lifting his head, "Sorry, Mr. Bryan."

"O'Bryan," the young man said as he sank onto the chair, "but just Brian is fine."

Beeson cleared his throat, lifted the file folder and read the label aloud, "Mr Brian O'Bryan. I see."

"A bit of Irish humor there wouldn't you say?" O'Bryan grinned as he leaned back in the chair and stretched out his legs. "I'm from a long line of Brian O'Bryan's. That Englishman Henry the Eighth has nothing on my family. When my great-granddaddy died his obituary read: Brian O'Bryan, son of Brian O'Bryan, son of Brian O'Bryan, son of Brian O'Bryan...."

Silently studying the young man in front of him, Beeson wondered if this chattering, red-headed character was a dolt or a smartass. He interrupted O'Bryan, "Let's get started. You're here because you want help finding employment."

"You bet."

"Looks like you've been with us for some ti...." Beeson paused when he opened the folder and scanned the information "...for several months."

"You're new here," O'Bryan said as he leaned forward and adjusted the name plate on the desk. "Howard Beeson, Occupational Counselor. Nice." He tilted his head and looked at Beeson, "But, where's Miss Gladys? She helped me lots of times. She's not available?"

Beeson inhaled slowly. "I was transferred to this office when Miss Kojak decided to take early retirement. I assure you Mr. O'Bryan I have a great deal of experience helping people find employment."

O'Bryan raised his hand. "No offense, Harold. I was just wondering about Miss Gladys. She was a nice lady. I hope she's okay. She didn't retire because she was sick or something did she?"

Possibly she didn't want to face you again, Beeson considered saying, but instead smiled and said, "No, no nothing like that. She's fine. I'm sure she's enjoying retirement." Returning his attention to the papers in the folder, Beeson continued, "I see that your last job was with a road crew. What exactly did you do?"

"I was a flag man. You know, the one that switches the sign from SLOW to STOP."

Beeson nodded, "Umm."

O'Bryan continued, "It was a miserable job at first because it was cold. It rained a couple of days, too, but we had to keep working because of a tight construction schedule. It was better when the sun came out and it got warmer."

"So that job ended?' Beeson asked after a few seconds of silence.

O'Bryan looked at the ceiling, "Nah, I got fired. It was a boring job anyway."

Beeson picked up a pencil and rolled it between his fingers, "Fired? Why was that?"

"When the sun came out, people opened their windows and put convertible tops down. It wasn't quite as boring then because I could see into the cars. I like people you know." O'Bryan stopped talking. He lifted the stapler from the corner of the desk and slowly wiped the dust from it before setting it back on the desk.

Beeson waited, "And?"

O'Bryan bit his lip then said, "Mmm, there was this good looking chick in a silver BMW convertible going by real slow. She looked at me and I looked at her. I kept looking and leaning on my sign and I guess my sign turned from STOP to SLOW as I watched her drive by.

"The cars that'd been waiting at my end started to go and the first one met a car coming from the other end. They didn't actually hit head-on because one of them swerved aside. So they just scraped one another. But the SUV that swerved," O'Bryan illustrated the action with his hands, "it plowed into the work area, slammed into a pick up truck loaded with sand and the truck tipped over. The boss man was too close to that truck and kinda' got buried under the sand. Not all the way though. He didn't get killed or even hurt bad. But he was pissed. After we dug him out of the sand he fired me."

"Humm, yes, well," Beeson was alternately clenching the pencil between his teeth and running it through the salt and pepper hair at his temple. He looked down at the open folder and said, "And before that job you were sent to cut grass at Fairlawn Memorial Garden?"

O'Bryan was rearranging items on the edge of the desk. "I quit that job. It gave me the creeps to be around all those tombstones and dead people; nobody to talk to, either. I like to talk to people, you know."

Beeson nodded, rubbed his neck, and held up a torn piece of letterhead, blank except for the printed heading MATTRESS MAN. "Does this have some significance?"

"Oh that," O'Bryan stopped rearranging. "I brought that to show Miss Gladys that I was looking for work on my own, too."

"You applied for a job at the Mattress Man store?"

O'Bryan laughed, "Yeah, I was cool. They wanted females to sell mattresses by sleeping on them in their showroom window downtown. So I got dressed up as a girl. I showed up in this slinky two-piece sleep outfit that I had stuffed in all the right places – if you get my drift. I stretched out on a mattress and did some moves I thought were, well you know, sexy. But I got careless and uncovered a leg. That was it. I had shaved my legs, but the guy saw my knobby-kneed-bowleg and threw me out the door. I didn't get the job but I sure had a good laugh."

Beeson rubbed both temples. He had an idea. There was a test he had once used at his previous location. He suspected this applicant was not the simpleton the other one had been, but using it would put an end to this charade of an interview. He leaned on the desk, cradled his chin between thumb and forefinger and glanced at the clock before saying, "Mr. O'Bryan, I think you should take an aptitude test."

"I did that for Miss Gladys," O'Bryan said as he aligned a paper weight and pen holder.

"Yes, I see that you did. But that was the basic aptitude test given to all applicants. I recommend that you take the more in-depth test that we now have available."

O'Bryan sat up straight and looked at Beeson.

Seeing a frown flash across O'Bryan's face, Beeson was quick to add, "You seem to have a creative side that may not have been previously evident."

O'Bryan shrugged then nodded, "Okay."

Beeson turned a page on his appointment calendar. "I'll need to make the arrangements for you to take the test, but I'm afraid my afternoon is already booked solid. Could you come back tomorrow?"

"Yeah, sure, I'll do that."

"Thank you Brian. How about tomorrow at 10 o'clock?"

"Okay Harold, I'll see you then."

They shook hands across Beeson's desk and left the area in opposite directions.

Beeson hurried to the café at the book store. After eating he began browsing the book shelves, his favorite pastime. He relaxed and forgot about Brian O'Bryan. He had planned to skip the display of reduced priced books without rummaging through it. But something caught his eye, a thin volume titled, <u>Counselors need Counseling: Lessons I Gave My School Counselors</u>. It was the author's name that stopped him. He picked up the book and turned to the back cover. There was a picture of the author. It was him, Brian O'Bryan.

Under the picture of O'Bryan in suit and tie was a description of the book that began, "Be prepared for side splitting laughter as you read of one student's hilarious experiences with his academic advisors and counselors." It ended with, "We look forward to this young writer's next book. If he can make searching for a job as amusing as his school antics, it will be a winner."

"Well, well, two can play this game," Beeson muttered as he tapped his finger on the photo.
"I'll be ready for you tomorrow. You, Mr. Smartass O'Bryan, have made my day."

Contact Dee at Senchakdauthor@aol.com Her stories have appeared in two online publications: The Shine Journal: The Light Left Behind and More stories at www.Windsweptpress.com

The WILD ROSE
By Bob O'Brien

The quietness of the night only added to my melancholy. My friend Brad and I were heading along the county blacktop as we had so many Saturdays before. In the predawn sky, twinkling stars were sending me the same coded message over and over again. "This is the last time. You will never get to do this again. This is the last..."

I called her The Wild Rose, or sometimes just The Rose, because her headwaters were close to Wild Rose, Wisconsin. I would never tell you, or anyone, for that matter, exactly where that spot is, but I will tell you this: Rose's cold-water springs are hidden in a scrub-brush meadow where trickles of water blend together, giving her renewed birth with every sunrise. Some uncreative cartographer, with absolutely no conception of the stream's challenges and without input from me, thought "Willow Creek" was a more appropriate name. But she'll always be The Wild Rose to me.

The Rose, like most of the women in my life, could be elusive, unpredictable, and temperamental, but if you approached her with patience, always moving slowly and with forethought, she could, on rare occasions, be convinced to give up her treasures.

A hint of light emerged in the east as we approached the field where we always parked. When I turned off the narrow dirt lane, dust followed my old pick-up into the brush.

Brad quickly cranked up his window. "Damn," he said. "We need rain in the worst way. I hope the creek has enough water to fish. Maybe we should just go get breakfast."

"Not a chance, Brad. I sure as hell didn't drag my butt out of bed in the middle of the night for eggs."

Brad smiled his impish smirk and I realized he was pulling my chain. "You gonna sit here and babble or are we goin' fishin'?"

"All right then--it's time."

We lumbered out of the truck, dropped the back gate, pumped and lit the Coleman, and slapped some of the dust off our paraphernalia.

I fished The Rose in jeans, a pair of old tennis shoes, a khaki hat, and for brush protection, a canvas hunting jacket that usually got too warm by mid-morning. Brad wore a long-sleeved shirt and over-patched waders that, I was pretty sure, still leaked.

We fished at first light because I had it in my head that worthy trout "spooked" easily once the sun was high in the sky. My self-proclaimed axiom, *the brighter the day the poorer the fishing,* was especially true on The Rose. Most fishermen seldom fished the late summer's low water, but Brad and I were never part of the "most fishermen" crowd.

Although we each carried a box of flies--wet, dry, nymphs, and a few small streamers, the bait we actually needed to catch fish--worms, crickets, grasshoppers and grubs--was packed in our wicker creels. All of those were personally dug up, trapped, or caught by one of us–probably me.

I don't remember why, but I always gave Brad the choice. "What's it gonna be–upstream or down?"

"I'll go downstream this time," he said with a coy glint. I knew he'd choose downstream. The week before, I managed to fool three nice trout downstream, while upstream, he only caught a barely legal single. The fact that I'd been fishing for these critters most of my life and this was only his second year, mattered little to his competitive nature.

Brad Jones was an art director in a small advertising agency. He became my trout fishing protégée, much to his wife's chagrin, after years of feeding me freelance artwork whenever his company needed an overnight layout. The challenge, and of course greed, motivated me to do whatever it took to show up the next morning with sketches in hand. I had fished alone most of my life until, one weekend when his wife and kids were off on some excursion, he asked to go along. It was nice to have a fishing buddy.

Before we parted, thunder rumbled in the west. "Is that what I think it is?" I asked, turning toward the sound.

"Yup, better take my poncho," Brad replied with a grin, knowing damn well that I never bothered to bring one. "Looks like a front's moving in." He pointed to a huge cloud bank that severed the morning sky.

I love fishing on rainy days; no shadows, my sounds are muffled, and fish venture out to feed on the new food supply washing into the stream. "I'll meet you back here about ten."

Brad gave me a little wave, pointed his rod forward, and like a lancer, charged off to do battle.

Plowing my way through nasty brush, I twisted, turned, zigged and zagged, until I reached the narrow path that led to the center of the first upstream hole. It was a hairpin turn where the current dug deep into the bank running under the spot where I knelt. I tried to be totally still for as long as my patience allowed, hoping the trout wouldn't notice I was on their roof. Ironically, while I was trying not to make a sound, the distant thunder was now closing in, booming all around me.

After flogging the water for ten fruitless minutes, I moved on to the next bend, which was one of my favorite spots. I got in position, close enough to flip a nymph-fly into its headwaters.

Crack. Whoa, I jumped back; lightning was dancing overhead.

Crack. The storm had arrived and there was nowhere to hide.

Crack . . . Crack. "*God, can you back off a tad,*" I whispered. He didn't. The rain started with a few big drops, then a few more, then He opened the floodgates and unleashed the wind. *Too much of a good thing,* I thought.

Apparently the lightning and thunder didn't bother the trout; a nice Brown took the fly after I bounced it deep into the hole. The trout tried to raise a ruckus, but I managed to nudge him to me and hoisted him onto the bank. On narrow overgrown creeks like the Rose, a net is virtually useless. To compensate, my leader was six-pound test; strong enough to hold most fish, weak enough to break when you got hung up on the ever-present roots, an integral part of the trout's lair.

With a trout in hand, I was content knowing I wasn't going to be skunked on my last day. I couldn't imagine the fish's brothers and sisters being dumb enough to make the same mistake so I moved on.

As I made my way to the next hole, water dripped from my hat to my nose and rolled down to my mouth. Even my underwear was soaked. Freezing cold water numbed my ankles when I gingerly stepped through the ripples to the grassy side. After a short walk I got on my hands and knees and crawled to the spot I thought would be most advantageous.

Ever so slowly, I dropped a weighted nymph-fly into the headwater of the hole. As it ran with the current, I anticipated the strike that was sure to come . . . it didn't. I repeated the exercise several times . . . the strike never came. Perhaps my little yarn and foil fly wasn't all that convincing.

I moved from one familiar spot to the next, all the while appreciating the stream's rugged, yet graceful, idiosyncrasies. Rose's straightaways concealed a brisk current that could be felt on your legs more easily than seen. She was like a slalom ski course, twisting and turning, weaving back and forth, digging deep under the bank at every turn. It was the bends, those pockets of protection, that the elusive Brooks and Browns called home. Year after year--I have no idea how many--I spent most Saturday mornings fishing The Rose. I watched her change from season to season, week to week, as God continually refined His masterpiece. My challenge was to recognize and adjust to the changes, evaluate exactly where the trout were, and present a bait as naturally as I could. Sounds easy . . . it never has been.

My grand finale romancing The Wild Rose--five hours passed too quickly. The cold rain showed no sign of letting up, the run-off water turned the creek cloudy, and my clothes were drenched. I had managed to pick up a second Brown, and I considered it a good day. Prolonging the end, I decided to fish one more hole before heading to the truck.

When I arrived at the edge of this final bend, I picked up an earthworm about to fall into the stream. He wiggled on my hook as I tossed him toward a little swirl at the front of the hole. Bam! A hard strike the moment the worm hit the surface. He was beautiful! Over a foot long, solid, and almost totally black from living far under the bank where the sun never shines.

When I got to the truck, Brad was grinning through the window. A "How'd ya do?" raced off his tongue.

"I picked up two early, and a real nice one on the way in." Knowing he couldn't stand to wait another second, I said, "Okay. Let's see what's in your creel."

He lifted the lid displaying four gorgeous trout, two of which were bigger than the one I considered real nice. "At 9 o'clock, I thought I was gonna get to go home whooped again," he said with a Teddy Roosevelt smile, "then all hell broke loose."

"You caught all four in the last hour, in the murky water?"

"Yup. Used worms with this." He held up a little silver spinner I'd given to him when he first started fishing with me. I remembered telling him it might work in cloudy water–I guess it did. Or, more likely, fish were apparently venturing out from beneath the banks to feast on the abundance of food washing into the creek.

"How wet are you?" I asked, noticing the rain had backed off to a drizzle.

"I take it you're not ready to throw in the towel?" Brad said, already knowing the answer.

"I'd hate listening to you tell everybody at the agency how you out-fished me."

"I'll give you an hour and a half," Brad said, "just so you can save your reputation. Any longer than that and my wife will be all over my case."

"Mine too. Up or down?"

His answer surprised me, "I'll go upstream this time; give you a shot at the ones I missed."

Thankful for an extra chance, I went downstream only a short way. I'd rather fish than walk, and this way I'd finish up close to the truck. In the hour that followed, The Rose dropped her protective shields just far enough to allow me the illusion that I was clever enough to fool a few of her precious occupants.

Once I pushed through the brush to the first bend, I used the tip of my rod to flip a limp earthworm into a swirl at the front of the hole. Hit–right at the surface–missed it. Trout, by their very nature, are too leery to be fooled twice, but out of desperation, I put what was left of my worm back in the spot where I originally cast. He must have been some hungry fish because, much to my surprise, he struck again. This time I was the victor.

As I methodically moved upstream, each bend gave up another trout. I now had seven. The rain stopped as I came to my final hole. It wasn't much of a hole really, just a slight turn with current running under overhanging grass. I'd never caught anything there before.

The worm-clad hook was quickly picked up by the current, then it started moving upstream at a very fast pace. I pulled the line taut and the fish ripped it out of my hand. Having no choice, I jumped in the water, tried to get low enough to get under the alders and follow wherever the trout might lead. My line went slack; he'd turned and was racing right at me. Stripping line as fast as I could, I saw him pass me to the right heading downstream. Eventually, I turned him and he was heading back up. When he got to the grassy area, I hoisted him up on shore. He flipped once and was off the hook, flopping toward the stream. Half in, half out of the creek, I tried to block his path but he jumped to the side. Reaching out to grab him, I managed to touch his back just as he landed in the water. Unfortunately, my momentum sent me tumbling in after him. *Was I really that inept, or was he just superior? Perhaps a little of both.*

As I crawled out on my hands and knees, I saw Brad standing a few feet back watching and shaking his head. "That had to be the Granddaddy of all Granddaddies."

"He sure as hell was a lot more fish than I could handle," I said. "I'm just glad he didn't drown me."

"I can't believe you're smiling," Brad said looking concerned.

"Brad, that was undoubtedly the most fun I've ever had out here."

"But you just lost the greatest fish this stream will ever see."

"That may be true, but just knowing he is out there is the reason we're willing to get up in the middle of the night and stand shivering in the rain for hours. I'm happy just having had a chance to meet him."

On our walk back to the truck, it didn't take long before Brad asked, "How many did you get?"

"Eight. How about you?"

"Nine," he said, failing to hold back a smile. I couldn't have been happier for him; he'd come a long way in two short seasons.

When I think back on that day, I can't help but wonder; by allowing me to touch her most cherished prize had The Wild Rose been saying, "farewell, my friend," or was it an attempt to lure me into cancelling my move to South Carolina.

Many years have passed since that stormy farewell to The Rose. I only seem to fish "fly-only" water now, and I don't eat what I catch anymore. No matter how expert the chef, trout doesn't taste as good to me as the fish that roamed The Rose. God took my friend Brad a few years after I moved away. He was such a good man; I'm sure he got to go upstream. I fish alone now.

I never returned to The Wild Rose; I never will. She couldn't live up to the image I've tucked away in the treasured memories section of my mind.

The Wild Rose–a loved but unconquered mistress. I miss her.

Robert O'Brien - Pawleys Island, SC 29585
proseNcons@live.com

The Rose – The Teacher
Time with The Wild Rose provided me with insight for most of life's challenges: It helps to get an early start. Work is hard, rewards are small, and time is short. Persistence and patience is no guarantee, but without them failure is assured. Enjoy loyal friends, they are special. You travel together, but you fish alone. Like the wily trout, all Gods treasures have been given to us to enjoy.

Society's Gift
By Patricia David
May, 2006

Existence.
You, Me, Us.

Evolutionary, conflicted, subjective,
Conjecture, science, experience,
Judgments.

Human behavior artistry -
Cause and effect.
random or planned.
Ethical or exploitation.

Look at you, me, us.
What do you see?

Fear, love, struggle, failure, success,
Skin color, differences, commonalities?

Seek richness, abundance, the sacred.
Grasp acceptance.

You, me us.
Society's Gift

Dance of Transformation
By Patricia David - March 2009

Country School House:
Five boys
Three Girls
Riding to school in the milk truck
A stroll through the woods Every Day
Happy times.

Junior high:
Baby boom- Suburban housing
Big City Student influx
Confusion
Adjustments
Painful Bullying
Name Calling
Detestable School!
Fleeing to the woods
Did anyone Notice My Pain?

My room:
A Haven.
Singing, Dancing, Poetry
My only Freedom

High School:
Science Fair Winner
Amazing accomplishment
Dancing With Joy!

"You will remember your Speech," she said coldly
On Stage in Front of the Assembly

Frozen -
Paralyzed - Unable to Begin
Teacher at Microphone Asking Audience to Wait for My
Memory to Return
Panic!
Peer Laughter -
Painful Taunting
Transported to a Place of Terror and Shame.
Fleeing again.
No woods or familiar streams -
The only refuge? a Restroom.
Sobbing -
A Deafening Sound
Teacher Lampooned - Laughed - Sent me home
alone on the back of the bus - silence
Where Are My Woods?

Adulthood:
Fear and Shame Formed me
however,
God's Grace and Personal Choices Transformed Me.

Performance Class:
Astounding discovery -
authentic Voice Returns
Liberation
I AM What I Am - I am enough!

Now:
Wife, Mother, Nurse, Therapist, College Instructor,
Grandparent, Author.
Everlasting gratefulness
the Dance of Transformation

Why??
By Patricia David 2009

Do baby birds fall from their nests?
Do clouds make recognizable shapes in the sky?
Does ice cream taste so good on a hot day and hot dogs only taste great at a baseball game?

Does love hurt sometimes?
Does pain build character?
Does loss lead to completeness?

Are people so afraid to be authentic?
Do we mask true emotion?

Do people avoid confrontation?
Do people spend so much time complaining and never complete the task?
Do people gossip?
Isn't there more humility?

Am I hungry Mom?
Doesn't daddy have his job anymore?
Do we have to live in our car?

Is there cancer, heart attacks, violence, mental illness?

Yet!

Do I always feel so much better when I help someone?
Does my heart sing when I hear, "How Great Thou Art"?
Do I feel joy when I toast the moon?
Do I feel an abundance of love when I'm with all of you?

Multiplication and Division
By Patricia David June 2009

Acquaintance, interest, friendship,
Friendship, romance, love,
Love, commitment, nuptials,
Multiplication!

Marriage, idiosyncrasies,
Baggage, disillusionment, tension, uproar,
Cold war,
Division!

Concessions, dialogue, tenderness, joy,
Multiplication!

Familiarity, desire, intimacy,
Abandon, union,
Multiplication!

Oneness, cell collision, explosion,
Life,
Multiplication and Division!

Pod, incubation,
Pain, Initial breath, worlds collide,
Division!

Utterances, needs, insomnia, shared responsibilities,
Multiplication!

Learning curves, acquaintances, friendships,

Multiplication!

Closures, commencements, departures,
Division!

Introductions, announcements, commitments, nuptials,
Spouses, in-laws,
Multiplication!

Retirement, logistic relocations, cell fragility,
Division!

Acquiescence.
Multiplication!

Cinnamon Buns and Beer
By Patricia David

Christmas preparations have all begun
The tree is quite beautiful, presents are wrapped
And
Oh those cookies- YUM!

Mama is Busy
Daddy seems quite grim
David and Anthony inspect the fireplace
Hey Dad is it really possible? - We know Santa's not very slim.

Anthony cries, "David, go get the yardstick
Our measurements must be precise
Oh gosh! It's not going to happen, David
So kindly take my advice."

No?
We have to calculate and re-measure
He has to make it down our chimney tonight
Because no visit from Santa
Means
We're in for a sad Christmas night.

Now David let's think about this.
It's ok to leave the front door agar
That way, it's for sure, you'll get your Eiffel Tower Kit
And
For me, my remote control car.
Wait- a- minute, Anthony

Wow, it's my favorite smell.
It's mama's famous cinnamon buns
And oh, her chocolate cookies -
The kind where we imprint our thumbs.

Let's forget the measuring nonsense
Hey, don't eat any more of those buns
You'll make Mama very unhappy
In fact I think we'd better run!

Am I in heaven David?
Look! The chocolate's dripping down my chin
I think our problem is solved though
His face turns into a grin.

It doesn't matter if Santa comes down the chimney
Or that he uses the front door.
If we truly believe in Santa's powers
It's not necessary to measure anymore.

BOY'S?
It's time to get ready for bed
Then we'll talk about Santa's snack
What should we leave him David?
He'll surely need his energy back.

Wow, Anthony, you've run out of ideas!
The answer is perfectly clear
We'll leave him my favorite – CINNAMON BUNS
And, how about a beer?

Bella's Mystifying Belly
By Patricia David - Jan. 1, 2009

It was New Year's Day, 2009.
I simply had to talk to our kids in Asheville, North Caroline.
The news was grim
Bella, their Yellow Lab, was sick again.
Tell me boys what did she do?
Does she have that nasty "Doggie Flu?"
Oh Nana, Bella ate a Huge bowl of Taco Salad
She's at the Vet's with Mama
It's the same old ballad.

Bella's belly is mystifying.
She eats socks and not so clean underwear off the bathroom floor.
She's like a vacuum cleaner and we're all kind of worried that
-
She won't be able to live with us anymore.

This dog tries to eat anything.
Let's see-
A toy truck
An antler from a buck
Mama's shoe
Daddy's shampoo
Anthony's toast
And something out of the toilet
Gross!

Wait a minute I hear the car
And oh, there's Bella with what?

It's a bucket, the one that Mama bought in Nantucket.

It's wrapped around her neck and she's oh heck.
She's sick again!
Mama, please take her back?
Bella can't stay home acting like that.

Now BOYS,
The doctor gave her medicine-to make her sick- by design
This Nantucket bucket saves me lots of time
So please let her rest
She needs to recline
Bella's been through this before
She'll be just fine.

There are so many things she must abstain from
Bella's Mystifying Belly
Is quite a conundrum

Incongruence
By Patricia David

Inferno
Rage
Sizzling coals
Covert
Abandonment
Scalded Seething Dimension

Dissociate

Smother
Acquit
Amended Quietude
Spatial Freedom
God, Chi, Divinity

Weep No More
By Patricia David - Nov. 2013

Over here –
No - over here.
Searching is not necessary.
I'm in the next room or out in the yard.
I'm on Litchfield's sandy shore.
I'm everywhere.
Don't search for me.
Don't weep for me.
I have captured the trophy.
I have won the greatest honor -
Absolute freedom
To do – HIS - work.

You are there
Now,
I'm everywhere.
Perhaps you'll think of me when you see a pink rose
or a swaying palm.
You will find me in the whisper of the evening breeze
or
the glow of a firefly on a warm summer evening.
I'm the ebb and flow of the waves along the beach.
I'm the face of the homeless in the park
I'm the orphaned child of Haiti, or India.

I'm the wounded soldier in a hospital room waiting for relief
from my pain
I'm the faces of the imprisoned be it material poverty, or
pain, or illness, or

incarceration,
it's all the same.
Nevertheless,
You'll find me there in prayer and in good deed.

So:
No more tears
No more grieving
And
No regrets

Instead:
More Laughter
More prayer
More love
More peace
More Joy
More Family

Pat is an author of three children's books: "HUGS, Inc.: The Amazing Adventures of Hope, Understanding, Guidance, and Support for Kidz with Cancer," "There's a Troll in a Bowl" (fundamentals of Vibrational Sound Healing), and "Winnie's Victory," (a story of Cancer recovery, animal rescue, and service to our Country's Veterans).

Contact Information: Email: gd0936@sccoast.net or patdavid4kids@gmail.com
Facebook: Pat David Huggable Moments and Pat David

Previously published:
Hugs Inc. - The Amazing Adventures of Hope, Understanding, Guidance and Support for Kidz with Cancer, published by Xlibris Corporation in 2011.

There's a Troll in Bowl, published by Star Publishing in 2013

Winnie's Victory, published by Star Publishing in 2014

Available: barnesandnoble.com, amazon.com, and the author at gd0936@sccoast.net or patdavid4kids@gmail.com, also on Facebook at: Pat David or Pat David Huggable Moments.

MOUNTAIN GIRL
Darlene Eichler

"She blew and she blew, and she blew the house in…the dust seeped into every opening, every pore. It choked and embraced. It smothered and stole the last breath. Some of the dust resisted settling, but wafted above the carnage, searching for fissures and breaks in which to creep and hide, in hope of growing to cause more destruction, infection, and decay."

June Marie Rose was born into this world in a coal miner's shack in Twilight, Kentucky. The year was 1918. A cold spring rain fell as this innocent baby began a journey that affected the lives of countless persons. And her mother, unaware of the perilous journey ahead, closed her eyes and slept. Her father looked down upon his sleeping wife and new baby, wondering how he would feed his growing family.

• 1934 •

She saw that the sun was beginning to disappear behind the mountain peaks. June ran home before the dark could catch her. By the time the screen door slammed her mother was blocking her way to the tiny attic room she called hers.
"Where have you been, girl? Didn't you hear me calling you?"
"Yes, Mama. I was just watching the men work on the road."
"I'm warning you, girl. If you stay around strange men you are headed for trouble."
"I'm careful, Mama!"

The little attic room was stifling. She opened the window as far as it would go.

Her thoughts kept going to the crew of young men who toiled under the hot sun all day. She had a favorite; he was tall, broad shouldered, and had an air of shyness about him. She dreamed of him bending down to kiss her on the lips, lifting her up to his level. It never occurred to June he would not be interested in this scrawny mountain girl with the black unruly braids and eyes as dark as coal. She had no doubt she could capture his heart, if only she could find the right dress to catch his attention. It had to be one that showed off her best features, her legs. Oh, what was the use of dreaming! She didn't have a decent dress, and she had no way of buying one. She drifted off into a restless state between sleep and wakefulness.

A determined sunbeam made its way through the grimy window. June rubbed the sleep from her eyes and reached for the alarm clock. The alarm had gone off earlier but she had slept through its tinny ring.

Dress? Then it came to her. She must find a way to get a pretty dress. She had dreamed about the dress. Or was it a dream? She ran to the dilapidated cardboard wardrobe, opening the knob-less door. It was a dream. There hung the two shapeless feed sack dresses and a tattered wool coat that was two sizes too small. Tears stung her eyes but she kept them from overflowing. She would find a way. The handsome, fair-skinned man was her ticket to a new life. A life out of this coal dust covered, soul-killing place.

The gentle breeze just brushed the silky fabric enough to bring it above her shapely calves. The CCC boys were working near the mailbox. Surely, the shy one would notice her in this dress of red, gold and the yellow of sunflowers. She had found a way. So what if she had stolen money from her mother's secret stash? Her mother would understand when she brought her husband-to-be home for supper. She tried to drown out the words of the preacher down at the Tabernacle of Faith. He said that God would bring down damnation on those who lied, stole, and fornicated, whatever that is. She was sure she had not done that. She had told little white lies, and now, she had stolen. Maybe this wasn't so bad. After all, it was her mother's money, and didn't her mother love her and want the best for her? Didn't she want her to get out of this hollow of poverty?

June heard her parents and neighbors talking about the Depression. She heard it at the company store, from her teacher at school, and preacher Caldwell even mentioned it in his sermons. They talked of closed banks, no jobs, and people losing their homes, the Dust Bowl, no food, and men jumping from windows in the big cities. It was sad to hear about these happenings, but June could not forget the black cloud of poverty that permeated everyone and everything in Coal Hollar. It was not only the lack of pretty clothes, food, a decent home, or a way to town, but it was the sense of hopelessness that weighed down one's soul. If it were not for her own determination she would have become hardened to accept this dreary life. But she had received a gene of stubbornness from someone that would not allow her to give up.

****

Nora Rose was a mountain woman. She feared very little and backed away from no one and nothing. She had a rich sense of humor and she could find something to laugh about even at the Tabernacle of Faith when one of the handlers was bitten. No, it really wasn't funny that his hand and arm swelled to twice its normal size. It was funny that Ned Thompson even thought he could handle snakes. He would go into a "hissy fit" whenever a yellow jacket got near him. Nora said that it would be safer for him to practice on moving mountains before he tackled snakes.

"And these signs shall follow them that behave; in my name shall they cast out devils: they shall speak with new tongues: they shall take up serpents; and if they shall lay hands on the sick, and they shall recover." Mark 16:18, the King James Bible.

It was a common practice for certain church members at the Tabernacle of Faith to handle snakes. Nora took her young children with her often. There were no babysitters in the community. Everyone who attended the church brought their children along. The younger ones usually hid their faces against their mother's soft belly. June found the rattlers mesmerizing as they squirmed and swayed in the handlers' hands. The serpents seemed to keep time to the steady beat of the twangy notes coming from the guitar and fiddle. The swaying became faster as the congregation's emotions were worked into a frenzy, their hallelujah's and amen's rising to the fly-specked ceiling. The two bare light bulbs seemed to be swaying as the shouts reached a crescendo. Preacher Caldwell began his sermon. He paced and he pounded the Bible, using his finger as a bookmark for his text: Romans 3:9-20.

Shouts and praises filled the stagnant air of sweat and tears. The swaying and dancing took on a life of their own. This was the part of the service June looked forward to for she was not in the service but dancing with her prince charming. She detested her world of coal dust covered poverty. She did not like Preacher Caldwell. Some of the girls, and older women, too, thought he was handsome. They hung on his every word and tried to be the first to compliment him on his sermon. Some went so far as to ask him home for supper. She wondered if they had more food than was in their house. Her mother would be hard pressed to stretch their beans and cornbread to feed a big, tall man like Preacher Caldwell.

His face reminded June of the serpents he handled. He had coal-black hair combed straight from his face and his forehead jutted out over his small dark eyes. His mouth, usually drawn up in a half pucker, gave him the expression of just tasting a crabapple. June thought maybe the women swooned over him because of his nice clothes. They weren't all that nice, but they surely were better than bib overalls and brogans. And he always, except when he was preaching so hard, smelled of cloves and witch hazel. The music was slowing. Those persons who had been hit by the spirit were coming out of their trances as friends and family frantically tried to revive them with fans from Carter's Funeral Home. The snakes were placed in their cages for safe keeping until the next evening. The preacher was praying that God's spirit would fall on all those who were full of demons. June felt as if he were talking directly to her. She entered into her world of escape to tune out the words that were as sharp as her daddy's pocketknife.

June rushed to reach the front of the church before Preacher Caldwell got there, but she was too late. He called out to her in that high pitched, sing song preacher voice. She turned to look him in the face, but before he could say anything, Miss Betty Fain was there between them, saying what a wonderful sermon he preached tonight. He acknowledged her with a faint smile and a nod of the head, but his eyes remained on June. Miss Betty was getting on in years, yet retained a keen awareness of when she was being put off. She moved on, and Preacher Caldwell moved closer. June held her breath and tried not to breathe in his scent of sweat. Seeing her daughter's dilemma, Nora swept up the church's short aisle in about three strides. She reached for the preacher's hand and gave him her best smile. She never "dipped" at church, so there was not a hint of tobacco juice. He responded warmly, asking her about her husband and other family members. June slipped out the door and waited for her mother in the dark shadows of the church house.

June was bored in school. This little ramshackle school building housed eight grades. Miss Dillon, the teacher, was no more than nineteen years old and she had eighth grade boys a head taller than she. She tried to keep the interests of all the students but it was a daunting task for one so young. June spent most of her time in her world of pretend, which kept her a quiet student, apart from the usual mischief in the classroom. She did not pay attention or turn in her homework. Her younger siblings, with glee, let Nora and Junior know when this happened. Her parents discussed these matters late at night when the tiny house was quiet. They never seemed to agree about what to do with their problem child.

Nora Rose was a problem solver. She was willing to compromise as she believed every situation had a solution. This was a quality one would not expect from this mountain woman, who occasionally allowed a tiny stream of tobacco juice to slide from the corner of her mouth. She had so very little with which to work. Maybe she solved her dilemmas before they grew too big, or she just had a natural talent of doing so. June was becoming a big problem. Indeed, Nora had to admit this was the toughest one God had given her. June had turned out to be so different than her siblings that at times. June felt she was born into the wrong family. She was not alone in these feelings. Both of her parents were at a loss to understand this tall, gangly and wild spirited daughter, but Nora had a solution. She believed that the CCC boys were God's answer to her prayers, not the whole crew, but the one who would make a fine husband for June. The CCC boys were the answer to many problems. They worked hard to build roads and recreation areas for the citizens' enjoyment. These strong healthy men were all of the age to marry and start families. They came into rural areas where single girls out numbered the single men. Most of the local males worked in the mines or had no means of employment. The majority of the girls were looking for a better life outside the mining towns.

Enter James Alfred Maxwell, 23 years old, Virginia born and bred. His family was made up of schoolteachers, ministers, and farmers who farmed the land granted to them by King George, III in the 1700s. He had grown up in a sturdy farmhouse with a swing on the front porch. Red geraniums grew in whitewashed pots beside the front steps. Life was not easy in these gently rolling hills surrounded by blue mountain peaks, but it was a land of milk and honey to June and her family.

June did not know her mother had a plan much like her own. Nora was aware her daughter spent a lot of time watching the CCC boys, but she would be surprised to know the extent of June's scheming. The first step was to know that she had been noticed. The chosen one kept his head lowered and his eyes on his work. A few of the others would sometimes give out with a wolf whistle. She pretended she didn't hear and walked, head held high back to her house.

She didn't know if the new dress had worked. He had not even raised his head; maybe he had not seen her. She had to come up with a better plan. The scene last evening at the Tabernacle of Faith kept running through her mind as she recalled how everyone rushed to help those who had fainted back to their senses. Passing out always seemed to draw lots of attention.

June awoke before the sun tried to peak through the dirty window in her attic room. This was the day she would try plan number two. She hurried down the rickety ladder to the big room which served as a kitchen, dining room and a bedroom for her little brother, Jack. She smelled the biscuits just coming from the oven and saw the thick, white gravy speckled with black pepper simmering in an old iron skillet. Grabbing a chipped plate from the wall cabinet that looked as if it wanted to slide down the splintery boards, she quickly broke open the hot bread and covered it in steaming pallid milk gravy. No coffee again today, as she lifted the apparently empty pot. That's okay, I don't need it. This will be a great day, she thought to herself.

The rusty pump out back squeaked and coughed as a tiny trickle of water came out into the old dented wash pan. June took a feed sack rag and a small cake of homemade soap from the kitchen and went into the quiet darkness of her parents' bedroom. Someday, she would live in a big house with running water inside and her own bathroom just off her bedroom. She would have silk under things, wonderful sweet smelling soap, and towels as soft as velvet. Her nails would be beautifully manicured and painted. June, stop daydreaming, she thought to herself. She bathed and put on the sensible cotton underwear her mother bought at the company store. They were old and a little tattered, but they were the best she had. As the silky new dress slipped easily over her lithe body, she remembered the bottle of cheap cologne on her mother's dresser. She opened the stopper, and the chemical odor sent her into a coughing fit. The cologne was so old. She pushed her feet into the too small ugly oxfords. They would never do; it would be better if she went barefoot. She looked under her parents' bed, and there were the black dust covered heels her mother wore when she was married. June slowly placed her feet in them, trying to scrunch her toes before they hit the end of the shoes. Having inherited Nora's tenacity to solve problems, she found some old rags in the closet for stuffing in the toes.

She started down the gravel road, walking with short steps and keeping her toes curled against the rags. She didn't see the work crew. Had they finished the work so soon? The road didn't seem to go anywhere. She walked on, each step becoming more precarious than the one before. As she rounded the bend, she ran into the shy one, who looked right into her eyes and smiled. She started to apologize but instead, her ankle turned, and she fell into his arms. He gently stood her up as if she were a china doll with feet too small to hold her weight. Before she realized what she was saying, she had blurted out an invitation to come to her house for supper. He said that he would do that…just tell him the day and time. Not wanting to let this chance go by she quickly said, "This evening at six o'clock." She turned and walked carefully around the bend out of sight, promptly removed her mother's shoes and ran home.

Her mother was going to be furious with her. What would they have for supper? It was near the end of the month, and there was very little in the cupboard and no money. She entered the house almost hoping that her mother would not be there. She was sitting at the kitchen table peeling little green apples, which looked loaded with worms and not worth the effort. June told her mother what she had done. She waited for the tongue lashing but instead she heard her mother saying, she would find something to cook. They would even have apple cobbler if she could borrow a cup of sugar from someone in Coal Hollar....

James Alfred Maxwell was a good eater. June was fascinated with the way he held his fork. He wrapped his fingers around it with his thumb on top, reminding her of a little shovel. He kept his head down just the way he did when he was working. James complimented Nora on the country ham (where had she found that?) and the flaky biscuits. The beans were leftovers from the day before, but they tasted even better with the fresh onion June had borrowed along with the cup of sugar.

Nora had gotten out her only tablecloth to cover the old wooden table which served as a place to eat, a place for homework, and daddy's work bench. There was even a small arrangement of black-eyed Susan's placed in a pint jar. James Alfred Maxwell seemed content as he leaned back in the best chair in the house. June had made certain the guest had the one with the strong cane bottom. He ate the warm, spicy apple cobbler and placed his spoon in the empty dish with a sigh of contentment. Both Nora and June felt certain that James Alfred Maxwell would be putting his feet under their table again.

Junior Rose and the two younger children were at the table to observe June's friend. They had been warned to be on their best behavior, even Junior. Sometimes his mouth could get a little smutty. The children were asked to eat lightly this evening and not to stare. They were bribed with candy they could not buy until the first of the month when the mines paid the men. They did get the giggles when Mr. Maxwell asked June if she had finished high school, but the stares they received from their parents told them silently to be quiet. The pause in conversation said more than June ever wanted James to know, but her mother came to her rescue again. Nora said that her daughter was a good student, which was true in the behavioral sense, but not academically. She explained that June had been taken advantage of by an older boy who should not have been in school. His family was the kind that would not hesitate to get even with anyone they thought had insulted them. Nora went on to say that she thought the best solution was to keep June at home with her. June did not dare look across the table at her daddy or her sister and brother. This story had some elements of truth, but there were more half-truths than the whole ones.

James listened intently, yet that was no clue as to what he would have replied. Instead of responding, he excused himself and said that he had an early morning. He thanked Nora for the delicious meal and said good night to the other family members. June walked him to the door and stepped outside in the twilight, hoping for more conversation from this quiet man. He said he was sorry she had left school because of a bad boy. He hoped she would consider returning. It was his belief that girls needed an education, too. He reached for her hand and said gently, "Please return to school." With that he disappeared into the night.

****

The bus trip was long back to Wythe County, Virginia. The call came just after midnight. The ringing of the telephone at that hour was always bad news. Bob Gray got there first.
"James Maxwell, it is for you."
James's mind raced from one family member to the next. What could have happened?
"Hello, this is James Maxwell. Who is calling, please?" He thought he heard sobs at the other end.
"This is your mother, James. I hate to tell you but your father died this evening. Come home, please."

Mr. Wade, the superintendent of the camp took him to the bus stop in town. He just made the last bus out for the next 24 hours. He said a silent prayer of thanks.

****

Back in Twilight, Kentucky, June had been wondering where James had gone. She looked everyday for the tall, muscular man. She hadn't gotten up nerve to ask any of the crew. Her mother had run out of patience with her. She wanted to know where this potential husband had run to. Had she and June come on too strong? She asked Junior and he laughed. He thought Mr. Maxwell was aware of what the two were up to.

"I won't stop until I get him," she screamed to the whole world. She calmed down enough to make a plan. She must go to Virginia. One of the crewmembers told her he would not be back and anyway the job would be over soon. I know when he says something he means it. I must go to see him before my love for him is gone. Wytheville, Virginia? Where is it? She asked the questions to friends and to strangers. No one had ever heard of Wytheville, Virginia. She knew who might know. Miss Dillon, her teacher. It so happened that she was from the next county. She showed June where it was located on the map. Now all she needed was a way to get there. Her daddy couldn't make the trip in his old car. Her mother kept telling her to forget it. Mr. Maxwell was not the marrying kind. She would show her. Who has the nicest car she had ever known? No doubt about it, Mr. Crump, the owner of the mines with his shiny, black Packard. When her mother heard what she was planning to do she put her foot down,
"No, you will not ask Mr. Crump. He is a dirty old man and you will not be alone with him. June Rose, you had better listen to me or you will be sorry."

Mr. Crump just happened to be in Twilight that day. No one seemed to

know why but it turned out to be a blessing for June. She thought he might be at Twilight's only restaurant, The Coffee Cup. Yes, there was his big, black shiny Packard parked at the front door. She pushed open the door and there was a table in the middle of the room with about six men plus Mr. Crump. She must have interrupted an important meeting by the looks on their faces. Mr. Crump stood up and offered his hand to her as she came nearer.
"And what do we owe the pleasure of a visit from such a pretty lady? There was just a hint of sarcasm in his voice.
"I need to talk to you, sir, just for a few minutes." June's voice could hardly be heard over the chatter the men were making.
"Why of course. Gentleman, carry on. I'll be back shortly." He touched her shoulder guiding her to a corner of the small room.
"What can I do for you, little lady?"
"I need to get to Wytheville, Virginia and I cannot afford the bus or train. I thought maybe you would take me in your fancy car."
"Well, now you do have a problem."
June couldn't tell by his expression if he was ready to break out in laughter.
"Let me think about this overnight. I will let you know in the morning. Meet me here at early breakfast time. By the way, child, what is your name? And does your daddy work for me?"
"June Rose and my daddy is Junior Rose. Yes, he works in the mines.
"Thank you little lady," and he went back to his meeting.

****

June was so early at the Coffee Cup, Sadie, the cook was just unlocking the door.
"What you doing here so early? Child, you should be home in bed."
"I'm not a child. I have plans to marry."
"Oh, I don't have time to hear them now, I have to go and get breakfast started."

The sound of an engine broke the early morning silence. Mr. Crump. He did mean early.
"Come on in child and talk to him while I get the coffee going."

Mr. Crump hurried from his car, a man on a mission.
"June I have some good news, I'm paying your way on the train and back to Wytheville. It has one stipulation, your mother and father must approve."

June's heart sank. Her mother would never approve. She realized Mr. Crump was waiting on a response.
"Thank you. I will talk to my parents and get back to you."

****

"Yes, mama. I need to talk to you."
Before you do that I think you would want to read this letter from James."
June grabbed it from her hand and tore it open.

Dear June,
This letter has been too long in the writing. I feel that I owe you an explanation after my fast exit. My father passed away and my mother needed me to come as soon as possible.

There is another reason I won't be back. I had a girlfriend before I joined the CCC and we grew apart. Since I have been home we are seeing one another again and we plan to be married....

The letter fell to the floor and deep, agonizing sobs filled the room.

The End

(CCC stands for Civilian Conservation Corps--established April 5,

1933 under an emergency conservation work bill by President Franklin Roosevelt--Civilian Conservation Corps-Ancestry. Com)

My other stories...

1. The Journey Home.	Nan Turner
2. View From the Attic.	Nan Turner
3. Promises To Keep.	Nan Turner
4. Return To Bridgetown.	Nan Turner
5. Rose's Song.	Nan Turner
6. Lily's Story.	Nan Turner
7 The Box In the Attic.	Nan Turner
8. Trunk Tales.	Darlene Eichler
9.Trunk Tales Updated.	Darlene.Eichler
10.Satan's Best Friend.	Darlene Eichler
11. Where's the Kitty.	Darlene Eichler
12. Emma Saves the Day.	Darlene Eichler

Books may be purchased from:
Amazon. com
Barnes and Noble.com
Contact--- dargeeic@aol.com

The Power of Faith, Family and Friends
By Sharon Shymansky Roberts

Sometimes there is tragedy. God never promised us an easy life free of toil and trouble. He did, however, promise us life everlasting with Him in heaven. But first we need to seek Him, even in our darkest times, for He is there with us.

5:35 am. Thursday morning. The alarm had just gone off. I remember Dan slapping the snooze button and then turning and wrapping me snugly in his arms for a moment or two. That comforting, secure feeling shattered with the intruding shrill of the telephone. Early morning phone calls are seldom good news. Dan answered, but I heard the speaker's words clearly and was out of bed and dressing before the caller had finished her message.

Cory, my middle son, had been in a car accident. It was bad. The caller instructed us to start for the hospital, but felt Cory would probably be flown to Med Star, the shock trauma unit at Washington Hospital Center in DC. She'd stay in contact with us on the cell phone. Hurry!

In an instant I was thrust into a mother's worst nightmare. Though I am a strong woman, when life comes at you that quickly, hurtling the real possibility of a son's death upon you, strength eludes you. At least it did me. I didn't fall apart; I didn't sob hysterically. I was just laid bare, right to my soul, helpless, defeated, afraid. For an instant, there was numbness…and then…I began praying. I prayed that no one else had been involved, and if they had, that they lived. I prayed for my son and for his son. I prayed for his brothers, and I prayed for strength for me. As we climbed into the truck to make the 35-minute drive to the hospital, I reached into the glove compartment for my husband's rosary, and I began saying the Hail Mary. Once, I glanced out the window and noticed the shrouding fog, the worst fog I ever remembered seeing, and I knew at least one of the reasons for the accident. The fog kept us creeping at a snail's pace, but throughout the trip, I continued praying the Rosary. I'd like to reassure you that prayer kept me strong, but I'd be lying. Prayer kept me busy, and it kept me hoping, but my insides were beginning to tighten and twist painfully. It's rather strange that you can spend an entire life never really knowing terror, yet the moment it lodges inside you, you recognize it instantly. Terror was the predominant feeling inside the truck cab, and only prayer kept it from suffocating me.

At the hospital, the nightmare became stark reality. Family and friends began pouring into the waiting room, and details of the accident began leaking through the numbness and escalating the terror. Head trauma. Unresponsive. Punctured lung. Skull and neck fractures. 45 minutes before he was found. Each additional detail added to the bleak picture, and I understood that prayer was truly the only thing I could do for my son, so I did it well. From the depths of my heart I prayed to Mother Mary. I knew she would understand the love a mother bears for her child, how no other love on earth is quite like it, and how heart wrenching the possibility of losing a son is. Even more importantly, for the first time in my life, I felt like I really knew and understood her pain. I kept praying. It occurred to me, during that early morning vigil, that if it hadn't been for my mom taking me to church and introducing me to my Lord, I would not have been able to do even this for my son. Thank you, mom. I remember wondering briefly what people who have not formed a personal relationship with God do for comfort and hope when they find themselves in tragic situations. I cannot imagine not having Him to turn to. About that time, our monsignor showed up, was admitted into the sacred halls of the emergency room, and gave a special anointing to my son. God had truly been informed – we wanted this young man saved!

The number in the waiting room was quietly growing. Each passing minute seemed to bring a new family member or friend through the doors. I had called my sister as soon as I had gotten the news, and she dropped whatever plans she had for the morning and drove through the terrible fog to sit with me. My sister-in-law, brother-in laws, cousins, aunts, uncles, nieces, nephews raced to the hospital as the day dawned. Cory's friends did as well. It seems humorous now, but the hospital staff called for a backup security guard, the numbers had grown so large. Quietly I glanced from face to face, and my burden was lifted a little. It was very obvious I was not alone in my fear and that knowledge, somehow, made fear easier to bear. First prayer, now family and friends. I was beginning to feel very blessed, even in the midst of this tragic event.

And then the news. He was alive, but he desperately needed to be transported to shock trauma. He couldn't be flown because of the fog and transporting by ambulance was risky. But, there was no choice. He had to go. I begged a ride in the front seat of the ambulance, and we were on our way. Even there, prayer, family and friends rode along. His cousin was on the hospital staff, and she sat at his head, gently comforting him, explaining to him, even though we were certain he could hear nothing. Friends from the rescue squad sat in attendance and another drove. I kept up the prayer vigil. It was a very long ride.

Shock trauma was both the height of the nightmare and the home of the angels. It was there I was allowed my first close look at my son. His face laid open to the bone in several places, the bloody, gashed head, the eyes swollen shut, the blood stained neck collar, the tubes in both lungs, the ventilator to keep him breathing. My handsome, physically fit, just turned 29 son was in the fight of his life, and I was helpless. Humbling. Very humbling. No matter how much we think we are in control, we aren't.

Quickly, efficiently, but compassionately, the doctors and nurses worked for hours on my son. In the end, God saved him, but their hands and minds were the instruments though which He worked. Meanwhile, the trauma waiting room was filling up. Even though the hospital was over an hour away from home and rush hour traffic was in full swing, family and friends came to wait. At one point there were over thirty people spilling out of the small waiting area into the hallway. My heart was full; even if the worst happened, I would not be alone.

But the best happened. My son, who had sped straight into a brick church (the irony is not lost on me, I guarantee you) wearing no seat belt - who lay enveloped by the fog for 45 minutes in his blood and vomit amid glass and bricks under a roof which miraculously did not collapse on him; who suffered a fractured skull a hairsbreadth away from his spinal cord; two fractured vertebrae in his neck millimeters from his arterial artery; a fractured face that stopped miraculously short of his orbital socket; a nose shattered clear through the septum and laid wide open; a pierced lung and another that had to be pierced to drain the fluid that was filling them both up; a broken rib right over his heart- this son was wheeled out of the hospital just seven days later. While he still has much rehabilitation in front of him, this son should not have lived. Look at his truck; look at the church; look at the pictures they took of him at the hospital. He was dying, but he was saved. Why? I don't know why; that is not ours to know. But I wholeheartedly believe God saved him for a purpose, and I pray every day that Cory opens his heart and listens, for God will be trying to show him the reason and guide him to a greater life than he has ever enjoyed, I have no doubt. How was he saved? That's easy. The power of prayer, the power of family, and the power of friends.

We have those powers within us. At any moment, on any given day, we are encouraged to turn to the Lord and offer up our prayers, our troubles, our hopes, our joys, our wants. We are invited to invoke the power through our faith. Each day, as members of an earthly family, we have the power to lift up someone simply because we are bound together by human ties. United, a family is a powerful force. Finally, there is the power of friendship. Friends are the people we choose to allow into our inner sanctums; we choose to tell them our fears and our dreams, and we trust they will support and love us for who we are, not because they have to as members of our family, but because they want to as members of our inner circle. Each of us is a friend, and that relationship with another individual is both precious and powerful; it carries a great obligation to use that power wisely for the good of our friends. You see, each of us is a powerful individual. Together, our individual powers can make miracles. Cory is living proof, and I am a grateful eyewitness.

It is my prayer that family and friends know how much we appreciate the time you spent with us when we needed you most. May you understand that the love you shared by taking time from your own lives to spend time with us in our darkness, that your words, your hugs, your kindnesses to Cory and our family all helped give us strength to face the future and helped heal my son's body and soul. When he felt the outpouring of love, he had no choice but to get better. I know he is thanking each of you in his own way as he works through his convalescence. This thanks is mine, from a mother's heart. I am forever indebted to each of you, and I love you all. For everything you did, thank you. And finally, to my mom who introduced me to my Lord. She led me to the altar and to the Bible. Where I took that knowledge and experience is my story, but she gave me the opportunity to develop my own personal relationship with the Lord. It is that relationship, sinner though I am, that sustains me during the hard times, that lifts me up and gives me hope for the future. I do not know how anyone survives life's trials without knowing Him in an intimate and personal way. I continuously work on improving my own relationship with Him, and even though I fail more than I succeed, I still try. I pray that my sons continue to seek him and to build their own relationships with Him for their benefit, and for the benefit of those they love, especially my grandchildren.

Contact: shroberts164@gmail.com

Preserved Reflections
By Mary Anne Benedetto

As a writer and memoir writing instructor, I am an ardent advocate of encouraging people to capture their life stories to pass along to future generations. When the opportunity arose to participate in a collection of written works by my **Beach Author Network** friends, I had a ping-pong style debate with myself about whether to write a short story of inspirational fiction or to share a few memories of my own that might inspire others to begin a memoir project.

Memoirs are my passion because stories left unpreserved are forever lost. I learned this the hard way when I stood on the U.S.S. Arizona Memorial at Pearl Harbor in Hawaii and remembered that my own dad was stationed there in the Army and was very much present when Pearl Harbor was bombed. From bits and pieces of dialogue with him during my childhood, I knew that he miraculously survived and went on to serve on Guadalcanal. Thankfully, his only physical damage was a severe case of malaria.

It was in that poignant moment of remembrance at Pearl Harbor that the lightning bolt of realization struck me, filling me with sadness and enormous regret that I had never captured my dad's stories. This experience made me determined to accomplish three goals: 1) be certain to interview my mother and compile her recollections, 2) to influence others about the importance of preserving the history of loved ones, and 3) to write my own memories for future generations. I recognized that once we are gone, there is no rewind button. It is our responsibility to preserve family stories.

While there are numerous topics that I suggest for memoir writers to consider, three typical examples are:

1-What is something quirky about your personality or your upbringing?
2-How did a particular historical event personally affect you?
3-Did you ever have to leave something behind? What was the ultimate impact?

The short stories shown below offer a candid glimpse into a few of my own life experiences, formulated by writing my answers to the above simple questions. **Evolving Tastes** confesses my peculiarities relative to food, **A Frightening Day in History** conveys my 9/11 story, and **Farewell to Connie** describes my childhood encounter with saying goodbye to something I desperately wanted to keep. It is my sincere honor to share these stories with you, and I hope that reading a few personal accounts from my life will encourage you to share your own memories with loved ones.

Evolving Tastes

On many levels, I have a history of quirkiness with food. My parents struggled to introduce me to a variety of edibles that would provide a balanced diet for my then scrawny, little frame. I was not having any part of it.

One of my earliest recollections on this topic is a memorable day when I was eight years old, and my mother made pancakes for breakfast. While that does not sound like a remarkable or memoir-worthy experience, there is a reason why it is unforgettable to me. The problem was not that I had an aversion to pancakes. On the contrary, I ordinarily liked them; however, not these particular specimens. For some reason, she prepared them with such colossal thickness that it was like chewing a mouthful of cotton straight from the fields. I took one bite and immediately resolved that I was finished with this meal.

Just to explain a little bit further, I have always been anti-condiment. Since childhood, I refused to eat ketchup, mustard, mayonnaise or salad dressing. It is impossible for me to supply any logic behind this. It has always been merely a personal preference. Because the anti-condiment list also included syrup, drenching these puffy pancakes in that sugary substance to integrate some degree of moisture was not an option.

On this day, I sat at the table just staring at the offending pancake on my plate. In an apparent attempt to force me to eat, Mom announced, "Mary, you are going to sit at this table until you eat your breakfast."

"If I try to eat one more bite, I am going to gag," I emphatically replied. I was not protesting merely to be persnickety. I sincerely meant it.

Mom just shook her head, and she and the rest of the family continued to devour their food. I remained stubbornly silent, determined that I would starve before I would eat anything with the density of a plush, terry cloth towel.

Eventually Dad, Mom and my sister, Pat, finished dining, cleared their dishes from the table and retreated to their respective activities. I was tenacious and was not about to budge. Once I became bored with my own inflexibility, I surveyed the dining room for a means of escape. Eyeing Mom's large sewing machine that took up residence in one corner of the room, I suddenly devised a viable plan.

Checking to be certain that no one would see me executing my solution, I quickly grabbed the pancake and stuck it behind the sewing machine. Then I marched into the kitchen with my empty plate and proceeded to wash the dish. Mom walked in, saw me at the sink and said, "You didn't throw that pancake away, did you?"

I replied with a perfectly honest, "No."

In my view, I had not done anything terrible because there was no sticky syrup on the pancake. I saw it as more like hiding a rolled up dish towel out of sight.

The following Saturday when my sister was cleaning in the dining room, she discovered a scary-looking lump of matter, stuffed behind the sewing machine. She knew my weird eating habits well enough to recognize what it was and dutifully threw it away.

There were other times when Mom served foods that I was never going to sample. Items such as liver and onions, chicken and dumplings, a special raisin sauce for ham (my dad always raved about how delicious it was), and on and on. She tried to institute a new rule that required me to at least taste one bite of each food item that was prepared. Once again, I refused and remained seated at the table until they gave up and removed the dishes and leftovers. I found that if I could "out-stubborn" them, I possessed the ability to sidestep the rule.

School cafeteria food was also a challenge until I discovered a la carte. In junior high school, I was given "x" amount of lunch money for the week. One day, I decided that I was not hungry enough to be interested in the menu offered on the regular lunch tray, so I purchased two items--milk and a piece of chocolate cream pie. Yum! That became my standard daily lunch, and I pocketed the difference. It is a miracle that I didn't become obese from my lunch routine that school year.

Then there was pizza. I hated it. I could not even stomach the odor of pizza. It seriously insulted my nostrils. It was not until I was in my early twenties and a dear friend, Lena, invited me to her house for dinner that I tasted it for the first time.

"I made a pizza for us," she announced with pride. How disappointed I was when she revealed this choice. I did not want to be rude, and apparently I was hungry enough to at least try it. Hmmm, what a revelation! This stuff was really great! I turned the gastronomy corner and became a lover of pizza--but only plain cheese or perhaps pepperoni. I could never eat a slice that contained multiple toppings, which brings us to yet another food-related quirk.

If it would not appear utterly ridiculous, I would love to eat every meal on a plate that contains dividers. I despise it when the peas touch the mashed potatoes or the green beans rub up against the steak. Even worse, you will never see me eat a cheeseburger. I love grilled cheese, and I love hamburgers--just not combined. No cheese touching meat. Nor do I like food that contains too many things mixed together, other than a tossed salad. So I am horrified by casseroles. This is really tough to admit, but when I order a biscuit with sausage and egg, I eat it in separate sections. The top of the biscuit is the first to go, then the egg, sausage next, and finally the bottom of the biscuit. There is no way that I could take a bite that would include everything at once.

If that isn't enough, there is more. I eat everything on my plate one item in its entirety at a time. For instance, I may start with the corn and then eat every bite of that vegetable before I start on the chicken. I devour all chicken before I dig into any other item on the plate. Everything has its turn.

Additionally, there is the texture issue. My husband, Fred, cannot understand why I do not like lobster or shrimp. It is all about the way the composition feels when I am chewing. For instance, baked beans are out of the question. They are far too mushy. In fact, if I have an urge for bean with bacon soup, I open the can, add the water, heat the mixture, remove all beans and eat only the liquid, accompanied by a few crumbled saltine crackers.

While I continue to be anti-condiment and eat no foods prepared with mayonnaise (which eliminates any number of items at a picnic), there has been some progress in my food-related idiosyncrasies. In my more mature years, I have learned to love broiled scallops, Chilean sea bass, broccoli sautéed with garlic, asparagus sautéed with shallots, eggplant parmesan, low fat vanilla yogurt laced with fresh fruit and a sprinkle of granola, and have graduated from insisting on a well-done steak that is grilled to the point of shoe leather quality to ordering a juicier, medium-rare version.

If you have a child or grandchild who is a picky eater, please be aware that there is hope. In time, their taste buds may mature and their sustenance expand. In the interim, just be certain that they are not subsisting on a daily meal of chocolate cream pie, and you may want to check behind the dining room furniture for foreign objects.

To my grandchildren Gabriella, Alexandria and Nicholas, and to my great-granddaughter Alessandra: If your children should develop peculiar eating habits, I guess we know in which direction to point the proverbial finger.

A Frightening Day in History

"Fred, we need to get back across the border right now before they close it," I adamantly announced to my husband upon learning that not only had the World Trade Center had been struck by a plane, but now the Pentagon had been hit. This was serious business, and we needed to return to United States without delay.

There was a brilliant blue sky on that peaceful, sunny morning of September 11, 2001, and it also happened to be our son Ken's twenty-ninth birthday. Fred and I had escaped our daily routine to spend a few days at a charming hotel in Niagara Falls…on the **Canadian** side. He was scheduled to play golf in the New York State Senior Men's championship to be held on the American side of the falls that same afternoon.

Our original plan was to proceed at a leisurely pace, locate a restaurant for a good, hearty breakfast, take a sightseeing walk and then drive across the border to the golf course. We were beyond ready for some relaxation, as Fred's dad was under Hospice care, and we had been visiting him at the Hospice Inn every day after work for about six weeks. Apparently, he was not yet ready to proceed from this life into his heavenly post as a newly assigned angel. Due to his dad's precarious health situation, we had debated about whether or not to make the five to six hour trip. Fred was reluctant to participate, but he had earned his spot in the tournament and finally decided that this was something that would give us both a greatly needed break.

I awoke in our plush, cozy hotel bed that morning with the persistent sound of an inspirational praise and worship chorus entitled "There's Something About That Name" repeatedly running through my mind. It simply would not stop. The lyrics were "Jesus, Jesus, Jesus. There's just something about that name. Master, Savior, Jesus. Like the fragrance after the rain. Jesus, Jesus, Jesus. Let all heaven and earth proclaim. Kings and kingdoms will all pass away, but there's something about that name."

Regardless of what I attempted to think about, that particular song dominated every ounce of my attention and continued to play over and over in my head. Fred was still in a deep sleep, demonstrated by a rhythmic pattern of snoring sounds, but I could not fall back to sleep with the repetition of the lyrics and melody passing through my brain. I finally crawled out of bed and showered. The chorus continued to repeat in my mind, and there was absolutely nothing I could do to hit the "off" button.

By this time, Fred was awake and ready for his turn in the shower. I tuned in to *Good Morning America* on television to see what was happening in the world, and within minutes, the tragedy began to unfold with Charlie Gibson announcing that a plane had hit the first tower at the World Trade Center, but the details were uncertain. Initially, they actually believed that it was an accident. As he exited the shower, I said, "Fred, there is something terrible happening in New York City." In frozen astonishment, we watched the television screen that featured shocking events taking place right before our eyes. There was speculation and almost a sense of disbelief emitted by the stunned news broadcasters.

Being someone who must eat on a regular schedule or I risk a headache and dizziness, we briefly left the room and television coverage to locate a restaurant that served breakfast. We tried to take a short walk, but in spite of the spectacular weather and lovely flower gardens surrounding the hotel, it was impossible to think of anything other than the strange situation occurring in New York. When we returned to our room, the updated news informed us that the Pentagon had also been hit. In that moment, I insisted that we pack up and get back across the border ASAP, as it seemed to me that entering the United States might become difficult if we did not leave right away.

In ghostly silence, we rode in the elevator to the first floor of the hotel with another couple who said they were immediately checking out. Just before the elevator doors opened, they told us that their daughter's location of employment was the World Trade Center. "I hope everything is okay with your daughter," I managed to say with a lump in my throat in sympathy of their obvious anxiety. I could not help being thankful that our son worked in the Albany area and not New York City. Seeing the number of hotel guests in line to check out, we made the split-second decision to simply leave. No goodbyes, no check out. It made no difference whether or not we would be charged for the nights we would not be staying in Canada. We felt a strong sense of urgency that we needed to take rapid action and return to our own country without hesitation.

Heading directly for the U.S. border, we had no difficulty crossing. Later that afternoon, we learned that some checkpoints closed very shortly after our departure and that those remaining open experienced long, arduous waits and extensive searches. The United States was, after all, under attack.

The New York State golf tournament committee deliberated about whether or not to go forward with the senior event, so we held tight, our eyes perpetually glued to the television in the clubhouse. It was like repeatedly watching the same footage of a scene from a gruesome movie. Sadly, the content was not fiction. Victims trapped on upper floors of the towers anticipated being engulfed in flames and chose to jump to their deaths. The enormous, fire-ravaged buildings did the unimaginable. In the blink of an eye, they suddenly imploded and became clouds of ash claiming not only the lives of their tenants and office workers, but also many responding police officers and fire fighters. Chaos. Confusion. Heroes.

Surprisingly, it was determined that the state tournament would proceed, but I cannot believe for a moment that any contender could focus on golf on that particular day.

Following the first round, we checked into a hotel on the American side of Niagara Falls, and the mood throughout the hotel was somber. Our little romantic golf tournament getaway had developed an unexpectedly grave atmosphere. Calling Ken on the telephone that evening, I said, "We wish you a happy birthday, but I am sorry it is such a depressing one."

On September 12, my husband somehow managed to achieve a hole-in-one during his round. Ironically, it was on the same hole where Tiger Woods had previously scored a hole-in-one during a Pewter Cup event. This was little consolation, however, given the devastation that had just hit so many lives and families. It was almost impossible to feel excited about it.

As we drove along the New York State Thruway during our return to the Albany area, the eeriest feeling hung throughout the skies. All air traffic had been suspended. We do not typically realize how busy our clouds and skies are until suddenly there are absolutely no flights…no commercial airliners, no private jets, no small aircraft. Just silence.

The chain of events that would ultimately end the lives of not only the victims, but many first responders as well, has a way of leaving a hole in your heart, even if you were not directly touched by this tragedy. American Airlines Flight 11 and United Airlines Flight 175 slammed into the World Trade Center towers. American Airlines Flight 77 hit the Pentagon. The passengers and crew of United Airlines Flight 93 prevented additional carnage beyond the scope of their own demise by courageously attempting to overtake the hijackers. Fearing those efforts, the terrorists violently crashed the plane into a rural Pennsylvania field. Seeing the stories of victims, their families, survivors, and how this entire escapade was meticulously planned had an effect on every American individual and permanently changed life as we once knew it.

There is usually some perceivable positive aspect in every negative if you take the time to inspect the entire scenario. The impact of these atrocious, irrational events of that frightening day resulted in bringing many people back into the practice of relying on their faith during difficult times, and church attendance soared immediately following this enormous loss of life on American soil. We may not understand the how or why when negative events occur, but we know that we are never alone if trust in God indwells our hearts.

I will always remember the song repeating in my mind that morning-- just at the exact time when this senseless and horrific terrorist plot was transforming into action. While the evil forces continue to strike fear in this world in which we live, I believe that I was given those words as a gift of comfort for that day and every day thereafter to remember to look to Jesus always, as His love is certain and God is faithful even as kings and kingdoms do pass away. It is a reminder that life can change in an instant and to always keep the faith.

Farewell to Connie

Have you ever considered a time in your life when it was necessary to **leave something precious behind**? Circumstances dictated that ties would be severed with either an object, a person, a place, a particular group or activity--perhaps with an entire way of life.

In my own experience, I can recall several occurrences that fit this theme, but my very first childhood recollection of leaving something of importance behind brings me to age nine--June, 1961. My fourth grade school year had been filled with birthday parties, good grades, delighted parents, a supportive church family and a group of girlfriends with whom a special bond had formed.

This final day of the school year at Hudson Elementary School in North Carolina was particularly significant because my life, as I had known it, was forever changing. On that sunny day in June, I was armed with my boxy, black Brownie camera, enthusiastically taking photos of my best friends Debra Craig, Kathy Kincaid, and my cousin Ann Jackson. I wanted to be able to remember them just the way they were.

Mom, my sister, Pat, and I packed our remaining clothing into suitcases and in two days would be setting out on a long distance adventure. We were moving to Arizona from North Carolina, and Dad was already there working and settling our newly rented home, anxiously awaiting our arrival by train into the Flagstaff railroad station.

Although I was nine years old, one of my prized possessions was a curly-haired, brunette, toddler-sized doll named Connie. Her height equaled about half of my skinny little frame, so transporting her from one location to another could present special challenges. In spite of the logistical difficulties, I stubbornly refused to allow Connie to be packed into the U-Haul trailer that Dad drove across the country. I simply could not part with her for the two month period that we would be separated. She would never have been able to manage without me. Who would oversee her well-being?

With every intention of taking Connie with me on the long train ride, I struggled to carry her with my other belongings as we trudged through the train station on our departure day. Mom was envisioning the difficulties that Connie would present during this trip that would take us all the way to Chicago, where we would change trains and board the sleek, modern Super Chief to transport us to Arizona. Where would Connie sit? She was large enough to take up a seat of her own, and Mom was not about to pay for Connie to occupy a passenger seat.

My Aunt Judy and younger cousin, Debbie, were there to bid us farewell, and Mom gently approached me with a suggestion. "Honey," she began. "Why don't we give Connie a new home with Debbie and Aunt Judy? You know they will take very good care of her."

I frowned, firmly pursed my lips, and gave Connie a loving glance. Somehow, even at the tender age of nine, I knew that Mom was right. After lugging this toddler doll all over the train station, I was well aware that dragging her across the country would be a daunting task.

"I'll give her to Debbie," I reluctantly conceded. The look on Mom's face was total relief.

Perhaps somewhere deep inside, I realized that I was reaching an age where being attached to toddler dolls was for younger girls and it was time to pursue other, more grown-up interests. That same day, as I sat in my assigned seat on the train that would take us to new explorations, I began to write in my red, locking, five year diary. It was the day I said goodbye to my former life and friends, left Connie behind (albeit in good hands) and discovered that it was actually fun, entertaining and valuable to <u>write about life</u>.

*****

Memoir Writing Tips by Mary Anne Benedetto

Consider this: What will people remember about you? Which stories of significance would you like to include for loved ones? Make a memory list.

You do not have to be a celebrity to write your stories, and you do not have to write about every breath you have ever taken in life. Choose stories of value to share with future generations.

Think about your goals for the project—for family only or publish for sale to the public?

Give up the excuses. Commit to the project. Find a location for writing where you will be uninterrupted, comfortable, inspired. Create a schedule for writing--put it on the calendar, give yourself a deadline, determine how many pages per week or how many stories per week or a particular word count per week. Set an attainable goal. Journal.

Think about your first paying job—one with a real pay check, and write the details. What was it? Where was it? How old were you? What were your duties? How did you get the job? What lessons did you learn from this job?

Think about significant firsts in your life-1st day of school, 1st memorable teacher, 1st date, 1st car.

If you aren't fond of writing, use a handheld recorder and tell your stories into the recorder as though you were sharing them with a friend. The recordings can then be transcribed into a priceless document.

Helping People Write the Times of Their Lives

Mary Anne Benedetto
(843) 215-4676
Email: info@awriterspresence.com
Website: http://www.awriterspresence.com
Social Media: http://www.facebook.com/mabenedetto
http://twitter.com/marybenedetto   http://www.linkedin.com/in/maryannebenedetto
http://www.maryannebenedetto.blogspot.com
Facebook Author/Speaker Page: http://on.fb.me/ZD4de1

Mary Anne Benedetto is a speaker, blogger, Certified Lifewriting Instructor and author of *Eyelash, Never Say Perfect, 7 **Easy** Steps to Memoir Writing: Build a Priceless Legacy One Story at a Time!, From Italy with Love & Limoncello* and *Write Your Pet's Life Story in 7 **Easy** Steps*! Her passions include special times with family and friends, helping people capture and preserve their life and pet stories, creating Christian fiction, golf, world travel and walking the spectacular South Carolina beaches.

SHORTS

The Girl Who Beat the Band
By Sarah Kelly

"M-m-m-Mary!" a girl on the sidewalk shouted when I went outside to play.

"You dumbbell," another one said.

Some of the neighbor girls were playing jump rope on the sidewalk and I tried to join in. They didn't want me there 'cause of my darkness and my stuttering.

It was 1922, near Christmastime, and my family and me'd just moved to Pittsburgh. There was me and Mama, my big sister Mamie, my grandma who I called Nanny, and Grandpa. We came by railroad which was real thrilling because it was my first train ride. The rhythm of the engine and sounds of the horn and bells was like music to my ears and put me in mind of the train that hooked up the colored and white parts of town back home in Atlanta. I figured maybe this train connecting Atlanta and Pittsburgh would carry me to a different world where people wouldn't be so separate.

After the neighbor girls teased me about my stuttering I ran back in the house and peered through the window. Those pretty white girls were laughing and playing Double Dutch with their jump ropes and having a fine time. I wanted to be like those girls.

But I couldn't. I could only be myself with my dark skin and peculiar ways. And my music. That's what saved me from misery. The music inside me gave me so much joy I thought I'd bust if it didn't get out. Problem was I had no piano or organ to practice my music on and my fingers were itching to play. All I could do was hum or sing to myself. But like my Nanny always said my singing sounded more like the night-squalling of an old alley cat. So most times the music stayed inside my head.

Back in Atlanta I spent most of my time at the store-front church where my mama played the pump organ on Sunday mornings. She'd go there every day to practice and always took me with her. Funny thing was as I watched her fingers move I somehow always knew what note she was getting ready to play. By the time I was three I tried to copy what I heard. Then I started playing my own music, the music that was in my head. It wasn't long before Mama let me go to the church on my own to practice. Got me out from underfoot she said. I got lots of grumbly stares for this from the neighbors since a girl's supposed to stay home and help her mama in the kitchen.

But I never got close to my mama and never wanted to be like her. She put the love of music in my heart but she also taught me hearts can be very cold. Hers sure was. So instead of clamoring for hugs from Mama I pestered her to let me go down the street to the church every day so I could play the organ which got me away from the drinking sprees. Mama and Nanny were the only drinkers. Their drinking was understandable seeing as all week long they washed and ironed for white folks. My mama who was admired for her beauty and her dainty figure almost became a hunchback carrying all those white peoples' laundry on her back. She fretted about that 'cause she was vain about her looks. So come weekends her and Nanny lost themselves in the gin.

The drinking didn't let up when we moved north. Turned out Mama and Nanny still had to knuckle under to white folks for us to get by. They washed and ironed all day just like they did in Atlanta and that's how we got on, same as we always had. Only it was so cold.

The coldness of Pittsburgh chilled more than just my body. I felt like a stranger in my new neighborhood and even with my own family. Seemed up north my darkness compared to the rest of my family showed up more than it did down south. Truth was Mama and most of my relations except for Grandpa had always made me feel different and treated me like dirt 'cause I was so dark. But I'd never felt such a powerful lonesomeness as I did when we moved to smoggy old Pittsburgh.

The day after the jump-roping girls teased me about my stuttering I decided to see if they'd let me join in their game of hopscotch. Just as their teasing started one of their mamas came running out of her house with a butcher knife, screaming, "Get out of our sight, you black vermin! You don't belong here!"

My body was shaking so bad I couldn't hardly move. I thought for sure I was done for.

"Leave the child be," came a quiet but firm voice from behind me.

It was Grandpa. He'd just arrived from his work at the laboring yard and I ran to him. He put his arm around me in a protecting way, still eyeing the lady with his steady look. Grandpa was a small man but imposing. When he spoke, which wasn't too often, people listened.

The lady's knife-wagging fist dropped to her side. She seemed all fuddled. "Well . . . I . . . that was right silly of me, wasn't it?" She laughed, kind of, more like a titter. "Here I was in my kitchen carving up a chicken when I hear a great commotion among the children. And I come running outside not even realizing I'm still holding on to this thing." Her eyes moved from Grandpa to me and her lips became more firmly set. "I'm right sorry if I scared you."

Truth was I was so scared my teeth were clanking.

The neighbor girls stood there with their mouths hanging open. Some of their mamas who'd been peering out their windows came clattering out of their houses to shoo their children inside.

Grandpa looked hard at the little crowd gathered on the sidewalk. "You folks stop bullying my grandbaby, you hear? She done you no harm." He squeezed my shoulder and steered me away from all the staring eyes. "Let's walk a spell, child."

He let go of my shoulder and I clutched his hand.

"Don't let ignorant folks frighten you," he said. "If my pappy could overcome his fears, you surely can."

I could see Grandpa was fixing to tell me one of his stories. I leaned close to him and listened.

"Pappy'd tell me at the end of each day he be toting his basket of cotton to the gin-house in fear and trembling."

"The gin-house," I said, "was that where they drank gin like Mama and Nanny?"

He frowned. Grandpa didn't hold with drunkenness. "No indeed, child. The gin-house where the cotton gin be."

"Cotton gin? What's that?"

"Cotton gin's a wooden box with a crank on its side that splits up the cotton fiber from the seeds. Slaves called it white man's magic."

"Was it really magic?"

"No, child. Gin mean engine. It just be an invention with different parts that works together for a single purpose, like any machine."

"If it was only a machine then what was your pappy so fearful of?"

"Well, if his basket was to fall short in weight he knew he had suffering coming. As he'd say it, the whippin' would follow the weighin.'"

I can't even tell you the feeling I had at that moment. My sorrow was like a dark pit deep inside me. I must've started shaking again 'cause Grandpa put his arm around me and held me close and chuckled real soft.

"It weren't all so bad, child. My pappy also tell me about the music. How when the sun just breaking across the fields the slaves would come from all directions singing and the fields a-ringing with their song. Hundreds of 'em lifting their voices like the heavenly host itself."

My eyes got prickly wet and I hugged him with all my might and he gave me back my hug. Grandpa's arms around me felt strong and comforting. I could feel the steady beat of his heart, like a drumbeat, and I was filled with fear that one day his heart would stop, and I'd be all alone.

Try as I might I couldn't keep myself in the bed. It was Christmas day, and Grandpa was waiting in the parlor, his cheeks spread in a grin over the surprise he had for me.

"A piano!" I squeaked, and all the fear I'd been feeling flew right out of my head.

"This here's a clever machine, Mary. It can work like a reg'lar piano, but it also lets you hear the music of famous players by playing their piano rolls."

"Piano rolls? What are those, Grandpa?"

"Come here and let me show you. Piano rolls are like magic. Each one holds a different song, played by the most famous piano players in the world. It's like having Jelly Roll Morton right here in our own parlor."

I was so excited my heart was bouncing like a pogo stick. We played roll after roll and watched the piano keys play themselves. Like a ghost was playing them. There were old ballads, waltzes, opera tunes, and marches. But my favorites were the jazz tunes—the boogie and rags which I tried to learn myself by slowing down the piano roll and pressing my fingers to the keys as they played.

Next morning I couldn't wait to get to my new piano. Now I could spend all day working things out and making my own sounds.

"Quit the racket!" Mama yelled from her bedroom. "It givin' me the bad head! Can't stand for no racket!"

I carried right on with my practicing. I put my hands over the keys as they played themselves and let the music's sounds and feelings run through me. When the piano finished doing its magic I played the song just like I'd heard it.

"Mind your mama and stop that bangin'!" Nanny yelled from the kitchen.

"I'm not banging!" I yelled back. "This is jazz music!"

"Jazz my foot," she said, walking into the parlor wiping her hands on her apron. "You can call that clamor what you want, but it's from the devil is all I know. You best play music that be more fittin'."

Mamie stood by the front door, all dolled up. She was sixteen and light-skinned and pretty. I wished I looked more like her but mostly I wished my sister would spend more time at home and not always be going off with her boyfriend Hugh.

"Where you think you goin'?" Mama asked as she staggered out of her bedroom.

Mamie rolled her eyes and sighed as she walked out the door. "Don't even start, Mama. I'm getting out of this house of horrors before it swallows me whole."

Nanny shook her head in her disapproving way. Mama went to the kitchen and I heard the gin bottle pop open. My stomach got snarly and sick feeling. After a time Nanny went to join Mama. I kept on with my playing and tried not to think about what was going on in that kitchen. The drinking made me sad, mostly because it kept Grandpa in his basement bedroom where he went to get away from the boozing. I wanted him in the parlor sharing in my music making.

Next day Nanny sent me downstairs to hurry Grandpa along so's he could get to work at the laboring yard.

"I don't know what's keeping him," Nanny said. "If he's late they'll dock his pay."

I ran down the basement stairs and was surprised to see Grandpa still asleep. Not even the faintest snore was coming out of him.

"Grandpa," I said, shaking him real gentle. "You best get up. Nanny says you'll be late for work."

He didn't stir.

I shook him harder and spoke a little louder. "Grandpa."

He lay still as a stone. My belly started to feel tight.

Nanny's voice sailed down from top of the stairs. "What in mercy's name is keeping you two?"

"Grandpa won't wake up," I said in a small voice.

Nanny trudged down the steps, groaning. That was 'cause of her aching bones which always got worse when Grandpa didn't get 'round to things fast enough to suit her.

"I had a might time gettin' down those stairs," she said, breathing real heavy. When she saw how Grandpa lay so still on his cot she bustled over and picked up his wrist. "Mercy on us!" she wailed, dropping his wrist and beating her fist against her big bosom. "He dead!"

Tears ran silent down my cheeks and my tight belly felt like it ripped open, leaving nothing but a big dark emptiness.

The shadow of Grandpa's death seemed like there was no end to it and blotted out all the happiness and safe feeling I'd known with him. It terrified me to think how I'd get through the rest of my life without him.

That was till I laid eyes on Max.

It was New Years Eve and Nanny said we had relations just come to town. "They's bereaved like us," she said, wiping the wetness from her eyes with the handkerchief that seemed like it hadn't left her hand since Grandpa died. "Your poor cousin Max. Such a fine boy and his daddy gone to glory in such a terrible way."

"What was the terrible way, Nanny?" I asked.

She shook her head real slow and wiped away another tear. "And that boy's poor, poor mama. I just don't know what's to become of her."

I still wondered about the terrible way but Nanny wasn't in mind to talk about it.

When Max and his mama arrived at our door later that afternoon my knees felt like Nanny's mashed potatoes that were simmering on the stove. The sight of him made things start hopping around inside me like I never felt before.

I didn't say a word during dinner 'cause I knew my tongue would get all tied up with the stuttering. After everybody ate and the grownups were still at the kitchen table talking Max asked if I'd like to go outside with him. I couldn't get out of my seat fast enough. Part of the reason was because the thought of being alone with Max made me shivery excited inside and the other part was I wanted to know what was the terrible way his daddy died.

Max and me put on our coats and went outside to sit on the front stoop. He didn't say anything for the longest time. He set his elbows on his knees and wrung his hands real slow, staring out into the street.

"I'm right sorry about your daddy dying," I said after a spell.

He looked at me and smiled his sweet handsome smile. The smile that did funny things to my insides.

"Well thank you kindly, Mary," he said. "I'm right sorry about your grandpa dying too."

"Thank you kindly, Max."

Max got quiet again and after a time I worked up the guts to ask him. "How'd your daddy die?"

He wrung his hands even harder and sighed real deep. "He owed money to some men."

"How'd that make him die?"

Max kept staring out at the street and his eyes were shiny wet. "The men he owed money to tied him to the railroad tracks and he got run over by a train."

I didn't know what to say so I just stared at him and felt my eyes get wet like his. He looked at me with a sad smile that was also a very brave smile. Then he wrapped both his hands around one of mine and held it tight against his knee. His sadness almost made me forget my own heartache. All I could think was how much I wanted his sadness to go away.

"How old are you, Max?" I finally asked, my voice real quiet.

"Fourteen. And how old are you, Mary?"

"I'm twelve. So I guess you'll be starting up at the high school Tuesday. That'll be my first day in seventh grade at the Lincoln School." I tried to sound cheerful but I don't think my voice came out that way.

"Yeah, I'll be at the high school. I don't know nobody there since my mama and me just got here. What do you say we meet up after school on Tuesday, Mary? I only live a couple blocks from here. Want to take a little walk? I'll show you where."

Did I ever. And he held my hand the whole time.

My first day at the new school felt like one big long wait. By the time the bell finally rang I was so wore out with the waiting I hardly had strength to move. But once I was outside I ran fast as my feet could carry me to Max's house. He wasn't there and neither was his mama so I sat on the front step jittering and waiting.

A while later he came gliding down the street on his shiny blue bicycle, his book bag hanging on his shoulder. My heart danced at the sight of him. I jumped to my feet and when he saw me he skidded to a stop.

"Mary!" he said, and a big handsome smile lit up his face. He walked his bike across the sidewalk and leaned it against the railing by the steps. He sloped his shoulder down and shook it to let the book bag slide off, which he caught with his other hand and hung on the railing post. My heart went to pieces at the sight of his fine strong shoulders. I wanted to hug him and press into him like I used to with Grandpa.

He just stood there and grinned at me. "How's your piano playing going, Mary?"

My mouth fell open. "How'd you know about that?"

His grin turned kinda sheepish. "Well, I came over to see you yesterday and when I got there I heard this beautiful music coming through your parlor window. When I peeked inside and saw you playing I couldn't hardly believe it. I watched you for the longest time and listened. I didn't want to bother you none 'cause you looked like you were concentrating so hard. Almost like you were in another world."

I was too filled with happiness to speak. Max understood about my music like Grandpa had. Now I was sure the strange feelings in my body parts meant I was in love.

I dreamed about marrying Max one day and for quite a time that's all I ever thought about. In my mind I pictured the cozy little house we'd share, far away from the smokiness of Pittsburgh. A safe happy place where there was no hurt and no bad feelings. I knew Max wanted this too.

I decided we should talk about the way I felt. "I figure we'll get married someday," I said to him, real bashful.

He just looked at me and smiled kinda sad. Finally he said, "My mama always say I can't marry no cousin, Mary. Our babies would be monsters."

Max must've seen the look of horror on my face 'cause he put his arms around me and held me close. "That don't mean we can't be friends, Mary. The very best of friends. And I'll always love you. You know good as I do that's what really matters."

But I wanted to be more than friends. I sniffled into his shoulder and nodded my head anyway so he wouldn't think I was being ornery.

From then on every time I saw Max I'd hug him tight and my heart would swell with love for him. But all too soon my swelling heart withered like a prune.

"Mary," Max said to me one day, his face real sad. "My mama's fixing to move us to Philadelphia. We're leaving day after tomorrow. So I won't be able to see much of you no more."

It was like the bottom suddenly dropped out of my world. I turned away from him and fought back the flood of tears busting to get out.

He turned me back around and hugged me tight. "It won't be so bad. I'll send you letters, I promise. And besides, we're cousins, right? We're family. It won't be long before we see each other again." Then he hugged me even tighter and whispered real soft. "And don't ever stop practicing that jazz music. The way you pour so much love into that music tells me it must make you feel real good inside. And if it makes you feel good it'll make other folks feel good too."

That's exactly what I'd always thought and now Max thought the same thing. I leaned my face into his soft cotton shirt and breathed in the wonderful smell of him. That boy smell that was like fire and salt and laundry soap all mixed together. Then I felt his shirt get soaked with my tears. The wetness felt warm. So warm it burned my face and made me bawl all the more. Max's arms around me should have been a comfort but now they just caused me more hurt. All I could see was another loss.

That night I was pinin' so much for Max I couldn't sleep so I got out of bed and went to the parlor to try to work out my feelings on the piano. The parlor was dark and I couldn't hardly see a thing. But I heard funny noises. I turned on the lamp and saw my sister Mamie and her boyfriend Hugh on the couch kissing. They both kind of jumped when the light went on.

Mamie looked at me real cross. "You're not supposed to be in here. Now get on out."

My eyes got salty wet and I ran from the room. I went down to the basement and curled up on Grandpa's old cot. I could still smell the scent of him and that smell made my tears gush out even faster.

"I'm leaving, Mama," Mamie announced later that week.

"What you mean you leavin'?" Mama asked, her words slurred by drink.

"I'm gettin' married." Mamie lifted her chin like she was making a dare.

Before Mama could say a word Mamie sashayed on back to her room. I was right at her heels. "Who you gonna marry, Mamie? Is it that cute sax player, Hugh Floyd?"

Mamie right near preened. "Sure is. You already knew, didn't you, Mary?"

I smiled. "Well I had a strong feeling. 'Specially after I saw y'all smooching in the parlor that night."

She was sitting at her dressing table fussing with her lipstick. The bright red kind that smells like cherries. I stood at her bedroom door shuffling my feet.

"Mamie?"

"Yeah?" She was staring in the mirror with her mouth open, spreading the lipstick real slow and careful.

I paused and looked down at my shoes. "I don't think I can live in this house anymore without you here."

"Where would you live then?" She smacked her lips to even out the lipstick.

I shuffled my feet some more. "Could I . . . do you think . . . I could move in with you and Hugh?"

Mamie put down her lipstick and kept staring in the mirror. Then she turned around to face me. "I don't know, Mary. I mean, Hugh and me don't even know for sure where we're gonna live yet. It'll probably be a real small place."

"I don't care. All I need is a little corner or something to curl up in."

She folded her arms and narrowed her eyes. "Let me think about it."

"Oh please, Mamie. Don't leave me here all alone with Mama and Nanny and their gin drinking."

Mamie's red-painted lips got tight like they always did when I took on like that. "Hush-up, now, I'm thinking."

I stayed quiet but I couldn't stand still. I hopped from one foot to the other.

I thought Mamie would get real cross. But she surprised me and all of a sudden smiled in a kindly way like she felt sorry for me.

"I'll talk to Hugh," she said.

Well can you believe Hugh agreed to let me live with Mamie and him? He'd found a little house nearby. He said he could afford the rent because of all his sax-playing jobs. After that he and Mamie got married right quick. In a place called a wedding chapel they said. Didn't matter where to me cause I was so happy I almost felt like I got married too.

Hugh even got some of his music friends to help him move my piano over to the new house. From then on I didn't go to school much. But I worked like a lumberjack at my piano playing. My piano became my school. I learned new things from it every day. And Hugh was a jazz player to boot. I couldn't get much luckier than that I figured. Living in the same house with a jazz player almost made up for not having Max around anymore. But not quite.

On my thirteenth birthday Hugh came home with a beautiful wooden cabinet in the back of his pickup truck.

"Come on over and help me carry this thing in the house, Jim!" he hollered to our next door neighbor.

I stood by the window and watched Hugh and Jim lift the cabinet from the truck and lug it into the parlor.

"What in the world is this thing, Hugh?" I asked soon as Jim was out the door.

"This here's a Victor Victrola phonograph, the very latest model." His face glowed with pleasure as he ran his hand over the cabinet's shiny surface. "Just look at the sheen of this wood. It's solid mahogany. And all the hardware's plated with real gold. Is that quality or what?"

I walked over to look at the cabinet more close. I didn't care about the wood or hardware. I just wanted to know how it played music.

"Let me show you how this rascal works. The man at the store explained it all to me." Hugh lifted the middle part of the curved top. "See this round flat thing? That's the turntable, where the record goes. And this long gadget is the tone arm, which a needle attaches to."

"What's the needle do?"

Hugh gave me his proudest grin then ran back out to his truck, grabbed a couple boxes, and rushed back in the house. Inside the bigger box was a stack of discs each in its own brown paper case. He slid the top disc out of its case and placed it on the turntable. Then he opened the smaller box which was filled with sharp little metal things. He took one out and hooked it onto the end of the tone arm.

"Look here real close, Mary. See those grooves circling all around the disc? This here needle tracks those grooves and sends music clear through the tone arm and into the horn underneath. Just listen to this."

He turned the crank a few times and the turntable started to spin. Then he laid the needle in the record's outmost groove real careful. First there was a hazy swooshy sound. Then music started to play. It was piano music and it sounded kind of muffled but I gasped in amazement all the same.

"Who's that playing?" I asked, breathless. It was the happiest, jumpiest piano music I ever heard.

"This here's who's playing." Hugh closed the record box lid and on the front was a picture of a very fat young colored man. But you hardly could notice his fatness for the huge grin on his face which was about the jolliest grin I'd ever seen.

"What do you think of Mr. Thomas Fats Waller, Mary? This here's his very first record, hot off the press."

"I can't believe his left-hand notes, Hugh!"

"That left-hand style's called stride, the best piano playing there is. Just listen to him vamp at that piano. He's the bee's knees, ain't he?" Hugh started to snap his fingers and do a lively two-step.

I felt a thrill inside and did the same. Hugh took my hand and we got in rhythm with each other.

"How old's this Fats, Hugh?" I asked as my hips swayed and my feet slid to and fro in quick little steps.

"About eighteen, I hear. So you best get hustling, Mary. You only got five years to catch up to his playing."

I was sure I'd catch up a lot sooner than that.

Fats became my new inspiration. Here was a real live young man not much older than me who already was famous with his music. And his music sounded so new and different. I loved Fats's boogie-blues style and worked hard at getting that magical feeling in my own playing. His powerful left-hand and the jumpy happy tunes his right hand played made me want to practice all the more. Every day after I listened to Fats I sat at the piano and tried to get that big full sound like he did.

And as I woodshedded away at that piano more and more, people would stop by to listen. Neighbors mostly but also people that just happened to be passing by. Even truck drivers. They'd all go wild when they heard me play, dancing on the sidewalk like they were at some night club. They'd even come up on the front porch and watch me through the window.

People kept saying I played like a man which was quite a compliment. Nothing was worse than being told you play piano like a girl. Nobody thought girls had any power. 'Specially colored girls who were supposed to spend their whole life keeping quiet and pleasing folks. And girls weren't supposed to play jazz. A fool idea I aimed to change.

So I practiced and practiced playing my left hand louder than the right like Fats did on the record. Soon it came to me why he did that. Because that's where the rhythm and the feeling is, like a drum keeping a steady beat. Like Grandpa's heartbeat. And like Max's.

Truth was my heart still ached 'cause I missed Max so much. He promised he'd write but he hadn't yet. That had me worried. What if I never heard from him again? What a burden that would be on my aching heart. I wondered if even my music could ever heal a hurt like that.

But I tried hard as I could to put Max out of my mind by thinking about Fats Waller. About his music and how it got me playing piano like I never had before.

I about fell over when Hugh told me the news.

"Fats Waller's coming to town to play piano for a week-long show and Mr. Harper the producer hired me to play sax with the band!" He'd just run in the door all breathless. I'd never seen him so excited.

But his excitement was nothing compared to how I felt. My heart near jumped right out of me. "Oh Hugh, when's he coming? Do you think I could go with you one day that week to meet him?"

"Hold on, Mary," he said, trying to catch his breath, "let me answer one question at a time. First off, he's coming right soon. And yeah, I'll find a way to get you in somehow."

"What do you mean find a way to get me in?"

Hugh moved closer to me and hushed his voice. "The place Fats is playing is a speakeasy, which means people drink booze there even though the Prohibition's outlawed it. You need a password to get in."

"A password? What's that?"

"A secret word that tells them you're not a cop trying to sneak in and bust the place."

"Oh." This speakeasy place sounded a little scary, but I knew it would all turn out fine long as Hugh was with me. And I'd do just about anything for the chance to meet the real live Fats Waller.

Hugh and me took the trolley to the speakeasy the very first day of Fats's show. Fats was easy to spot. There was no missing him. He was so big he about filled the place. But his face didn't look jolly like on the record box. He sat at a table spread with blank music paper and watched with a real serious look on his face while Mr.

Harper rehearsed the dancing girls.

Hugh grinned at me then winked and went off to get set up with the band. I stood staring at Fats, afraid if I opened my mouth all that would come out would be one big stutter.

Finally Mr. Harper yelled, "Okay, Fats, we're ready! Write us some tunes for this dance number!"

Fats started writing with a fury and it seemed he'd never stop. He must've wrote six tunes while he sat there at that table. Then he went up to the bandstand where the piano was and played all this new music for Mr. Harper.

I snuck up closer to watch his hands. He was wild. He was all over the piano and it seemed the piano didn't have enough keys for him. Truth was it scared me to watch him. So I closed my eyes and listened real hard. And a strange thing happened. Just like back in Atlanta when I watched Mama play the pump organ I could hear what note Fats was going to play next. Like telling somebody's fortune. Then I could see what I felt in my heart and I knew what was happening with Fats's music.

Soon as Fats stopped playing Hugh went over to him and pointed at me. "See that little girl down there? She can play everything you wrote today."

Fats looked down at me from the bandstand then broke into a merry laugh. "Go on from here, man! You telling me this little gal can play more than Chopsticks?"

"Can't nobody play piano like Miss Mary here," Hugh told him.

Fats grinned his big old grin. "I don't believe it. Come on up here to the piano, Baby Doll, and show old Fats what you can do."

I about froze from fright but somehow I made my way up to the bandstand and sat at the piano.

"Okay, Baby Doll," Fats said, kind of snickering but friendly. "Let me hear those little fingers make some big sounds."

I put my fingers on the keys, took a deep breath and started to play. I don't know how but somehow, like magic, I played everything I'd just heard.

After I finished I looked up at Fats and he was staring down at me like he'd been knocked in the head. He picked me up right off that piano bench and swooped me in the air, roaring like a crazy man. "You smash those keys near hard as I do, Baby Doll!" Then he put me down and looked at Hugh. "Where'd she learn to play like that? You teach her?"

"Naw, she learn by herself. Don't need no teacher training, that one."

"Just like me, I guess," Fats said, grinning down at me. "That's how I learned, teaching myself. And you play like me, Baby Doll, always playing your left hand louder than your right. That's where the beat and the feeling is, you know, in your left hand. Just like keeping a steady drum beat."

I didn't tell him I already knew that. But my shyness eased up a little and I grinned back up at him.

Then he did something that almost made me fall on the floor. He told Mr. Harper to hire me for the week. He wanted me to play that very night while folks were coming into the speakeasy and finding their seats, before the band and Fats started their show.

My heart thumped with such a commotion. But there was no time for jitters. Folks were already starting to stream in and sit at the little tables that were scattered around the room. And Fats had disappeared somewhere to get ready for the show.

I sat at the piano and played without fear during the audience's settling down time since everybody was talking and drinking and not really listening. After a time Fats came out to the piano and everybody in the room stood up, clapping and cheering. I scooted on down to one of the little tables fast as I could and joined in the clapping. Then I sat and watched Fats work his wonders.

Suddenly in the middle of his piano antics Fats turned his head and looked right at me with his big sparkly grin. "Come on up to this stage and show these fine people how you can play piano to beat the band, Miss Mary!" His roaring voice sailed through the big hall and hundreds of pairs of eyes turned to me. I about keeled over.

"Get yourself right up here, Baby Doll!" he yelled again while his magical fingers kept vamping away at the keys. "Show 'em how the little piano girl can smash these ivories hard as a man!"

My belly did a somersault. Then another one. Could I do this? I forced myself to stand and start walking up to the bandstand.

Soon as I got to the stage Fats stopped playing, stood up, grabbed my hand and pulled me onto the piano bench. My fingers were shaking but I started to play and before I knew it Fats was on the bench beside me playing one his roaring strides underneath my steamy blues tune.

The audience went wild, cheering and laughing. Everybody was on their feet dancing and having a ball. When Fats and me finally finished, both of us panting and sweating and grinning, the folks in the audience clapped and whooped like they'd never stop.

Fats had me play piano with him every night that week. I wished Max could be there. But him not being there didn't hurt nearly so bad as I thought it would. I thought I needed Max. Now I knew I needed music more. Especially jazz because now I knew what jazz meant to me. It was my bridge to other people's worlds. And to their minds and hearts. And I knew jazz would always be my most faithful friend. It would live in my heart forever, and it would save me.

Sarah Bruce Kelly

"The Girl Who Beat the Band" is based on the true story of jazz legend Mary Lou Williams.

Also by Sarah Bruce Kelly:

Vivaldi's Muse, winner of the Tyler R. Tichelaar Award for Best Historical Fiction

Jazz Girl: A Novel about Mary Lou Williams and her Early Life

The Red Priest's Annina: A Novel of Vivaldi and Anna Girò

sarahbrucekelly@gmail.com
facebook.com/sarahbrucekelly

TRAIL'S END
Richard Lutman

The life Dan Reeves knew best was over. Someone else would have to stay in the line shack for thirty a month and found. He'd saved enough to put something down on a ranch. Then he'd be his own boss and away from the bastards like his boss Biff Thomas.

The cattle drive had been the last for the seventy-year old who sold his ranch unexpectedly and decided to live with his daughter, Sarah Jane, in Denver. The little tease liked to stand next to one of Biff's hands, sometimes close enough for their arms ever so slightly to touch. He'd seen her type before, bored with nothing better to do. Even the toughest cowhand was aroused by her perfume. Someday she'd get what was coming to her. Dan wished he could be around when it happened.

He had been with Biff for five years, long enough to hate the old bastard and his daughter who needed to be disciplined. Biff liked to curse and spit at the new hands and thought nothing of giving them a good beating. Those who quit were never forgiven. Those he fired swore revenge.

For a day or two Dan had sat around with the other ranch hands and talked about what they were going to do now the cattle drive had ended. Some would stay with the new owners, while others moved on. A few of the younger hands dreamed about finding Sarah Jane alone. Dan's dream was to buy a ranch in Cutler's Valley about fifteen miles east of the town of Devlin where he was now headed.

After four days of riding all Dan wanted was a mattress and a long night's sleep with a roof over his head. He'd had enough of nights on the hard ground in his bedroll. It would be good to climb off his horse, get a room, and later after a wash down or bath, treat himself to a restaurant meal, a few drinks and a woman to be with.

It was late afternoon when he reached Devlin. The town

smelled like cow dung and his bottom itched from being in the saddle too long. He didn't care how he smelled or looked. His horse picked its way down the main street. He wanted to feel the town's rhythm. His future was at stake and he needed time to think. He was a tall muscular man with dark hair and blue eyes the endless, lonely ranch work, too often marked with violence and disappointment, had combined to leave their marks on him. He looked older than his thirty years. His slight limp was the result of being thrown from a horse. The long scar down his left check came from being tangled in barbed wire.

Facing the rutted, dusty main street was a church, general store, a hotel, bank, and a stable. A few houses had flower gardens in front. What a contrast he thought. The town was full of noisy revelers.

Decorations and banners announcing the fifth year anniversary of the town adorned the buildings and fluttered above his head. He continued down the street, the excitement of the celebration in the air. Celebrations always brought in the women. He could use one right now no matter how bad he smelled.

He guided his horse toward the hotel, swung down and stretched, ironing out his muscles, then brushed the dirt from his clothes. For a moment it felt funny to be standing on the ground. The hotel was weather beaten, but solid looking with a large porch.

The lobby stank of unwashed bodies. The clerk at the desk was reading a newspaper.

"Got a room?" asked Dan.

"Full up." Said the clerk, not looking at him. "Not a room to be had anywhere. Town's five years old today. Never thought we'd make it. But Devlin, he never gave up. Wouldn't let us either. He's a man to be reckoned with. Like the Devil himself when he gets mad. When the history of the West is written you mark my words, he'll be in it."

Dan reached over, grabbed the clerk and shook him. "The hell with you and your hotel." He strode back outside, fighting to control his anger. A town should be shaped by the people in it, not by one man Dan thought. He began to dislike Devlin the way he disliked Biff Thomas. The chalky dust stirred up from the street by the light breeze strung his eyes.

He led his horse toward Devlin's Golden Lady, tied it up and headed inside where he stood for a moment adjusting to the dim light.

The odors of whiskey, cheap perfume, and rancid, sweaty bodies filled the room. Pictures of scantily clad women hung on the walls. Behind the bar was a large smoky mirror. Instinctively he knew the man at a table against the back wall with his legs straight out in front of him was Devlin. He was a big mustachioed man who looked to be in his late forties. A cane had been hooked over a nearby chair. Dan stopped when he saw Devlin engaged in a heated conversation with a well-dressed man who kept turning his white Stetson around in his hands. The two men behind Devlin were tense and alert for trouble. One was square shouldered and solid looking with a crooked face. The other, rangy and shifty-eyed. One or two of the customers looked up from the bar, then went back to their whiskey.

"Market's dropping, Tom," said Devlin.

For a moment Tom stopped turning his hat.

"I need ten thousand, Paul." His voice rose to desperation.

"You owe me over seven now," said Devlin.

"I've got a man in Wellington with four thousand head of stock." Tom clenched his fists.

"Then sell."

"You know I can't do that," said Tom. His jaw tightened and he looked around the room, for a moment catching Dan's eyes. There was a look of desperation in them.

"And I can't risk ten thousand on the gamble the market will go up and you'll get out from under," said Devlin.

"I've been down before and I've always climbed back," said Tom.

"Not this time," said Devlin.

"Why? I'm asking you why? After all these years we've known each other, you owe me at least an explanation."

"We've all got our troubles, Tom. I'm sorry." He focused his eyes on the man in front of him.

"You've been waiting for this. You've never been sorry about anything."

"You have it all wrong," said Devlin. Dan noticed the forced concern behind the words.

"You dirty son-of-a-bitch," said Tom. "How much longer do you think you can push others like me around?" He drew his pistol and aimed it at Devlin. "Tell your men to put their guns on the table. This is between you and me."

The bar patrons stopped as if caught in mid space.

Devlin signaled the two men behind him and they placed their guns on the nearest table.

Dan instinctively stepped forward, grabbed Tom's arm from behind and knocked the pistol to the floor then kicked it away. Devlin flipped up his coat and leveled his pistol at Tom.

"Now get out of here," said Devlin. "And don't ever come back. Ever. You're finished in this territory."

"I didn't mean it, Paul." Tom sounded close to tears. "I don't know what happened to me. Please. I've never done anything like this before. Please."

"I hate men like you." Contempt crossed Devlin's face. "You disgust me with your whining."

Devlin made a slight movement of his head. The two men took hold of Tom's arms and dragged him outside.

"You'll pay for this. You hear me. You'll pay."

"The next round's on me," said Devlin to the bar patrons. Someone let out a whoop and the patrons swarmed the bar.

"Obliged. Name's Devlin. Welcome to my town," he said extending his hand. Dan shook it. The grip was powerful. His face hard and cruel. Sharp piercing eyes darted around the room as though he were expecting something to happen that he didn't want to miss.

"Dan Reeves. Just finished a drive."

"Sit."

Dan sat as Devlin studied him. Dan returned his gaze.

"Whiskey?"

Dan nodded and took the glass offered him. The two men returned. Dan saw blood on the man with the crooked face. The other brushed the dust from his clothes then rolled a cigarette.

Dan wondered who else Devlin's hired hands had taken care of.

"The big one's Steve," said Devlin. "The other's Jake. Boys, meet Dan Reeves."

The two men nodded.

"I owe you," said Devlin.

They drank again, Dan took the whiskey slow. After the days on horseback he thought he had never tasted whiskey as good.

"I don't know what got into Tom. He seems to forget who it was that made this town what it is and gave them a chance. They just can't understand."

Devlin gave Dan a hard stare that made him uneasy.

"Well, Mr. Reeves, what do you know about dancing?"

"Dancing?"

"It's been a while since I was on the dance floor," said Devlin. "But my wife Judith likes to dance. She means a great deal to me and I want her to be happy. I'd like you to take her to the dance tonight. Then we can talk about the future. This town needs men like you."

But not men like Devlin, Dan thought. Maybe he'd better move on and find a ranch somewhere else. If he stayed he knew he'd have to face Devlin at some point. He wasn't afraid of him, but didn't like the odds he'd seen.

Devlin leaned forward and put his hand on Dan's shoulder and squeezed it.

"It's important she has a good time. She's a very beautiful woman and I know the effect a beautiful woman can have on a man." His face hardened.

He poured out a shot for each of them. Then without waiting for an answer he drank his down.

"I'll tell her the good news. I'm sure she'll be delighted to hear I've found her a dancing partner."

What kind of a woman would marry someone like Devlin? He figured he'd find out soon enough.

Devlin rose clumsily to his feet, pressed his legs against the table, then took the cane in his hand and shuffled toward the stairs, motioning Dan to follow. He stopped for a few moments before climbing to the second floor. Once at the top of the stairs, he rested against a chair placed outside a door, then knocked. The door opened. A woman with brown hair stood in the doorway. Her blue shirt was open to a strong looking throat, revealing an expanse of browned skin.

She stepped aside as her husband entered leaving the door open enough for Dan to see half the room. Had he left the door open on purpose?

Devlin sat heavily on the bed. She gave her husband a look Dan couldn't read.

"You bastard. You've been drinking." She turned away and walked to the bureau.

"I've found someone to go to the dance with you tonight," said Devlin. "A harmless cowboy. He helped me with some trouble downstairs. I want to pay him back."

"No," she said.

"You're going and that's it." Devlin's cane slammed against the head board.

She laughed.

"What's so funny?"

"You are," she said.

"What do you mean?"

"Will you run him out of town when it's over? Like you've done before." She turned to face him.

"I owe him for saving my life," said Devlin.

"I wish he hadn't."

He raised his cane as if to strike her. She didn't move. Her eyes bored into him.

"If it wasn't for me and this town where'd you be?"

"The hell with your town."

"I should have let you rot in that rooming house."

"Then why didn't you?"

Devlin took a step towards her, then put his hands on her

shoulders and squeezed them.

"You're hurting me." She turned and hit him. His return blow staggered her back. Dan fought the urge to burst into the room.

"His name's Dan Reeves."

"I don't care what his name is," she said.

He took hold of her wrists with one hand. He forced her to her knees. Then struck the cane against the floor next to her.

"All right," she said in a weary voice. "All right."

He tossed her wrists aside and sneered at her. She stood up fighting the sobs that shook her body.

Devlin crossed to the door and motioned to Dan. He wondered if it was only the whiskey that made him feel edgy. What would it be like to push him down the stairs and watch him die? He paused in the doorway, first looking at Devlin then his wife. Blood oozed from the cut on her lip.

Her brown eyes were lit with golden sparkles. Her perfume reminded him of crushed clover.

She held out her hand and he took it. It was cold.

"Judith." Her straight forward look unsettled him.

"I want you to wear the blue dress with the white shawl," said Devlin, who had stopped by the door. "The one I bought you in St. Louis, you look good in it. I like two things in this world, Mr. Reeves, fast horses and good-looking women. When I die I want to be made into a beautiful woman's saddle."

He lowered his body into the chair. As she closed the door, Devlin's cane blocked it.

She took his arm and led to the other side of the room. She motioned him to talk in a whisper.

"Paul's very particular about who his friends are. Those he can't control, he frightens away or beats down. He's a cunning man. Don't misjudge him by anything he says. When a town like this grows, it's supposed to take a lot of time. Paul changed all that. He saw the possibilities and couldn't wait to start, no matter what the cost. He was driving too fast over a narrow road and thrown from a wagon. He had the horses shot and the wagon burned. If I were you I'd head on out of here."

He looked at her and knew he couldn't.

By seven o'clock the sounds of the dance in the school house spilled over into the night. A straw-colored moon hung between the peaks of the mountains, while on every side fireflies swayed back and forth as if moving to the same music as the dancers.

Devlin had positioned himself where he could survey the room. He nodded at passersby and sometimes shook his head when he was spoken to. A long table had been set up against the wall. In the back of the room a fiddler played "Billy in the Low ground" with a long seesawing elbow and called out the dance in a whiskey voice.

"Swing your partner. Now your corner. Do-si-do your partner. Do-si-do your corner. Allemande left with your left hand. Grand right and left around the hall. Now promenade all."

Dan led Judith back to their square, bowing to each other and the others in the square as the dance ended.

He followed her back through the open doors to the large porch. Steve and Jake watched from the shadows.

He realized the blue dress made her look more desirable than any woman he had ever seen. Her eyes teased him. Her hair was soft and inviting, and he wanted to run his hands through it.

"Take me away from here."

Her face was close and full of enchantment. Her lavender perfume made him giddy. He couldn't stop himself and kissed her softly, lingering over her lips. Her arms went around him. She kissed him fiercely and pressed so close to his body he couldn't move.

Jake leapt at Dan knocking him to his knees. Judith stumbled and fell. Dan shook his head trying to clear it. Steve came at him fast. Dan's fist struck upward and caught Steve in the stomach. He bent over then slumped to the ground. Dan was off balance from his blow to Steve as Jake saw his chance and drove his knee into Dan's chest. The blow staggered him backward. Dan steadied himself and struck Jake with a short jab. His head rocked back, and he stood long enough for Dan to measure him and send another blow against his face. Jake lost his balance, and fell sprawling.

The fiddling broke off and the dance came to a stop. Devlin was on his feet, pistol drawn. Steve's hand flashed for his revolver. Before he could shoot Judith stepped between them. Steve hesitated and Dan knocked the revolver away. He grabbed her and they ran into the night toward the horses. Devlin's shots shattered the darkness around them.

After riding through the night they stopped to rest by a creek that ran in a silver thread to the mountains. Even the murmur of the water and the songs of waking birds couldn't make Dan forget what happened at the dance. He wondered what it would be like now they were alone where nothing could interrupt them. She owed him for helping her escape from Devlin.

Over the distant ranges, a small black cloud poured a dark mass of rain on some isolated spot. The sky was listless, flat looking, and bright. The air was laden with sulphorous smoke as lightning began to flash. The wind rose and the leaves shook. The first drop thumped on the earth, and another, and another, exploding the dirt into little craters. The lightning and rain moved closer, breaking the sky open.

The rain increased. The drops stung their faces and made it hard to see. They rode into deepening darkness.

The trail fell away into a steep gully of a creek. The horse's hooves slipped and Dan grabbed for her reins. The horses toppled both of them over into the gully. Dan hit his head. Judith let out a cry. Before he passed out, Dan remembered stones glistening in the roaring rain.

The tops of the hills on either side of the creek were sandy with short, tufting grass. The morning breeze was fresh and sweet. Gophers whistled and insects rose from the grass in thick clouds to torment them.

Dan had lost track of time, but knew they had been walking for several hours by the position of the sun. The horses were nowhere in sight. At the bottom of the next hill a small deserted town clung to the prairie. Weeds grew in the main street. Several cabins, a livery stable, general store, saloon and church stood in a solitary row. Dan hurried to the first cabin, which had been built next to a small grassy mound.

"Hellooo. Hellooo."

There was no answer, only the sound of their breathing.

"Hellooo. Hellooo."

He banged on the door.

"Where is everybody?" she said.

"This could have been a plague town or maybe the townspeople just gave up and left. Towns like this are cursed."

She looked at him.

He pushed against the door and it swung open. Sun streamed through the windows. He looked around then opened a cupboard. A tin of coffee and several cans of beans had been placed on a shelf. She stood next to him. Her musky odor excited him.

He bent to kiss her. She slapped him.

"You bitch."

"Just like a man. You see a woman like me and all you want to do is make love to her. Get out of here. I want nothing to do with you."

His eyes blazed as he opened the door. Devlin stepped out from the side of the cabin. The single whipping throw of his pistol discharged. The shot spun Dan around. His body lost its vibrant tension. He slumped. His head drooped forward. Then he swayed and fell. Judith screamed. Her face reddened. Anger and hate choked her. She swung at her husband. He ducked, laughing. She swung again.

"Did you really think you could get away?"

"You disgust me. You're nothing but a lousy cripple."

He regarded her blankly then raised his pistol and shot her in the heart. She fell quickly to the ground, reached out towards Dan and fell still. The red blossoming from her chest like a rose.

The wind blowing through the street was like the sound of a fiddler playing faster.

"Trails End" is a Western Noir. A western is defined as being set in the frontier between 1870 to 1890. My novel "A Patch of Dirt," scheduled for publication in 2016, is a contemporary western noir set in present day Montana.

Website: www.wordrealm.net
Facebook: https://www.facebook.com/Richard.lutman.92
Twitter: https://twitter.com/Wudeeplo
wudeep@sc.rr.com

Published works:
I Like A Little Bit Of The Handsome Americans Myself (Novella)
The Holy Terriers: A Dogoir (Non Fiction)
Iron Butterfly (Novella) ...and 21 short stories

Chapbooks:
Altered Images, To Be With You Forever, When I Moved The Earth (a narrative poem)

Novelette:
The Nut Tree

This story was previously published in *Beyond Imagination*

A Special Dinner
By Maureen O'Brien

    I was running late for work but was consumed with a need to check on Mom. I don't know why. Just some intuitive thing which, over the past two weeks had been happening often.
    Maybe it had something to do with our recent phone conversations. What had happened to the long, news filled, chats we used to have? Just yesterday, she had dismissed me again. "Marcus, I really can't talk right now. I have to go Sweetie." She seemed to be so busy, always on the go and in a hurry to get somewhere. What was she up to?
    I waited after ringing the doorbell but when there was no answer, I let myself in. The door was unlocked. Mom doesn't believe in locking doors. She always says if someone breaks in to rob me, he'll probably look around, feel sorry for me and leave something instead.
    I found her in the dining room where she was putting the finishing touches on her table setting. I couldn't believe my eyes. A vintage lace tablecloth covered the table I had enjoyed as a child. Fine china dishes were set for three. The centerpiece was an arrangement of colorful hydrangeas which I was sure, she had picked from her prodigious garden. White cloth napkins, shaped into swans were peeking out of cobalt blue wine goblets. She stepped back to admire her handiwork. I detected her whispering something but couldn't make it out.
    "Hey Mom, sorry to barge in on you. Hope I didn't startle you but I guess you were so busy you didn't hear the doorbell. By the way, your table looks beautiful."
      She didn't appear at all startled. Paying little attention to me, she continued to rearrange the flatware. I had never seen so many

different size forks on our dining room table and what were those little knives for.

"Well," I announced, "Set a pretty table and they will come."

I don't think she heard me over the blaring television. Matt Lauer of The Today Show was going on and on about how terrible it was that Lindsey Vonn would not be able to compete in the Sochi Olympics.

"Oh Sweetheart," Mom said, "What a nice surprise. But isn't this just awful? That poor girl has been training so hard and now her knee went out again. I swear it makes me want to cry. Can you imagine?"

Something was really off here. Mom had never been particular about setting the table. Most times the dishes didn't match. She called it her eclectic touch. I was sure she had never owned a lace tablecloth. The wine goblets—where did they come from? I had to get to the bottom of this and so I repeated my comment in question form, "Set a pretty table and they will come?"

"Well, aren't you the cutie. What movie did that come from? Something about baseball, wasn't it? That handsome Robert Redford starred in that, right? Lindsey doesn't play baseball, dear. She's a skier. Don't you watch the news?"

There was no doubt that Mom was losing her hearing. She refused to wear a hearing aid, insisting that she could hear everything and anything worth listening to. Dad had always called it selective hearing. It must be genetic. My wife described me the same way.

I decided on a direct approach. "Mom, I was just wondering why you're going so festive with the dinner table. Are you expecting someone special to dine with you tonight?"

Giving me a quick peck on the cheek, she walked into the kitchen and started loading the dishwasher. Running water and clanking dishes combined with Mom humming a tune. Mom doesn't know the words to any songs but she loves music so she hums a lot. Her friends call her "The Hummer."

I checked my watch and realized that I couldn't hang out much longer. To be honest, my patience was wearing thin. "Mom, are you keeping something from me. Who is coming for dinner?"

Mom let out a big sigh and threw her arms wide open. "Come over here Sweetheart", she chortled. "Give me a big hug. And then, we have to go wake up the boys."

"The boys? Did I hear you say boys, Miss Nora?" The deep, gentle voice was accompanied by heavy, plodding footsteps coming down the stairs. A boisterous, hearty laugh followed, making him sound like Santa coming down the chimney. He slipped into the kitchen as if it had been his routine for years.

His size was astonishing. He took up the entire entrance to the kitchen. Deep crevices lined his face as if chiseled from red clay. His thick, bushy eyebrows were so expressive, they seemed to be engaged in a conversation all their own. He was so homely and yet handsome at the same time. His clothing was shabby but clean and he was freshly shaved.

He extended his huge hand to me, "You must be Marcus. I've heard so many good things about you. And now, if my memory serves me right, I think I promised you a gourmet breakfast, Miss Nora. Can you join us Marcus?"

"Well, this all sounds very cozy Mister...Mister. I didn't get your name, sir. You may have heard good things about me but I know nothing about you. So if you, and you too Mom, could fill me in here, I would appreciate it."

I felt ambushed. Stone-faced, with my arms crossed on my chest, I turned and stared at Mom, demanding an explanation.

"Okay Sweetheart, it really is quite simple. I've been volunteering at the St. Joseph's Shelter for the last three months. That's where I met George and his son, Jason. They've been homeless for seven months now and well...Father Flynn called me last week. You remember Father Flynn, don't you? Anyway, he mentioned that the shelter was bursting at the seams. They just don't have enough room for everyone who needs a roof over their head and a hot meal."

"Well, that *is* pretty simple Mom. So you just decided on your own, without consulting me, that you would open up our home to people you barely know?" A pregnant pause. "That was a question, Mom."

"Yes, I know that was a question, dear. And here's the answer. First of all, I've gotten to know George and Jason quite well. They've been doing most of the cooking at the shelter and boy, can they cook. George was the head chef at the Ritz Carlton in Boston, but it came under new management and well…And Jason wants to follow in his dad's footsteps, so he has a full scholarship and has been attending The Culinary Institute in the city. Quite a resume don't you think? Secondly, and more importantly, this is not as you called it, *our home*. This is my home and I can do whatever I want to do in my own home. Sorry to sound so harsh dear, but I don't feel you're being very understanding."

Stunned, I watched Mom parade over to George and wrap an apron around his ample waist. I remained, silently in place, the place I had been put in.

Mom tented her hands and turned to face George. "I don't know about anyone else but I'm starving. All I dreamt about last night were the Eggs Benedict that were promised me for this morning. But George, first come look at the table I've set for us tonight. You promised me a five-course dinner so I went to the thrift shop and bought---well, just come and look for yourself. And then you can go wake Jason up."

I remained in the kitchen, fiddling with the salt and pepper shakers. My mother's assertiveness shocked me…I couldn't recall ever seeing her like this. My mind traveled back in time. I recalled the day I arrived home with an injured bird in my coat pocket. I was about seven years old and my father was adamant that we were not keeping it. Mom's words came back to me now. In her inimitable sweet style, she turned to my Dad and said…Well of course, we will keep this little bird, dear. And we will nurse it back to good health and then let him fly away. But not until then.

Mom has always been assertive, I thought. Maybe I need to stop being so overly protective. After Dad had passed away, I thought it was my job to take care of her. It was obvious to me now that she was quite capable of doing that herself. Okay, what better time than right now to let her start doing just that.

I ambled into the dining room and watched as Mom told George a little story about each of her Thrift Shop purchases. George was smiling, nodding his appreciation of all her selections. "Shouldn't someone wake Jason up?" I asked.

George winked at me and erupted with laughter. "Believe me, that won't be necessary. Fry the bacon and they will come."

"That includes me, George. Work can wait. I can't wait to taste your Eggs Benedict."

I turned toward Mom, my arms wide open. "But first things first, Mom. I sure could use that hug right about now."

Please see my contact info under the story "Forgiveness."

The Battle of Bear Creek Bridge
By Dee Senchak

Another Saturday afternoon with nothing to do, so I head for Bear Creek. It's a nothin' kind of creek with a nothin' kind of a bridge over it that doesn't compare to the concrete and steel bridges in Pittsburgh; but at least things move here, unlike everywhere else in this dumb town. I jump across the gully. The gravel slides under my feet and I slip into the water. If Dad hadn't been transferred, I could be at a Pirates game right now instead of sitting in ankle deep water looking stupid. This is one time I'm glad I'm alone.

Reaching under me, I pull up a cave man's hardball; a stone all smooth and round, well, lopsided round anyway. I toss it onto the bridge, kick a couple more stones loose, and pile them on the bridge. There are plenty of smaller smooth stones in the creek bed so I toss a bunch of them onto the bridge too. Then I climb up on the bridge and with my engineer's eye - Uncle Fred always says I'm going to be an engineer like him - I stack two smaller stones on the big stones and start building an army of stone soldiers on the rusty bridge railing.

My army looks good. I hop up and wrap my legs around the narrow metal railing of the bridge, rest my belly and my chin on it, and examine the troops. These guys will talk to me as much as the kids at my new school. They don't.

But looking at my army ready for battle, I forget where I am and start to feel good.

A car slows down as it goes by. I smile so they don't think I'm dead or something. They step on the gas and leave me in a cloud of white exhaust smoke. Great Camouflage! And just in time, too, because I can hear the enemy on the other side of the hill.

When the smoke clears, I can see heat waves at the top of the hill. The enemy is on the move; heading toward us.

The stone soldier closest to me wobbles just a little as I poke him and give the command, "Get ready men."

I press my cheek against the rusty railing. There's a slight buzzing in my ear. Signals bounce through my 12-year molars like Morse code dots and dashes. The message: *My power will topple your army.*

"Prepare for battle," I shout as vibrations jiggle my belly.

The enemy is charging toward my army at full speed. The stone soldiers begin trembling. A hundred lions are roaring in my ears. The vibrations in my belly grow to rumblings that shake my whole body.

"Charge," I yell at the top of my lungs and keep my mouth open to keep my teeth from clattering together. The enemy is on us. My stone soldiers are shaking and bouncing like roaches on a roller coaster. A couple are teetering on the edge of the railing. I press my knees tightly to the bucking-bronco-bridge and watch my stone army break ranks. They bounce apart. Some roll onto the bridge. Some roll off the other side and go Ker plunk, splash into the water. Then my head starts to bob too much for me to know if any of my soldiers still have their heads on.

The enemy's final volley comes in a whoosh of warm air that blasts what's left of my army off the bridge. I put a hand out to catch them. Then I hop down and scoop up all the stones that fell off the bridge into the creek.

I have to work quickly now. I need to rebuild my army before the next 18-wheeler comes charging down the hill and across this great bridge.

Please see my contact info under the story "Mattress Man."

Three Knocks
By L. Thomas Cook

The moment I stepped into the Gospel Diner the aroma of fried foods, decades old, hung in the air. The overwhelming scent, and the sizzle of Crisco, welcomed me home. As a teenager, I'd spent many an afternoons in this place mainly because it was the only diner in Gospel City.

It seemed frozen in time. The linoleum black and white checker squared floor with yellow streaks from over waxing, the white Formica surface of the breakfast counter scratched and chipped on the edges, and the booths with duct tape where age had ripped the cushions. The overhead florescent lights flickered with an occasional crackle giving the few customers in there a pallor look. Was that something new? I climbed onto a wobbly stool at the counter. A middle aged man with shaggy black hair and familiar face I couldn't recall, sat at the end leaving six stools between us. He nodded expressionless in my direction.

"Just coffee," I said to the waitress with a name tag that read Janie.

Behind me in one of the booths sat a couple unlike any others in town. The man wore a leather biker's jacket, an eagle patch along the sleeve. Across from him was a woman with snake tattoos. Both in their thirties. They were examples of the occasional strangers who drove through town on their way to someplace interesting, stopping only for directions or a quick bite to eat. I caught glimpses of them in the mirror. Their movements slow and absentminded as they sipped from their cups and stared off.

I became lost in their sleepy trance until startled when an old, bearded man stood next to me. An odd coldness ran up my left leg as he brushed against it when he lifted himself onto the stool.

He introduced himself as Trapper Crane, confessed his age to be 78, and smiled inflamed upper gums. From what I could see of this wide-open gesture, he was missing teeth from the incisors to the molars. I think he noticed my attempt to hide repulsion because he explained that the "Dang dentist in town is a no good cheat. The dentures this dang fool no-good rat snake made pinches my gums and makes me talk funny." He smiled again with drool trickling from the left corner of his mouth either unaware of the saliva or not embarrassed by it – I'm leaning towards not embarrassed. Every word spoken with spittle, he leaned a little closer to me, and grinned cockeyed. I caught a whiff of something stale, maybe mold, that and the way he glared, as if he held the ability to look through me, gave me the creeps.

I shifted on my stool wishing it wasn't bolted to the floor so I could move away, although I don't think it would have helped. He pressed me for my name.

"Shelby Buttermen," I said while avoiding his eyes. "I just got back to town."

"No fooling?" Trapper slurped back the saliva that soaked the corner of his mouth. "You any relation to the Buttermens' that lived in Gospel City fur…" he scratched his head under the stained and dirty John Deer cap he wore, "fur near as a hundred some odd years as far as I can recall?"

I sipped my coffee while I silently prayed he'd go away. The waitress behind the counter seemed to take pity. Not much older than me, her hair was pinned up in a bun that was out dated along with her overuse of mascara and rouge. A nice smile, she refilled my cup and rolled her eyes in Trapper's direction.

"Trapper Crane," she said, "you best not be making a nuisance of yourself with my customers. They far and few as they is."

Trapper chuckled like an old cowboy from T.V shows I watched as a child. A kind of 'Hee hee' country twang except it was missing the 'darn tooting.'

"Don't get your panties in a knot, Janie," Trapper said. "We just sitting and chewing the coffee grinds. Ain't that so, Shelly?"

I offered a quick nod to Janie indicating I felt safe enough, for now anyway. She grinned and said, "He's harmless," before she moved down the counter line.

"So is ya kin to the Buttermens'?" Trapper asked again.

I nodded and added cream to my coffee.

Trapper slapped his knee and laughed. "Well I'll be."

"Did you know them?" I asked.

"Nope," he said and gummed a piece of toast he had soaked in his coffee.

I looked sideways at him ready to call the waitress back, pay for my breakfast, and get out of there. People like him were the reason I left Gospel City and headed to New York. I longed for intelligent conversations, well-read individuals, and deeper meanings to life than sitting around a diner with the same replicated farmers who filled the town for generations. They always smelled like manure and moist dirt. Their hands calloused and fingernails caked under with dried up river mud.

"Heard 'bout them though," Trapper said. "Nice folks." He winked. "What brings you back here?"

"I'm a writer," I said as if that would explain it.

"Writer of what? Them there fancy books?"

"Fancy books?" I tried not to laugh. "Well I don't know if I'd call them *fancy books* exactly. I write fiction. Mostly mysteries. But I'm thinking about writing a nonfiction on life in the country versus the city."

"That so?" He gulped his coffee. A drip rained from his lower lip lost forever in his full faced gray beard that probably hid crumbs of fried chicken from years ago.

"I should get going." I signaled for the waitress.

"Hold on." Trapper took hold of my wrist. "You sure 'bout the kind of story you want to tell?"

I shivered to the bone with his hand wrapped around me. The creeps turned to fear. Or, was it dread? His grimy hands, the dark eyes, the light washing him in shadows, played tricks on my imagination. Pulling my arm back, I tried to relax my nerves. "Do you read, Mr…?"

"Trapper. Call me Trapper. We ain't exactly strangers."

"Excuse me? What does that mean? I just met—"

He laughed that cowpoke chuckle again. "What I mean is, I know something 'bout your family. Ain't any Buttermans' left in Gospel City. 'Cepting of course you, here, now. Kind of odd coincidence since it's the anniversary and all."

"What anniversary and all?" I turned my stool to face him.

He shrugged and brushed his hand down his curly, bristled beard. "One of them there legends I guess most folk would call it."

"Urban legends?" I snorted. "I don't have time for that and I don't believe in them."

He gazed at me with dark brown eyes cloudy with age or was it something else that came from deep inside? The chill I felt since he appeared grew stronger. I avoided his stare and slipped off the stool. "I need to go. It was…interesting meeting you, Mr…Trapper."

"Go where?" he said to my back. I turned to face him again and wished I hadn't. The flickering light gave me a headache and cast a bluish-green tone to his skin. "Ain't ya curious to hear 'bout your ancestors? I'd think a writer would be mighty curious. 'Course maybe you heard the stories and don't want to hear them again or…" he lifted his dull eyes to me, "you don't remember them."

"I've heard plenty of urban legends." Who hadn't heard of Bloody Mary or the legend of the young girl hitchhiking on the side of the road? I never really knew how the stories got started. Maybe from some truth exaggerated over time or from tales told to children to make them behave. "And I heard more than enough stories growing up in this town."

"I could tell you a story or…or do you want the truth?"

A huge part of me told myself to run. Another part was glued to the floor. If I truly am a writer, I should listen, right? Besides, what could an old pig farmer, or whatever the hell he was, tell me anyway? There was no reason for the nervousness I felt. At best, maybe I could turn this lame tale into a decent story and jump start my career. At worst, I'd waste an afternoon.

I smiled. "Okay, Trapper. Go ahead. Tell me the story."

"Not just a story." Trapper grinned toothless. "How 'bout you come with me. Seeing for yourself helps."

Leery, I said, "Go where?"

"Just to the edge of town." He stood to a full six feet, took a last sip of coffee, and winked at the waitress. "Be back soon enough, Janie."

The edge of town was an easy walk from the diner. Beyond the

Gospel Diner who's claim to fame was *The Best Grits in the South,* there wasn't much left to the town of Gospel City, at least not as I recalled from my childhood.

There was always the main route off highway 64 that led people around the farms and into town. With less than eight hundred people who worked the farms or one of the few businesses along Main Street, the town had little to offer except for a white steeple church, grocer, gas station, post office, and southern style homes with long front porches. At night, people had sat on those porches fanning themselves and talking to neighbors who strolled past. The smell of jasmine often filled the air along with the jingle of ice cubes cooling a glass of sweet tea or lemonade.

In my teen years the town bored me. There was nothing to do. I dreamt of going to New York or some other big city, to college, and having a career where I could travel and see the world. What happened to that dream? I had barely made it out of town before life seemed to fly by in the preverbal blink of an eye. And now here I was, back again and with nothing much to show for it.

While time might have felt as if it stood still for me, the town of Gospel City had aged in ways I wouldn't have believed. The main street into town had become a dusty, underused road. The center of town that once offered cool, green grass, benches, a fountain, and a memorial to those lost in war, was just a patch of weedy dirt. The monument stone etched with dead soldiers' names was unreadable from weathered wear. The fountain had crumpled. The benches gone just like the filling station with only an old gray slab to mark where the foundation once was.

The post office was boarded up. So was Fraser Grocery Store. Even the church windows were sealed with washed out green panel shutters nailed shut. The entrance to the cemetery where oaks and crepe myrtles once grew like stately statues providing shade as a welcome to visitors, was transformed into dead trees and fallen limbs. The black, rod iron-gate wobbled when Trapper pushed it open. Weeds up to my knees bent as I followed him inside where lines of tombstones, some as old as the 1700's, drooped sideways as if the will to stand straight had been stolen from them.

"What happened to the town?" I said as I passed one blackened rain streaked stone after another.

Trapper removed his cap. Bald on the top, the few strands remaining on each side of his head blew softly in the breeze. "Never was much of a town, Shelly. All you youngins' used to say that."

"But the houses. In town. They used to be so beautiful. The Manderville house on Main was the nicest one of all and now the front porch has fallen in, the windows are busted, the bushes are overgrown. Why?"

"Folks moved away. Farming died off. Generations of families died off. Other folk headed for Marion County."

Trapper and I walked a path through the old cemetery. As it led further to the back in an undeniable straight line, a trail, worn into the ground by so many visitors over time, had killed the grass. All around us were sagging rows of gray markers cursed by the elements. Nothing with living colors for miles. Even the azalea bushes that once bloomed vibrant pink were reduced to dry sticks poking out in every direction like the brittle fingers of a witch.

"We get looky-loos every now and again," Trapper said as he strolled by tombstones and ran his finger over the tops. A slight morbid grin spread across his lips and a chill covered me with the strange sensation that in his own way, he touched the stones as if to say hello.

"Looky-loos? I don't understand."

"Folk come to check out the story. See if it's true." He laughed his cowboy laugh at me and the questions on my face. "Imagine that. Shelly Buttermen done forgot the story?"

"My name is Shelby," I said with irritation I wanted him to hear. "Why are we here?" I didn't bother to wait for his answer. I turned on my heels and headed back. "I really don't have time for this or some stupid story that takes place, obviously in a damn cemetery. Talk about clichés. I write mysteries not spooky stories that have been done to death – no pun intended. I think I have the perfect beginning for my non-fiction. Why cities produce more educated, non-superstitious intelligent people than the rural backroads of America."

"She's right here," Trapper said.

I turned and he was standing alongside a blacken-gray stone. The gravestone was squared at the top and chipped in the right corner. A name, easy enough to read, was in scripted deep into the marker. A dusty trail encircled the grave. I assumed it was created by parades of people who for some reason navigated to that spot more than any others I could see. But why?

"Lucy Buttermen," Trapper said and squeezed his cap between his hands. "Your great-great aunt."

"Lucy," I repeated in a hush. "I do…vaguely remember something about her."

"She the one responsible."

"Responsible for what?" I hesitated, but gave in and came closer.

"She the one who brung the few living here. The ones looking for some story to tell others. They the ones think it fun to say they come to Gospel City Cemetery and lived to tell the tale. 'Course, some do live to talk or there'd be no point. Story would sure as die off as the rest of the town if they didn't. But then," he shook his head while he stared down at the grave, "others ain't so lucky." Trapper lifted his cold eyes to me. "You recall the legend, now don't ya, Shelly?"

I drifted my glance back to the resting place of this person who was supposed to be my deceased relative. Other than being told we shared a blood line, I felt no connection to her, or did I? It wasn't easy growing up in town with the story of Lucy Buttermen hanging over my head. I must have pushed the tale away, but standing here, in this dismal place where holes had been dug and filled for eternity with death, it slowly came back to me.

"It's okay, Shelly. I know it weren't easy for ya. I'll say it for ya." Trapper took a small step back but remained in arms-length to the gravestone. "Folk say if ya come here, especially on a full moon, you call Lucy's name and knock three times on her stone, she'll rise and whisper in your ear."

"Your fate," I said so softly it surprised me that Trapper heard.

"That's right. Your fate to live or die."

Another urban legend I never wanted to accept when I was young and one I still wasn't ready to believe. I scoffed a sickly breath. "That's ridiculous."

"Is it? Still ain't willing? I'll tell you from the beginning. I'll tell you the truth of it."

I heard Trapper say the date and with those words, his voice slipped away. I retold the story transported back as it played out in front of me.

March, 1861. Lucy Buttermen was eighteen years old and her head was full of dreams. Her family owned a farm just three miles outside of town. Three hundred acres of rolling hills, ponds, and white fences to hold in the horses and pigs they raised. While much of the state of South Carolina made its fortune in rice, the Buttermen family knew their wealth lay in providing meat and work animals to others.

Lucy wasted little time on such matters. There were plenty of slaves to do the work and, as the only daughter to Richard and Eliza Buttermen, she had better ways to spend her time. Her three older brothers would one day run the farm and, as her father told her often enough, he would provide her with a few modest acres as a diary for marriage, and, the time to think marriage, was here.

She would giggle her girlish charm at her father and his old ways and then beg to go to Charleston for the socials and extravagant parties saying if he wanted her to find a worthy husband that would be the place to do so. Richard Buttermen found it hard to resist. Since his wife died when Lucy was just five years old, she was the image of her mother and just like her, Lucy loved the big city of Charleston and hated the small, antiquated town that had been the home of Buttermens' since the eighteenth century.

Lucy's desire was to leave this pathetic place and travel north, perhaps to New York, where there were libraries and universities, museums, and style. Her father saw no need to send a girl to any university, a waste he said, but she held the hope to somehow convince him just as she convinced him every few months to allow her to visit her cousin in Charleston.

The home of her cousin Mary was a modern, Victorian style house. A grand, three-story, white painted home with deep evergreen shutters, stain glass windows, a huge wrap around porch perfect for summer evenings, and surrounded by azaleas and wax myrtles, live oaks, and rose bushes. It sat in the middle of town among rows of other elegant mansions built for plantation owners from the sweat of slave labor.

Early spring was mild in Charleston and parties were common for almost every weekend. Mary Buttermen was the second of four daughters to Lucy's uncle Douglas, her father's oldest brother. His wealth came from the land he inherited and that he used to grow rice. Richard, although envious, had no choice but to use the land he was given for other means. Not located anywhere near the marsh, his land was meant to farm vegetables and raise pigs and horses. Often kidded by his brothers as the 'pig farmer,' he forced a laugh, but under his breath cursed them all.

Lucy sometimes heard the cruel jokes and felt ashamed. It was one of the reasons she hated Gospel City, the farm, and all that it entailed.

But there was no time to think of those things. Her father would spoil her with lacy dresses if for no reason than to prove to his brothers he was just as successful as them. Richard adored Lucy's beauty, her charm, and how, when she entered a room, others noticed. She was his princess and he was sure one day she would wed an important man – perhaps a governor destine to be president. That would show his brothers just what a 'pig farmer' could produce.

When Lucy arrived in Charleston, her cousin Mary greeted her with open arms. Several trunks filled with fancy dresses were brought into the house by servants as Mary explained all the parties lined up for the next few weeks.

Neither young girl were concerned with the state of the country. They paid no attention to the threat of war with the north or President Lincoln's call to end slavery. They focused only on the cadets who promised to attend the parties and the sons of politicians who would never let any opportunity to meet young women go missed. There were also the gentlemen of the university back in town after the holidays. They were men of philosophy, true thinkers, and many of them filled with different ideas about the world. And then there was the northern breed. Some of them from respectable families. Some there on scholarships. Either way, most of the wealthy, truly old southern families didn't approve of them – which is what made them a sinful treat for young ladies looking to rebel.

    The night of the first party, Lucy met Jerimiah O'Dell, a Catholic boy from Massachusetts, and in his third year studying architecture. Although he wasn't wealthy and his politics on the matter was controversial, he and Lucy bonded right away as if they were old souls reunited. He filled her head with stories of places he'd run off to living on the road and taking jobs just to buy bread. She found that exciting. His tales of the gothic ruins of old countries he'd seen in his travels was romanticized along with his desire to construct elaborate buildings in big cities. His dream, like her, was to live in New York and be part of a new world with new ways of doing things.

    For the next two weeks, Lucy and Jerimiah spent every possible moment together. Cousin Mary even helped to sneak Lucy in and out of the house so no one would know. But all there secrecy was in vain. Once Richard Buttermen received news from his brother that his only daughter was seeing a Yankee, non-Baptist, dirt poor student whose family held no position or wealth, he was furious. He arrived in Charleston determined to bring his daughter home and stop the foolishness.

    But the unthinkable happened. The south seceded from the north and in April, 1861 Confederates fired upon Fort Sumter. The fate of both the North and South was sealed.

All men were expected to take up the fight. Jerimiah was no different. He was expected to pick a side and take a stand – except that was not Jerimiah's plan. His plan was to flee a country at war for matters that didn't affect him. He chose to leave the country and, even with little money, intended to bring Lucy with him.

Richard Buttermen had arrived in time. Carrying a hysterical Lucy over his shoulder like a sack of grain, she screamed and fought her father every inch of the way. He managed to get her into the carriage and make it back to Gospel City just as the sun rose.

Three days went by. Richard decided to join the army and fight for the Confederacy he loved. Lucy refused to leave her room, plotting to run away the first chance she got.

That chance came one night when the moon was full and eight days after Jerimiah had managed to send her a message through Cousin Mary.

My love, the note read, *tonight I arrive and our dreams will come true. When you hear me call your name and knock three times, you'll know it's me coming to take you away and love you with all my heart. Be ready. This is our fate. All my love, Jerimiah.*

On that evening, Lucy heard her name whispered and eager, waited for the three knocks. Once they came, she smiled and gathered her things, ran down the back stairs and into the waiting arms of Jerimiah O'Dell. Her father, she explained to Jerimiah was busy with soldiers and talk of how to protect the town of Gospel City as they fought to save the south.

But Richard was no fool. He used his sons to spy on Lucy and when his youngest rushed in to tell him that 'the northern rebel was outside stealing Lucy,' Richard grabbed his loaded musket and tore out of the house. The three soldiers he knew well as neighbors followed.

Jerimiah held Lucy tight in his arms. "Lucy, my love," he spoke in her ear, "this is our fate to be together. No one can tear us apart. Not war. Not your father. You are mine."

They kissed to seal the bond and prepared to climb into the carriage when Richard shouted for them to stop.

"You," he screamed under the silvery light of the moon, "are not leaving with my daughter."

"Papa," Lucy said, her voice quivered, "I love him."

"You know nothing of love," Richard shouted back.

"This is my fate," Lucy cried. "Our fate."

"This is not your fate. He's nothing. He has nothing. He's a traitor to the south and the north." Richard aimed his gun.

Jerimiah shielded Lucy from the shot. She screamed in horror and pulled Jerimiah into the carriage. His blood ran hot in her lap where his head had dropped.

Lucy whipped the reins and the horse galloped. Another shot fired. The horse reared up. Lucy gained control but after the next shot, the horse startled so badly it ran into the ravine and broke free from the carriage that crashed into a tree.

Jerimiah and Lucy were thrown to the hard ground. Lucy stumbled to her feet and reached Jerimiah. Lifting his head into her blood stained lap, she leaned close to him and felt his last breath warm on her cheek.

She screamed and begged her father when he dragged her away from Jerimiah's lifeless body. She looked back at the sight of her love and crumpled into a broken pile of tears.

Eyes blurred, she glanced up at her father with hatred dripping along with the cries. She snatched his pistol from his belt and held it pointed at his head.

Her words spoken in a calm, venomous tone, she said, "I will decide fate. Mine and yours."

Hands shaking, an evil look upon her face, she aimed the gun directly at Richard.

I placed my hand over my mouth. "Oh my God. She shot her father?"

"Whether she would have or not," Trapper said, "no one knows. One of her father's friends shot her first. Richard dropped to his knees swearing she wouldn't have done it, but who knows for sure."

"And that's why?" I choked back my own tears, but one by one they fell on the grave at my feet.

"Family buried her here. Wouldn't even let Jerimiah be put in the same cemetery. Richard said he didn't deserve the dirt of the south let alone being near his baby girl even in death."

"That's why the legend is that if you call her name and knock three times, she'll appear?"

"She thinks its Jerimiah. And when she finds it ain't, she gets mean. Real mean. She takes her vengeance like most spirits ripped from life do."

"There's no real proof of that," I said.

"Still fighting the truth, Shelly? Go ahead then, tell her and him." He pointed to other tombstones around us. "And that one and all of them buried here that there ain't no proof."

"This is insane. You're telling me these graves are filled with what?"

"The ones she killed."

"No. I don't believe it. Any of it." I took two steps back but when I saw the name on the stone to the left of Lucy's grave, I froze. "Janie?"

Trapper was behind me. His breath on my neck could have easily been ice. "I wondered when you'd get around to noticing. She come here like all them others thinking this was all just folklore. Just bull crap. She found out. Called Lucy's name under the full moon and knocked three times. Lucy raised right up out of the ground and whispered in Janie's ear. What I can't say for sure, but that girl run out of here like a streak of lightening bit her. Soon as she got to the road, a carriage come round the bend, ran right over her."

"Is the woman at the diner…Janie, is she that woman's great granddaughter or something? A relative?"

"What you think?" Trapper eyed me. "Gospel City don't exist no more, Shelly, you knows that. Deep down, you knows that. No one come here no more 'cept the looky-loos. Only souls bother to be in this town are the ones laid to rest here."

I shook my head, trembled, and stepped back again. My foot hit on a rock. I glanced down at another gravestone, the name and date worn thin by the elements.

"That there is Gus. Man you seen at the diner eating grits like he couldn't get his full. One at the end of the counter. You seen him, Shelly, I knows you did. He come here same as the others to laugh and find proof. He weren't laughing when he fell down his stairs and broke his neck."

"How is this possible? I just arrived in town…" My mind was foggy. How did I arrive in town? Shaking away the doubt, I said, "I've been away and now you're telling me…I saw the town. The people."

"The town?" Trapper laughed. "What town is left? It's a damn ghost town. And the people? Only the ones at the diner. And if you look closer, you'd see they ain't breathing. They just a bunch of restless souls rising up from the grave and wandering into the diner, forgetting everything like it weren't possible. Wishing it weren't possible and knowing in the end, they be the fool to provoke Lucy. All just so they gets to prove something. Happens more around the anniversary. Look here." He guided me by the arm to another grave. "This one killed his self. That was his fate. And this one and this one, they all died calling for Miss Lucy, tempting fate, making her think they was her Jerimiah. Now some that come here, they don't die. They live to tell the story. If not, what would be the point? 'I seen a real ghost town,' they tell others. 'I walked a cemetery to find a ghost,' they brag. Fine by us. Got to have looky-loos come and other's to keep the story alive. Like I said, sooner or later almost every one of them fight the truth. You weren't the first to wander into the diner. It was just your turn I guess."

"What in the hell are you talking about?" My hand shook from fear, rage, both. "You're lying," I screamed.

"You just like all of them. You know you are, Shelly. And it be my job to set you straight."

"None of this is true," I shouted louder while I shook from the inside. How? I pushed him back ready to run, but something unseen slapped me forward. I tripped onto a weedy grave. This sunken spot, where not even the grass took hold, right beside Lucy's with a name etched in the stone read: Shelby Buttermen.

I broke into tears. Shaking my head like a mad woman trying with all I had to deny it. But, I knew.

"It was night. I was all packed and ready to leave this damn town the next day," I said as I stared at my inscription. "I was finally going to get out of this horrible place. I came here just to shut up everybody. To stop the taunting all those years growing up. To show everybody I wasn't afraid of some stupid story. To prove it was nothing but an urban legend. A silly folklore that meant nothing.

"I called Lucy's name and knocked three times. The wind picked up but nothing happened and I laughed. I laughed and said I knew it was all a stupid, dumb story. And then there was a white mist. Thick, smoky white air surrounding me. I felt a chill on my neck and the whisper. She said…she said it was my turn. I ran as fast as I could, jumped in my car, and headed down the road. I saw something in the middle of the road. A woman maybe? I don't know. A voice whispered to me. 'I tried to leave this damn town and couldn't. Why should you?' I looked in my rear view mirror and she was there. In the backseat. Her eyes were white orbs. Her hair black. Her skin gray. She held up her hands covered in blood. I lost control of the car, slammed into a tree. I went through the windshield." Running my hand through my hair, I felt the shards of glass and pulled some free. They glistened in my open palm.

The air left my body with a gasp. "I…I died? It's not possible."

"It's not a story, Shelly. It's the truth. I know for fact 'cause you was right there when she come to me." Trapper nodded at my shock. "I come here too. Just an old fool filled with the devil's liquor. I stood right yonder at her stone, called her name, laughed at her. And then I knocked three times. When I turned, she was right there, in front of me. Dressed all in white like the bride of a demon. A look spread across her face. Pure evil. Her eyes were hollowed out white shells. The front of her dress covered in blood. She tipped her head to the side like she was studying me. You sat on top of your stone, a wavy spirit, just looking at me. I couldn't move. I couldn't breathe. Miss Lucy whispered to me."

My mind tried to fight it all but the more he spoke, the more I saw it as it happened. "What did she say?"

"Run." Trapper lowered his head. "I ran all right. Ran out into the road and a truck come from nowhere. Slammed into me. I lifted clean out of my body. Floated till you took my hand and said now I knew the truth."

He strolled over to a plot with a headstone that read: Morgan. He brushed away the dried leaves and dirt to reveal the rest of the inscription: 'Trapper' Crane. 2004. Age 78. Rest in Peace.

His feet disappeared up to his ankles into the ground of the grave. "Moon be full this night, Shelly, and it being the anniversary of Lucy Butterman's death, plenty of looky-loos be calling." He pointed over to the far corner of the cemetery. "We got space for more. Not all will have the same fate. Got to have them to tell the story. But some? Well, whatever she whisper sure to happen. You best get some rest too, Shelly. You know the story. We live the tale over and over. If you don't hear nothing else, hear this. You, me, all them others, this here is our fate. We are the truth."

L.Thomas-Cook

www.lindathomascook.com

lthomascookwritesnow@gmail.com

www.facebook.com/linda.thomascook

On sale now: *In Your Eyes: Santini & Jamison Vol. 1* available on Kindle and Amazon.

Coming Soon: *Forgiveness*: A paranormal suspense published by DeerHawk Publishing

SHORTS

Flight From Fright
Faye Bradley

There are times in life when we look back on what we did with friends and wonder, "What in the world were we thinking?" One Friday night back in 1956 with my friend Josie was such a time.

Landing in Seattle, I was excited to catch up with my girlfriend after decades had passed since we were thicker than glue in high school in Wilmington, Delaware. Josie and I had dinner together in the hotel that warm summer evening as we caught up on the 'old times'. A long way from home on the east coast, Seattle was Josie's residence for the past number of years.

My husband and I had flown in from South Carolina for an overnight stay and were heading off the next morning to salmon fish in Campbell River on Vancouver Island, British Columbia. Josie and I - both much older and, of course, so much more mature now after having gotten married and having raised children, began to catch one another up on the past twenty years. We talked about our parents, siblings, children and grandchildren, zeroed in on good memories, weddings, graduations, and the passing of loved ones and classmates and remembered some of the adventures of our youth.

One such escapade will always live on in our minds. It was a beach trip we took that Friday night in 1956 that still stirred lots of emotions in both of us as we tipped our wine glasses together, shaking our heads at how crazy we were back then.

Graduating from Wilmington High that year, Josie and I were offered the management of a private swim club for the summer. For my school friend and me, it was a dream job. Located at one of the nicest private schools in the country - only about ten miles away, we were given a room in the female dorm with the other students and beds on their sleeping porch, giving us the choice to spend the night when we did not want to drive home.

In those days, we were required to sign in and sign out by writing our names in a log book, putting a phone number beside it where we could be reached. Josie smoked - and got caught a few times with her cigarettes, so, rather than giving up the bad habit, her choice was always to leave the campus whenever she could. If the pool was not open in the evening for one reason or another. If it was too cold. If it was raining. Anytime we were not needed, Josie wanted to leave. She had her mother's car to use that summer and we thought we were so grown up with our new-found freedom.

The two of us loved our jobs. We had full control of the pool, supervising rowdy kids, teaching swim classes, overseeing the maintenance of the pool and calling the shots as to when we thought the pool should be open or closed. The pool had to be emptied completely at least every two weeks, then we washed it down with scrub brushes and cleanser. This took a day. Fed by a spring with a hose, it took the pool forever to fill and we felt it was far too cold to swim in for the next couple of days after it was re-opened. Others argued that it was 'just right' and we had to negotiate, usually giving in to an avid swimmer or family on a hot summer night.

Having taken life saving courses since the age of fourteen, it was especially exciting for me to do something related to my passion of being around the water. By the time I was a senior in high school, I was teaching swim classes and Junior and Senior Life Saving at the YWCA and at the Boys Club in the Wilmington area so the job managing the school's pool and swim club was a perfect fit – and an honor.

Josie and I also had our Water Safety Instructor certifications from the American Red Cross so the school felt we were well qualified. It was quite a responsibility for two seventeen-year-olds and we thought we were pretty big deals that summer of 1956. Such big deals that one Friday night - not long after we started working there, we took our fake ID's and set out to visit a popular resort hangout at the beach to listen to what we heard was some of the best music on the east coast. Leaving our jobs at the swanky private school up in Hockessin, we decided to drive to the beach, stop by the Fenwick Island Light House Diner on Fenwick Island, Delaware for a sandwich and a Coca-Cola and then drive along the coast to Rehobeth Beach. We each told our parents that we were going to one another's home for the night, and then wrote down some phone number on the log sheet. Who's number, I can't remember and, of course, there were no cell phones in those days. We just wanted to spread our wings. Only two hours away, we felt we could get back in time to go to work the next day with no one being the wiser.

I spent my summer vacations with my family on Fenwick Island and felt I knew my way around the sparsely developed shoreline that made up the long barrier island. Divided into beaches with names like Lewis, Rehobeth, and Bethany, Fenwick stretches all the way from Ocean City, Maryland in the south to Cape Henlopen State Park in the north.

The island also has a township called Fenwick Island, Maryland and one called Fenwick Island, Delaware. While they both have the same name and are just across the state line from one another, our family preferred the one in Delaware. The Maryland township of Fenwick seemed too congested for our tastes although it was nothing like Ocean City, Maryland - twelve miles to the south, where the boardwalk seemed to go on forever. Dolly's famous taffy, fancy hotels, amusement rides, every kind of beach shop one could imagine, homemade ice cream and boys out looking for girls to 'pick up' were just some of the attractions. There were even slot machines.

No thank you. We did not even consider going down there in spite of the fact that I had relatives in Ocean City who owned a grocery store and the best meat market around. I enjoyed many a visit with them although, not tonight. No, we wanted to live it up on our own and then get back in time to be at work by ten o'clock in the morning to open the pool for the day.

Our plans worked out well as we got out of town, driving southeast to the beach with hardly any traffic on what turned out to be a fine summer evening in June. I admonished Josie several times to roll down the window of her mother's 1940's two-door Chevy as she smoked. So, there she was, flipping ashes out the window as she drove along on our way to have dinner at the famous Lighthouse Diner and then to hear music in Rehobeth at the Bottle and Cork.

I had tried smoking several times in the past but always ended up coughing and not liking the taste. It seemed to burn my tongue and was bitter - not to mention that I knew my father strongly disapproved of any of his four daughters even thinking about trying a cigarette. A few weeks earlier, I had a dream come true when I met Florence Chadwick face to face at a nearby pool where the famous swimmer was working out before her next planned attempt to swim the English Channel. In awe as I watched her train, she swam for hours on end attached to a rope to build up her endurance. As a strong swimmer myself, I used to swim past the breakers in the ocean ignoring my father's calls for me to turn around and come back in closer to the shore. I would swim against the current for about a mile or so and then practically float back. I ignored the fear of sharks or under-toes back then. I wanted to be a long distance swimmer from as far back as I could remember so I knew smoking would ruin my breathing and any chance I might have at being like Florence Chadwick.

I would swim in any pool I could get in and tie a rope around my waist just like Florence Chadwick so I would not have to make all those stupid turns. She inspired me and then it became a secret goal of mine to swim across Chesapeake Bay. It was a goal that I held close to my heart – faithfully swimming two miles a day.

Hungry, we arrived at the diner on Fenwick Island and jumped out of the car, noticing maybe only three other cars in the parking lot. By now, it was nearly nine o'clock and was starting to get dark. Our plans from here were to drive north along the beach to our destination and join a group of our peers for a fun evening. At least we wanted to think of ourselves as their peers. The truth was, we were still under the age limit to get into a night club. Both of us had successfully scratched the 8's in our birth years to look like 6's - which was possible in the 50's since the drivers licenses were not encased in plastic like they are nowadays. We were not sure if it was going to work although it had been successful for us once before by just nonchalantly flashing our licenses under the plastic covering of our open wallets.

Josie was more mature in ways that I only dreamed of. She was more developed in the right places and carried herself boldly, catching the eye of many a guy as she passed by. Our girlfriends envied her and she had to endure the guys' wolf whistles in our official one piece Speedo swim suit while on duty at the pool - especially the week we had the All-State Boys Football Team there.

What a headache that turned into for us. They did not respect our authority and felt they did not 'need' lifeguards and pushed us to our limits. They thought they were being 'cute' by tossing all of the lounge chairs into the pool. At the end of our rope, we banned them from the pool for a day, reporting the incident to their coach. He made them apologize and put each chair back in its place as we stood by proudly directing their activity. After that, they just flirted with us only to make themselves look silly in our eyes. After all, they were a year younger than us which helped to make us feel superior.

Back to the story. The two of us sat down in a booth at the Fenwick Island Diner and ordered our dinner, talking about the evening ahead and were completely oblivious to customers sitting nearby or even those coming and going. As we got up to pay our bill, we noticed two men - not boys or guys near our age, but two older men, eyeing us. Nervous, we paid the bill and went to the car as we tried not to look too uncomfortable. Once outside, we wasted no time in getting out of the parking lot.

Pointing to the road across from the restaurant, I suggested we drive along the beach to avoid making it obvious that we were heading directly up the highway to the Bottle & Cork - which was a pretty well known destination in the area for music and dancing. As we pulled out of the parking lot, we noticed the men getting ready to leave. Uneasy, Josie fumbled as she quickly shifted gears trying to drive away as I was frantically pointing for her to take the beach road straight across the highway. The car stalled out at the stop sign.

Cranking it back up, she sped forward, crossed the highway, then turned down the next street that paralleled the ocean. Even though it was dark, we could see the damage that Hurricane Hazel did to the area only two years earlier as we drove along. Many of the oceanfront homes had been washed out into the sea and those left were old and, although they looked like they could stand just about anything that may come in the future, most of them probably needed a fresh coat of paint.

Many families had rebuilt after the storm and it seemed like it was going to be a boom town before too long with rows of new homes still under construction – although this time up on stilts with carports underneath. The new beach homes had dishwashers and washing machines and even indoor bathrooms – something that was not the norm before the hurricane had brought with it the addition of many modern conveniences. In fact, I remember when I was little having to use an 'out-house' behind our cottage in the tiny, laid-back, pristine community of Fenwick Island, Delaware where there were only dirt roads that had to be scraped a couple times a year to smooth out their ruts.

Looking into our rear view mirror, we saw the lights of a car approaching about two blocks away. We feared it was 'Mr. Mustache' and the other man with stringy hair that we saw at the diner. It was about all we could remember of these two older men who were probably in their 30's. Josie stepped on the gas and, before I realized what she was doing, she pulled into a vacant carport driving as far in as she could get and then turned off the ignition - and the car's lights. She then quickly pulled me down in the seat. The two of us clung onto each other as I started praying out loud. Sure enough, a car passed by a few seconds later. It could have been a minute or so, but it felt like it was right away. It seemed too soon to be any other car than the one driven by the perverts who we felt were looking for us. Huddling in the car below eye level we could not tell.

So, here we were. Two terrified girls in a carport of a deserted beach house in an area that was not highly developed and with no street lights. Now what? We waited. And waited. No other cars drove by. It must have been an hour that we waited. Nothing. No one. It was so dark and most of the beach houses in the area were vacant. Back then, most folks did not go to the beach until the first of July. This was when summer started and, unlike now, school did not even let out until just in time for the 4th July when everyone would go to the beach to enjoy fireworks, bonfires to cook hotdogs, eat watermelons and jump into the ocean to wash off.

Okay, maybe we only waited fifteen minutes, but it seemed like an hour. Both of us were shaking from this near disastrous experience and hastily agreed that our big night at the Bottle and Cork was not to be. All we wanted to do by now was drive home. Slowly, Josie backed out of the carport and there were no cars were in sight. In fact, there were no cars driving in any direction. No cars parked anywhere. It was eerie.

Josie quickly drove back to the main highway and we started inland as we looked this way and that way, still convinced that the men were lurking somewhere - ready to stop our car. We both started praying that we would not see them as Josie kept driving faster and faster. Finally I had to tell her that she might get stopped by the police and then we would have another set of problems if our parents found out we went out-of-town. With this, Josie settled down to the speed limit and concentrated on our ride back to Wilmington and the safety of our homes.

While it looked like we were going to get through this trauma, another faced me. As we talked and talked - with Josie smoking up a storm from being so stressed, I announced that I had to go to the bathroom "No way..," Josie replied. She was not going to stop. Even if I could find a well-lit place like a Howard Johnson's with twelve – or even twenty, cars outside, she was not going to stop. Even if it was lit up like a Christmas tree, she was not going to stop for anything or for any reason. She told me that I would just have to wait.

I looked around - knowing that Josie's mother did not keep the neatest car in the world. There were old newspapers, an empty shoe box and some other junk in the back seat. Next thing Josie knew, I was climbing over the seat. Telling her not to worry, I found a small plastic bucket her mother used to gather tomatoes out of the garden. 'Why would she have a bucket for tomatoes in the car,' I thought, but who cared, I needed it - and right now! The craziness of this served as an ice breaker and broke the tension of the night as we started laughing. We then began telling jokes and relaxed as we headed home.

Getting back in the middle of the night, we could not go to either of our homes – or the school, so we parked down the street from Josie's house and tried to sleep. About six in the morning - when the sun finally came up, we drove around for awhile before finally going to my home after we saw my father leave for work at seven-thirty.

Walking in, Josie raced to the bathroom to freshen up as much as she could. With only one bathroom in the house, I went into the kitchen and kissed my mother on the forehead.

My dearest mother - cleaning up the breakfast dishes, turned and eyed me and said, "You look like you've been up all night..." I meekly smiled and said that Josie and I just wanted to come by before heading back to our jobs to have a nice breakfast. My mother - never one to question her youngest daughter, just smiled and put on more bacon and started fixing some scrambled eggs, knowing we girls had probably been up to no good.

Available at Jekyll Island Museum, Jekyll Island, GA
Barbara's Fine Gifts, Myrtle Beach, SC
PirateLand Campground, Myrtle Beach, SC
Inlet Sports Lodge, Murrells Inlet, SC
Clock Tower Books, Georgetown, SC
And Ebook through Kindle, Amazon, Nook, etc.
Hardback through Amazon and Barnes & Noble

Follow Faye Bradley through Facebook
Fayebradley32@gmail.com

Freddie's Frozen
By Pat David

I'm a frozen frog in Fairbanks, Alaska.
I'm beseechin' yah Summer
Will yah make it a little faster?

God made me strong enough to survive the cold
But
This never endin' shiverin' is gettin' mighty old.

I'm stuck in a swamp by the railroad tracks.
Oh how I miss playin' my Tenor sax.
Can't move, nor ribbit, can't even ride my bicycle
CAUSE
My mouth and eyelashes are drippin' with icicles.

I see a train comin' round the bend
All it takes to save me is a little help from a friend.

Gee Whiz, Mr. Engineer, come on! Take notice?
Yah need to look out yer window at the swamp. NOW, really focus!
I'm the small green amphibian covered with ice on this log.
Please Mr. Only YOU can help this frozen frog.

He didn't even look.
That guy's a schnook.
By hook or by crook

SHORTS

Truth be told
I'm gonna' get out of this miserable cold.

Here I am AGAIN spendin' another night alone on this
forsaken log.
Oh how I long for singin' with my friend Bob.
We'd ribbit all night until our lips were blue
One night, a neighbor sick with the flu,
couldn't take our harmonizin',
how we ended up in a mess of Kudzu
wasn't surprizin'.

Kudzu?
That vine grows in the South.
A place where it's warm
Well shut my mouth!

South?
Warm!
A place where - all y'all, darn tootin, ain't, and bless yer
heart,
are an art form.

You see folks, I'm a frog from a bog in N'Awlins, Lousiana.
Oh how I miss singin' and plaiyin' my sax all night from my
neighbor's veranda.
Bob and I would eat masquitas, and spiders, and especially
those crunchy, earwigs.
From a bottle of our neighbor's White Lightnin',
I'm afraid we took quite a few swigs.

So, yer probably wonderin' why in the world did I ever want

to come here?
Hey, there go a Moose, a snowshoe rabbit, and look a Reindeer.
A trip to Alaska? What was I thinkin!
I bought a one way ticket without even blinkin'.
And now
I'm frozen with my whole BODY shrinkin'.

Everything's frozen, even my brain
One good thing though
No weight have I gained.

Somethin's happenin'. My, my, what's that?
Well what do yah know, it's a warm and very WET, splat.
Splat-- splat-- splat splat splat-
Hey, the ice on my back is startin' to crack
My legs are movin'
My heart is pumpin'
It's rainin' folks
Now ain't that somethin'!

Here comes the train again
And
It's goin' in a Southern direction.
Hey Mr. Engineer
I need to make this connection.

I'm gonna' jump as high and as fast as I can
Then
Ribbit very loud
Yep, that's my game plan.

Toot Toot - Ding Ding
He saw me
Thank you Lord!
"Hey young man, come aboard."
"Come sit next to the boiler
where it's cozy and warm."
"You're a lucky young man
cause
Another Alaskan freeze is comin' fast as it can.
Yup,
Weather Man warns it's sure gonna' be quite a storm."

"If Id'a had to stay in that Alaskan swamp much longer,
I know I woulda' gone insane.
Instead, I'm safe and warm in this cab, eatin' a candy cane,
Just listenin' to the clickety-clack of this rusty, old freight train."

"Hey young man open your eyes."
"Take a look out your window -
Those are Rocky Mountain skies."

"My wife packed me a lunch with a key lime pie.
I suppose you're used to lots of bugs or even a horse fly
But
My lady's a real good cook. Of this I cannot lie.
Come on dig in, passing this up would most definitely be a crime."

"Look! Mr. Engineer there's a moose on the tracks
With the screech of the brakes
and a sudden whack -

The two of us have fallin' flat on our backs.
I'm a little banged up
but
He ain't movin'.
He's all cut up and his blood is oozin'."

The train is derailed on the side of a mountain.
I could ribbit very loud but there's no use in shoutin'.
We're all alone
No radio. - No phone.
I have to get help
Mr. Engineer, please don't moan?

These railroad ties were made for hoppin'
I can feel it - the temperature's droppin'
This N'Awlin's frog has to hurry
Please God get me there soon cause I'm in the middle of a nasty, snow flurry.

I'm comin' up on a railroad trestle
Oh gosh, it's really wobbelin'.
Keep goin' Freddie , just a few more feet and you can stop this uncomfortable hobblin'.
My oh my, a push car's comin'.
This frog's legs are sooo tired of jumpin'.
My heart is pumpin' awful fast
Don't know how much longer this runnin' can last.
Dear Father above make them stop?
Please, please, please, my chest is about to pop.

SHORTS

"Hello little fella'
Ain't you a bit out of your
stomping grounds?
There's nothin' around here not even any towns.
What's a frog like you doin' way out here?
No bugs for you to eat, only rabbits, and mule deer."

"Please help me up into your car?"
Our destination isn't very far.
You see, a freight train derailed in which I was ridin'
and
I think the engineer might be dyin'.

"Frogs can't talk."
"Now this is a quandry'."

"Shucks fellas, on the contrary, my Momma always told me
that I won the Lottery."

"Please watch out, here's that wobbly trestle."
"It's so scary, I betcha' the builder never used a level."

"Just a few more curves and we'll be there shortly."
My friend the engineer needs rescuin'
By now, his wounds must be festerin'.
This cain't be the end of the story!"

"You're right young man, I must confess."
Golly gee this train's a mess.
Here's your friend
He may be hurt, but he's still breathin'.
Some medical attention he's gonna' be needin'."

"Can you talk Mister?
Oh heck, just whisper.
We're gettin' you ready to go to the hospital
Where you'll get the best care possible,
Cause
The doctor there is my big sister.
Oh my, they sent a chopper
Those folks know what they're doing, they'll treat yah real proper."

"Now that my friend's on his way,
I have to say, "My travelin' days over.
I need to get to N'Awlins
cuz
I'm tired of bein' a rover."

"My amfibious friend you're most definitely in luck."
"My cousin Jake drives a semi truck."

"Please call and ask if he'll rescue me?"
"I promise to be very good you wait and see."

"One problem though,
He has a dog.
"He's his protector
His name is "Road Hog."

"A dog, that's no concern my friend.
My neighbor back home has coon hounds in a big pen.
All y'all should hear us in the Spring.
I'd be playin' my sax and then I'd sing.
Those dog's keep a howlin' till my ears ring."

SHORTS

"I miss my home so much!
In this cold weather, I simply cain't adjust.
Please call yer cousin.
I promise not to do any fussin'
Heck, if he likes donuts, I'll even buy him a dozen."

"He's on his way and you're in luck.
He's got plenty of room in his eighteen wheeler truck.
He's gonna drop you off in Louisana.
His destination is Texarkana."

"We'll take you to the local truck stop
Then it's on the road without a stop.
He's gonna' tell the local cop,
"Got a special passenger here
who loves to hop."

"Thank yah friends.
All y'all are special men.
There was a time when I thought I was done for
Please come see me in N'awlins, this I must un-der-score
Cause
Freddie the Frog is frozen NO MORE!"
RIBBIT :-)

Please see my contact info under "Society's Gift."

For Your Amusement
By T. Allen Winn

I'm not sure why I came here, not really; well sort of, maybe. No one made me. No one dared me. No one even knew I was coming; well almost no one. That was a very bad mistake on my part. Not telling someone about it and coming here in the first place; and not coming here alone. I didn't have anything to gain and certainly not anything to prove. Yet, I couldn't help it. I had to come. I had to know, but what did I really expect to find, to learn, to experience. What do I know about such things? I'm not a chicken but what does that really gain me now? The blame for what has happened is my fault and I can't undo it, take anything back. Boy how I wish I could. I should have heeded the warnings of my elders, but instead I did the opposite. Opposite is always more exciting, more fun, or it was until now. I just don't want to be here anymore. I now know things no one should ever know. I'm not sure I'll ever be able to tell anyone though; not that I want to keep secrets; it's just that I'm not sure I'll be allowed to leave. I still hear those screams. I should have come here alone. No, that's all wrong. I should not have come here at all.

Lake Shawnee Amusement Park Archaeological Dig 1988 West Virginia

"We have another one," stated Marshall Student, Alex Ross.

"That makes what…thirteen now," asked his Concord College co-excavator Geri Stevens. "Why are you looking at me so strangely?"

"Take a look for yourself."

She peeked into the shallow grave. "This definitely confirms our suspicions then. We'd better contact the professor; she'll not want us to touch anything until she examines the evidence."

"As we've suspected since the sixth one, this is no ordinary burial ground, is it?"

"You do realize we're going to lose this dig once the professor publicizes her findings."

"I think we all knew it was heading in this direction whether we wanted to admit it or not. What's your best guess on what we have here, Geri?"

"The obvious, someone has been using this site recently, but no one person could have been using it for the suspected time span. That would be impossible."

"I really hoped we'd be able to see this through whether we find any more or not, but I'm afraid this just became a crime scène investigation and we're history. This is beyond a native American burial spot, that's for sure."

"Do you ever wonder about all those reports, Alex?"

"What…the ones about the amusement park being haunted?"

"Yeah. I've felt it. Haven't you?"

"More than I'd ever admit to anyone else but you; we've stumbled into more than just an Indian burial site or even a murder investigation, there's something beyond bizarre about this place."

"You've experienced it too, haven't you, Alex; admit it?"

Alex nodded. "Children laughing, sometimes crying, those swings moving when there was no wind…"

"And the Indians chanting…I never knew you had heard it too."

"Not saying it out aloud somehow made it not be real. I don't believe in ghosts."

"I used to not, but now; I don't know what I believe. Let's go. Suddenly this place is really creeping me out."

"The Lake Shawnee Amusement Park has always creeped me out, but our scholarship depended on our being here, but not any more…let's go before something really terrible happens."

Mercer County, West Virginia 1783

Mitchell Clay and his family were the first Europeans to settle in the area. Mitchell had been a veteran of the Battle of Point Pleasant, often referred to as Lord Dunmore's war, the Revolutionary War. He had purchased the Clover Bottom property on the Bluestone in 1775. While life in any new frontier was harsh, they had made do and had lived there peacefully, Mitchell and Phoebe raising their kids and prospering. That August day in 1783 began as routine as any. The Clay family had completed their annual small grain harvest and Mitchell tasked his sons, Ezekiel and Bartley, to construct a fence around the grain to contain it. He then departed on a hunting trip; supplying fresh meat for the table was always a welcome escape from the rigors of farming the land. The two brothers went about the business of doing what their father had asked, wishing they had been allowed to go hunting but accepting they would have their turns soon enough.

Everyone had assigned chores. There were no idle hands within the Clay clan. The females of the family were at the nearby river washing clothing and linens. Summer weather made this more pleasurable than during the winter months, but still, the daughters did not embrace their assignment. They knew better than to vocalize their discontent. Complaining got you nothing but possibly more chore assignments. Bite ones tongues and bear it; the washing had to be done and ultimately this was viewed as a job for the women folks. It was not up for debate or argument, end of story. The girls made the best of it, laughing, singing and taunting each other with splashes of water.

The sound of nearby gunshots in the direction of their homestead prompted them to cease what they were doing and run home as fast as they could. They were ill prepared for the scene unfolding before their very eyes, immediately finding themselves in the middle of a vicious Indian attack. Tabitha Clay, eldest of the sisters, spotted one of her brothers, Bartley, lying motionless on the ground, a savage straddling him, his head being held in the attacker's grip, the Indian in the process of removing her brother's scalp. Acting on pure adrenaline and enraged instinct, Tabitha rushed her brother's attacker. She leapt on him, grabbing the Indian's arm, attempting to stop him from completing his bloody task.

Unable to dislodge the knife, her adversary got the upper hand on her. A vicious struggle began, young girl against a more powerful renegade. Tabitha did her best, attempting to dislodge the bloody knife but size and strength prevailed. Focusing his attention on the young girl, the Indian stabbed Tabitha. To his surprise, she was much feistier and determined than he could have ever envisioned. Tabitha this time managed to wrest the knife from the Indian. Her victory was short lived, he again getting the upper hand and snatching the knife away. He showed her no mercy and eventually literally chopped the young girl to pieces. Her brother, already dead, she, too, had succumbed to the savage attack perpetrated by the band of eleven Indians. After their rampage, the Indians departed, but not before taking the scalps of the dead siblings. Ezekiel was mercifully spared the carnage and was kidnapped instead for reasons and purposes unknown.

Phoebe Clay unable to help or prevent the slaying of her two children and theft of a third had remained hidden with her other children. She emerged unharmed after sensing the coast clear. She brought her two dead children into the house and laid them on a bed. Liggon Blankenship, passing through, stopped by the cabin. He listened to the woman's frantic tale; saw her dead children as proof of what had happened. She begged him to help in rescuing her son and shooting the perpetrators. Instead, the cowardly Blankenship, turned tail and ran, telling every settler he came across that the entire Clay family had been massacred by the Indians. Phoebe then took her remaining children and fled, seeking refuse at her nearest neighbor, James Bailey.

Mitchell Clay, unaware of his family's tragic encounter, had been haunted by a dream the night before; one where his family had been brutally attacked by Indians. Troubled and dogged by its vividness, he felt compelled to cut his hunting trip short and return to check on them. There had been no Indian threats but the dream tormented him still. Upon his return he stumbled onto a grisly sight. Evidence of the brutal attack from his worst nightmare now stared him in the face. Running inside the family cabin he discovered his children, Tabitha and Bartley, freshly scalped and lying dead on the bed. Fearing the worst possible consequences that the remainder of his family had been taken in the raid; he decided to follow the trail while still warm and rescue them if they were still alive.

Mitchell eventually caught up with the Indians but when they realized he had followed them, they overpowered him and stole his horses. By the grace of the Good Man above, Mitchell was not killed. The Indians then headed towards Ohio. Under the leadership of Mathew Farley, a search party made up of Mitchell's two remaining sons and two future sons-in-law and neighbor, James Bailey, set out to find the murdering savages, but not before burying the dead children.

They were able to track and locate the eleven who had perpetrated the heinous attack near present-day Boone County, on the Pond

Fork of the Coal River. At daybreak the trackers attacked the unsuspecting, killing two and wounding a third. The wounded one attempted to flee but was killed by Charles Clay, brother of the slain, as he begged for his life. They recovered Mitchell Clay's horses but found no sign of the kidnapped Ezekiel Clay. Angered by the senseless murders of the children, two members of the party stripped the skin from the backs of two of the dead Indians and later made razor straps from the hides. Sadly they would discover that Ezekiel had been taken to the Indian town of Chillicothe, Ohio, and burned at the stake. Later, the Indians returned to the site of the battle and erected burial cairns for their fallen comrades.

Archaeological Dig 1988

Alex Ross and Geri Stevens sat in the warmth of an excavation tent near the entrance of the amusement park awaiting the arrival of Professor Joann Monahan and Detective Trevor Mendenhall. They reviewed various notes and bits of history attempting to role play being a crime scene investigator or possibly even a paranormal investigator. In 1900, then owner of the property L. D. Coon had found an Indian hatchet that probably marked where the battle had taken place. The two amateur sleuths were tittering between revenge as the motive for the bodies being found and a curse. Both were difficult to support with tangible evidence; except, neither could discount what they had experienced and heard at the dig. The place could be haunted, if you believed in such nonsense. They could never disclose this to their professor or the assigned detective. Such talk might compromise their scholarships.

Reviewing the genealogy of the Clays they looked for clues that might explain the significance of the gravesites and pattern of repeated use. Phoebe Belcher, born in Bedford County, Virginia, had married Mitchell Clay in 1760. They had seven sons and seven daughters. Daughter Mary had married Captain Ralph

Stewart, noted Indian fighter and Revolutionary War soldier. Alex recalled that he had once met a Danny Kuhn at Marshall who was related to Mary Stewart. He had considered tracking him down to inquire of any strange events surrounding the Clay or Stewart families after the Indian massacre. Research so far had not uncovered any skeletons in the closets of any family members that might explain the current situation. Still, something dogged the students, what were they missing.

"I've got something," announced Geri. "It was in the stacks of news articles Professor Monahan had acquired.

Alex examined the article Geri had passed to him. "So, in the 1920's a businessman named Conley T. Snidow purchased the old Clay family farm. He was the originator of the amusement park. C. T., as most called him, bought it with no knowledge of the Clay massacre, not that the event should have had any influence on his purchase. The park featured a spring fed swimming pool, dance hall, occasional Wild West shows, carnival rides, water rides, a racetrack, concession stands, and cabins for guests to stay in. It seems it was quite a popular summertime retreat for thousands of coalfield families."

"Did you read the part about the two deaths?"

"So what? Those were documented, both accidents, one on the swings and the other in the swimming lake. What are you getting at, Stevens?"

"Come on Alex, don't you find it disturbingly ironic that more children, white children at that, dying on the supposedly Indian sacred grounds?"

"Indian spirits seeking revenge you mean? I'd lean toward Clay ancestors seeking revenge on Native Americans the more likely scenario."

"How can you say that after the Clay family members took strips of skin from the Indians' backs to use as razor straps and then, on top of that, reports indicate that the morbid trophies stayed in the family for years afterward."

"They must have buried the hatchet so to speak. It is documented that the Ohio chief of the tribe allowed Clay to claim Ezekiel's body and return him home to be buried with Bartley and Tabitha. Their bodies were exhumed and moved to the hill behind where the farmhouse stood to be buried in shallow graves with their brother. Maybe three of the thirteen are them."

"Once we know more about the cause of the deaths and their nationality, then maybe we can connect some dots. You're just speculating way too much."

"If this thing turns into a criminal investigation, which more than likely it will, we might never know those answers. The police will root us out for sure."

"What's taking them so long? They should have been here by now," spouted Alex.

C.T. Snidow's Dream Comes True

1926 – 1950's and Beyond

The young lad had absolutely no fear of the water. He was a regular tadpole according to some of his elders. While he loved the assortment of rides, there was no better escape from the hot summer days than the park's spring fed swimming pool. While his friends preferred the Ferris wheel, the swings or any number of other rides, he was content, even if alone, as his vivid imagination kept him occupied. While pretending to dive for sunken treasure, he became aware of the presence. A chill rippled over his body, as he paused, dog paddling in the deepest section of the pool. He twirled about expecting to see someone else but the pool belonged to him, as it had for the past thirty or so minutes. Just as he was about to shrug off the feeling, the water became a bubbling inferno near the shallow end. He waited for the kid responsible to surface but no one did.

The large circle of bubbles began moving in his direction. Mesmerized he paddled in place, eying them, still expecting another kid to pop up any second. None did. The bubbles quickly encompassed him, tickling at first, bursting all about his face, him reacting by slapping his hand on the surface and laughing at whoever could hold their breath so long. Then the fun stopped, the maker of the bubbles materialized. Alone in a spring fed pool and with amusement park sounds as the backdrop, no one can hear you scream.

It was late afternoon and the frantic mother stopped any of the amusement park attendants that would listen. She had been unable to locate her young son. She had dropped him off at the park that morning, but he had not been where she had instructed him to be upon her return. Children can become easily distracted, especially among all the activities offered, she had been told countless times thus far. No one seemed overly concerned except her. Her persistence prevailed but not the outcome she had wished. She spotted something floating in the deep end of the pool.

Circling to that side her worst fears were confirmed. Her screams had been heard over the carnival's routine sounds. Her son's lifeless body had been plucked from the crystal clear water, his death ruled as a drowning. No one attempted to explain the odd purplish markings on both his ankles nor could doctors explain the minuscule amount of water in his lungs. Drowning just didn't add up. Due to bad publicity and an unforgiving public, the preexisting pool had become too much of a liability and was filled with sand to prevent any further accidents.

Over the next few years rumors swirled of other missing children, reportedly homeless drifters, none of them substantiated, and there had been no new tragedies involving residents of the surrounding communities, that is, not until in the early 1950's. The cute little girl in the pink dress with ruffled sleeves could not get her fill of riding the whirling swing ride. Swings rotated in a circle at high rates of speed, the kids strapped in, feet dangling freely. The operator of the attraction helped the girl onto her swing and then after no other children showed up, engaged it for her paid turn. Soon afterwards an almost dark presence enveloped the atmosphere, the ride's operator oblivious to all that was about him. The same blinding demeanor had inflicted a truck driver delivering soda to a nearby refreshment stand. The sole occupant of the swings died instantly when the swing and the truck made contact. No one recalled actually witnessing the incident. The park or curse or whatever you might wish to call it had claimed another innocent child.

The park fell on hard times after the second child's death; jinxed, cursed, unsafe, attendance plummeted. It eventually closed; C.T. could no longer afford the albatross hanging around his neck. The abandoned amusement park's reputation continued, former workers spreading all sorts of rumors about odd happenings. Some of them were relieved to no longer be employed. Often unbelievable tales were told after one too many adult beverages had been consumed at local bars loosening their tongues. Town folk gave the park wide berth except for thrill seekers, looking to confirm if rumors were just that. With those visits came more stories of ghostly encounters. Mischievous trespassing kids were the culprits for the most parts and their exaggerated claims were discounted as being the over active imaginations induced by drugs or alcohol.

Gaylord White had worked at the park in his younger days and could tell his fair share of abnormal encounters. He had admitted to having odd feelings of someone behind him touching his shoulder or his arm. No one would be there. Unexplained feelings of a presence there were not uncommon, at least not to him. Oddly, even with all these peculiar encounters, he eventually bought the old park in 1985. White had planned to subdivide the land and sell residential lots. That was before he began finding all sorts of artifacts and stumbling into too many supposedly Indian burial sites. He figured people wouldn't take too kindly to having houses built on top of an Indian graveyard. He instead opted to give the amusement park another try. Cursed and damned, he had no better luck than his predecessor. The dream died after a three year stint.

Hindsight, he should have known better, considering what he had personally experienced there. He recalled, to those who would listen, his main experience. It occurred while he was on his tractor clearing the brush from the field after he had purchased the property. He saw the full apparition of a young girl in a pink dress with ruffled sleeves. He believes that this girl was the spirit of a girl who was killed on the rotating swing ride in the early 1950s. Gaylord claimed that he parked that tractor and left it there for the young girl since she seemed to like watching it so much. He had also reported hearing what sounded like chanting on the property as well.

Historical or Criminal, Under Further Review

1994

As predicted, the dig had been history once Detective Trevor Mendenhall dug into the mystery surrounding the thirteen discovered juveniles. It had indeed become a crime scene investigation. Professor Monahan, backed by both colleges, battled endlessly to stay involved and informed, arguing that thirteen might be a handful of three thousand Native Americans buried on the property. Even with the suspected existence of Indian settlements curiously in a circular arrangement on the property before the first white settlers arrived, the investigation and judicial system shut them out. Alex Ross and Geri Stevens graduated but never forgot what they had discovered or what they had personally experienced. This was more than a mere dig or just an innocent deserted amusement.

Mendenhall and his team of criminal investigators agonized for years over the findings. The thirteen bodies found in one mass grave had spanned over an estimated hundred eighty year stretch. The deepest body had been dated at or around 1800. Stacked like cord wood, each body thereafter had come to rest in fifteen or sixteen year intervals, all except for the last two. Both had been placed there no more than five years before the 1988 archaeological dig began. It defied explanation; thirteen bodies had been buried precisely in the same plot for nearly two hundred years. The children, seven girls and six boys had been alternately placed in the grave except for the last two. Even more bizarre, no cause of death had been determined for any of them. Each appeared to be eleven or twelve years of age.

Obviously the site of the Lake Shawnee Amusement Park had indeed been constructed on a Native American settlement. There was no disputing the evidence to support fact. Mendenhall had struggled with the most important evidence of the case thus far. All thirteen kids had been Caucasian. That made absolutely no sense, not on a Native American burial site. A serial killer had to be discounted. A killer couldn't possibly commit murders over nearly a two hundred year span. Besides, the lack of cause of death didn't support murder or a serial killer. None of them had been identified or accounted for as missing, puzzling given those over the past three decades. How do children end up in an unmarked mass grave in a small town and there be no evidence of their existence or disappearance. With resources and funding running thin from the years of attempting to solve the crime or lack thereof, it teetered on the verge of being categorized as a cold case. The mere thought of walking away from it frustrated Mendenhall.

There should be a trail; those two kids in 1983 shouldn't have just gone missing without some mention of it. How could that be so? The coroner had identified them as identical twin eleven year old boys. Twins dying at the very same time should be a significant event on someone's radar screen; zilch, nothing but dead ends. Dead end, the mere thought of that term infuriated Mendenhall. Then there was the Clay Indian massacre of 1783, the brutal murder of three kids, the more recent amusement park deaths and all this talk about the place being haunted or cursed. He didn't believe in such rubbish, so called paranormal activity being observed at Lake Shawnee; individuals claiming to have experienced orbs in photographs, disembodied voices, Native American chanting, unexplained sounds, and the long forgotten carnival rides moving on their own. He dealt in fact, not fiction and fairy tales; spooks haunting Indian burial grounds were just a way to extort money from innocent people.

Even so, Mendenhall had consulted a local paranormal expert, an acquaintance familiar with the park's history. The contact claimed to have visited the location and confirmed he had seen a full apparition of a male subject in the car in the nine o'clock position of the Ferris wheel. He supported other documented encounters that the swing seats moved on their own when no wind had been apparent, had cold and hot spots. There was no denying it, the paranormal expert believed what he had actually witnessed had happened. It didn't convince Mendenhall though. Ghosts didn't bury those children and how could the burier of the first child have possibly known to dig the original depth of the grave so precisely as to allow twelve more to be buried on top with room to spare. Closing the case might be a blessing in disguise for the detective. No, that was a bold face lie. No case had ever stumped him. No case had ever haunted him like this; haunted, wasn't that an interesting thing to think.

Out of the blue, he received a phone call. The voice on the other end said he held the key to the mystery, all the answers but no solutions. When he pressed the caller, he hung up. There was urgency in that voice. Mendenhall leaned back in his chair and rubbed his hands through his oily hair, thinking how much the caller sounded like a kid. He almost wanted to shrug it off as a prank call but his gut pleaded with him not to do so. He had run out of motives, answers and time; his gut ruled this one. Wishfully he willed a return call, a second chance to work through the predicament with the obviously stressed out person. He had learned long ago that a watched phone never rings. As if on cue it did, almost causing him to flip backwards in his chair. Heavy breathing, then the same voice spoke again, sounding even more frustrated or just plain desperate. This time Mendenhall remained quiet after saying hello and then encouraging the caller to speak his mind.

Lake Shawnee Amusement Park

August 1983

Joseph waited until dark to sneak inside the old park. He could just as easily have done this in the daylight. No one cared about the defunct amusement park nor did it have any security in place to thwart trespassers. Most avoided it at all cost. Not Joseph, the mere chance to encounter a ghost excited him. He had been obsessed with going inside since he and his twin brother Ralph arrived in town just three days ago. His bother had thought his decision to be totally idiotic. He didn't share Joseph's obsession with the unknown. The boys were two week's shy of their twelfth birthday. They had been on the run for nearly six months, having escaped an abusive situation with a step-father after their mother had died of suspicious circumstances. That seemed a lifetime ago, the horrors of Kanawha County a distant memory.

The boys were resourceful, having survived in the world of the homeless, not easy for juveniles. Tough life lessons had prepared them for the worst circumstances; perseverance at all cost. Joseph had stolen a flashlight from an unlocked truck and now wandered through the eerie old park alone, senses on high alert, licking at the chops to see a for real spirit. He paused at an old Ferris wheel, not sure why, but there was something about it that was almost hypnotic. Rusty old swings nearby beckoned him to take his rightful seat. Through his vivid imagination he could pretend riding it around and around. He had never felt so alive and free as he did tonight in this enchanted park.

Something caught Joseph's attention, movement from the corner of his eye. He switched off his flash light, the full moon providing enough light to scan the amusement park landscape. Some Native American tribes referred to the full August moon as the Green Corn Moon or Sturgeon Moon. Joseph wasn't privy to that fact though; he had no Indian blood flowing through his veins. He held his ground, barely blinking and hardly breathing, waiting for the next glimpse of what shared the park with him. He had high expectations that he was about to witness his first supernatural experience, a troubled ghost roaming the grounds. He was disappointed when he quickly identified the interloper.

"Joseph, where are you hiding; I know you're here, no need to try to spook me," yelled his twin brother, Ralph.

Joseph cursed slightly and silently. His lame-brain brother was going to ruin everything. Why hadn't he just stayed back at their campsite like he said he would? He didn't believe in these sorts of things and non-believers had no place in situations like this. Any wondering spirits would receive negative vibes for sure.

"Joseph Stewart, where are you hiding your sorry butt," he yelled even louder, "And I still don't know why you picked Stewart as our last name. I liked our real name better, our mom's name. Come out; come out, where ever you are."

A sudden chill enveloped Joseph and he shivered to shake it free. Were his ears deceiving him? He could faintly hear what sounded like drums, more precisely, war drums, like those you hear in the western movies just before the Indians went on the warpath. He was about to yell out to his prank playing brother when the chanting started; a multitude of voices, something his brother would be incapable of pulling off alone. Then the worst of all scenarios occurred. He heard his brother's unmistakable scream and then all went deathly silent once again. What did all this mean, he wondered, and what should he do about it?

He remained frozen in place; odd for one who had dreamed of such an encounter forever. Encounter, what did encounter mean? He hadn't physically encountered anything but perhaps his brother had. It had to be some sort of elaborate hoax. No, his brother couldn't have had time to pull this off; he had just mentioned his intentions for coming to the park a few hours ago and his brother had not been out of his sight until he left for the park.

Joseph Armstrong 'Stewart' decided he wasn't going to solve this mystery from his present vantage point. He fought the urge to yell his brother's name, opting to proceed quietly and cautiously instead. Possibly there were other perpetrators in the park pulling off this ruse, intent on doing them both harm. With that in mind, Joseph retrieved a piece of rebar he discovered on the ground, perfect length for delivering a homerun if he confronted hostiles. Hostiles, odd, he had never thought in those terms before.

He approached the old carnival midway where his brother had vanished, still the flashlight not engaged. Just before he rounded the corner, the war drums fired back up, only louder this time, the sound almost blanketing him. Seconds later the chanting began, too close for comfort. Unnerved, Joseph hauled ass. He didn't stop running until he had found shelter inside what appeared to have once been a hotdog stand.

I'm not sure why I came here, not really; well sort of, maybe. No one made me. No one dared me. No one even knew I was coming; well almost no one. That was a very bad mistake on my part. Not telling someone about it and coming here in the first place; and not coming here alone. I didn't have anything to gain and certainly not anything to prove. Yet, I couldn't help it. I had to come. I had to know, but what did I really expect to find, to learn, to experience. What do I know about such things? I'm not a chicken but what does that really gain me now? The blame for what has happened is my fault and I can't undo it, take anything back. Boy how I wish I could. I should have heeded the warnings of my elders, but instead I did the opposite. Opposite is always more exciting, more fun, or it was until now. I just don't want to be here anymore. I now know things no one should ever know. I'm not sure I'll ever be able to tell anyone though; not that I want to keep secrets; it's just that I'm not sure I'll be allowed to leave. I still hear those screams. I should have come here alone. No, that's all wrong. I should not have come here at all.

A child crying caught his attention. Peeping over the open front of the rickety old building, he scanned the immediate area seeking the origin of the crying. There, sitting on the swings he had earlier occupied was a little girl wearing a pink dress. She was shaking her head no, and she was pointing somewhere behind the hotdog stand. Joseph could clearly make out her words being mouthed, even though he couldn't hear the words being spoken, *run, run, leave now.* Too late, much too late, they were upon him. He had nowhere to run. All he could do was mimic his twin's screams.

Lake Shawnee Amusement Park

August 1994

Detective Trevor Mendenhall still rattled by the brief phone call, stood at the entrance to the park. He should have told someone he was coming here but he feared he might incur interference from his superiors, growing impatient with him and the time he devoted to the case. The abandoned park was just too forbidding in the darkness, not that Mendenhall feared the dark or the boogeyman. There were far worst encounters on the everyday streets but, still, this placed oozed something intangibly out of kilter, something he couldn't quite put his finger on, similarly to that phone call. The pleading voice, childlike but yet not, had beckoned him here, saying he could stop it; stop what though?

Mendenhall perused the out most perimeters first; the night hardly required the assistance of his flash light due to the brightly shining full moon. He still wasn't sure why he was here or exactly what he expected to find or prevent. He treaded across land that used to be a spring fed pool in the early days of the park, veering past an old race track, before heading towards the Ferris wheel, a common ride in most every park or traveling carnival. Various games of chance dotted the midway. He remembered as a kid tossing rings, shooting hoops or throwing baseballs at milk bottles. Just as he approached the last venue, The Pick-up Ducks, he saw a tiny figure dart past a concession stand. He sprinted in pursuit and saw the figure disappear inside a ticket booth. He slowed his pace, no need to hurry, there was no place for the person to hide or escape now. Force of habit, he readied his pistol.

The detective switched on his flashlight and eased the squeaky door open. No one was there, impossible. Movement, no, more of a creaking board alerted him to check behind a huge waste receptacle located under an overhang at the ticket booth window. A pair of dark eyes reflected in the beam of his light. He pushed the receptacle aside with his foot, never breaking eye contact, to expose a little boy. He scrunched back in the corner, trembling and crying. He held out his hand to the youngster, announcing he was a policeman, flashing his badge. The boy accepted his gesture. Both stepped outside the booth.

Through a few simple questions he had learned his name was Chester McCoy, eleven years old, he was here alone, but had not come here of his own free will. His parents and he were on vacation and had stopped for gas. Chester had been asleep inside the camper being pulled by his folks. He had vaguely remembered being picked up and carried then waking in this strange place, dazed and confused so it seemed. The boy had not been the caller so that mystery remained unsolved. Then he said the craziest thing; he had been running and hiding from Indians. When asked could he describe them; he couldn't. Chester hadn't exactly seen them but he had heard them. Realizing that he was becoming distraught, Mendenhall halted his questioning and changed the subject. Hand in hand, he walked Chester McCoy back towards the amusement park entrance where his vehicle was parked. He assured the lad that he would reunite him with his parents.

Just as they reached the exit to the park and after sending Chester through the turnstile, Mendenhall heard the unmistakable beating of drums and chanting. He placed young Chester McCoy in the back seat of his car and told him to stay put and keep the doors locked; he'd be right back. He then followed the sounds echoing from deeper in the park, convinced these were most likely his kidnappers. Possibly they had snatched the boy to use in some symbolic Indian ceremony; maybe another intended eleven year old victim to go along with the previous thirteen. Mendenhall was confident he was about to solve this odd serial crime and put an end to the child murders. He came close to calling it in and requesting back up but this was his case. Nobody else had really cared but him. He could just imagine the look on the captain's face when he served it up on a silver platter; crow would leave a bitter taste for sure.

Halloween 2014

A handful of people had begun gathering just before dark, many conversing and anticipating the adventure ahead. Thereced was a mixture of believers and nonbelievers but thrill seekers just the same, each wielding various versions of flashlights, required along with the price of admission. Capitalizing on recent publicity and exposure, just maybe the place could be profitable for a change. In October 2005, the park had gained national attention when *ABC network's Scariest Places on Earth* had filmed the location. A psychic contracted by the network had refused to stay on the property due to what had been described as a spiritual energy being too strong. Film crew workers would not enter the filming location alone at night due to eerie feelings.

Local lore had been played up, mentioning that one of many ghostly spirits was still at play in the abandoned Lake Shawnee Amusement Park near Princeton, West Virginia. Specifically the young girl dressed in the pink ruffled dress that had died on those swings was billed as one of the spirits still haunting the park. It certainly had prompted a renewed interest for thrill seekers after *Discovery Channel's Ghostlab* and the *Travel Channel's 'The Most Terrifying Places in America'* had spotlighted the park on segments.

Alex Ross, now in his mid forties, waited his chance to venture back into the park. Standing in line alone with the strangers gathered, his thoughts returned to 1988 and he reminisced to himself about he had experienced here. Alex had never been able to let go; personally haunted by that day they had been pulled from the dig and prohibited from finishing what they had started, what they had rightfully discovered. The original investigation had been handled too tight lipped to suit him, like there was something to hide. He graduated, moved on for awhile but couldn't shake it. Eventually he began his own investigation from the sidelines, attempted to piece together a puzzle too bizarre to wrap his brain around, thirteen children buried in a single grave over a span of nearly two hundred years. There was rhyme to the reason and he had been damn determined to solve the mystery. A clearing of a throat followed by a bump from behind returned him to the present. He turned to confront the rude and impatient person but instead broke out in a grin.

"Geri Stevens," he said.

"Geri Gordon, married with three children; instinct told me I might find you here, Alex."

"Alex, it is, married, then divorced, no kids and destined to be a reinvented recluse."

"Well what can I say; this place dug its claws into me way back when and it hasn't turned me loose either."

"Same here, I've never been able to get past what we experienced during the dig and not having closure I suppose. Do you think tonight will bring closure?"

"Not a chance but I'm here just the same. What about you?"

"I have a theory, some facts, some conjectures, but I think it would hold its own if allowed as evidence."

"Do you care to share with an old colleague?"

"I thought you'd never twist my arm. So here goes…"

"Mitchell and Phoebe Clay, as you may recall, had fourteen children, seven boys and seven girls, three of which were lost that terrible August day in 1783. The Clay men and a posse hunted down those responsible and then brutally delivered justice to several Native Americans. From those events an evil presence evolved, possibly on its own or by Indian intervention, but evil just the same. It took up residence on this property, the parcel of land where it all began and where those who countered with despicably bloody results still resided. For the next nearly two hundred years it ruled."

"It, what do you mean by it?"

"I will get to that soon enough but, for now, let me lay out my case my way. You and I discovered the grave containing thirteen. It has been confirmed that the thirteen bodies had not been the result of one event, one burial. It spanned at least a hundred eighty years, in intervals, as best as can be determined, every fifteen to sixteen years. No single person could have been responsible for all the deaths. Forensics confirmed all of the children were approximately eleven years old and healthy, no sign of criminal activity, and the cause of death could not be determined in any. Thirteen dead, seven girls and six boys, correct?"

"Yes, the last was figured to have happened as recently as 1983."

"Yes, the twelfth and thirteenth, but not the last," confirmed Alex. "Do you recall the detective's name, the one who booted us from the dig? Let me refresh your memory; Detective Trevor Mendenhall, he couldn't wait to get us out of here. The man was an opportunist and he wanted to crack what he perceived as a career building case, wide open. I've talked to other policemen in the department and all said he was obsessed with the case. In 1994 superiors with the department had decided that enough time, money and energy had been spent on those never to ever have been identified children. They were shutting down the case. Our detective didn't take too kindly to that from what I have been told. "

"It sounds to me as if you've suffered a bit of obsessive behavior too, Alex."

"No denying it, guilty as charged. From the best anyone can piece together, because Mendenhall never shared his intentions with anyone; the detective ventured out here one August night in 1994. His car was found in the parking lot locked and abandoned the next morning. After an extensive search inside the amusement park, outside and the adjoining countryside, the detective was never located. They even brought in cadaver sniffing dogs, still nothing. He just vanished into thin air so it seems and to this day he has never turned up dead or alive. It remains on record as a cold case."

"There's more, right?"

"Theory, but yes; the Clays, Mitchell and Phoebe, had fourteen children and I believe these deaths were symbolic scarifies, but by whom or what I really am not sure. Consider the facts though, seven boys and seven girls and in that grave were the bodies of seven girls and six boys."

"One shy, do you think we discovered the gravesite before the fourteenth was placed there?"

"Maybe, or maybe the discovery really had no impact on the outcome. Detective Mendenhall's body was never recovered."

"I don't follow. The others were children and the detective doesn't fit the scenario, other than being a male."

"Possibly Mendenhall was destined to be the grand finale, the last male. He had ties to this. I traced his bloodline and his family tree had deep imbedded roots."

"He was related to the Clays?"

"No, Edward Hale was his ancestor."

Geri shrugged, "I don't get it."

"Hale was a member of the 1783 search party lead by Matthew Farley. Hale allegedly shot and killed the very first Indian that signaled the beginning of the vicious fight. Mendenhall, for whatever reason, ended up here and I think he was claimed as the fourteenth and final sacrifice, considered to be the most important, the direct link to the one who drew first blood."

"But first blood was drawn at the hands of the raiding party with the murder and scalping of Bartley Clay."

"Native Americans don't see things the same way we do. In their eyes the search party bushwhacked and killed the braves for revenge. The Indians justified their attack as defending land that belonged to them. In their culture there is a clear difference. Remember, we both confessed we heard that chanting."

"So you think Indian spirits got their revenge?"

"No, I have no fact to support murderous ghosts. Maybe this is a case of one generation passing on the responsibility to the next, a required sacrifice every so often."

"Do you think those other thirteen had family ties to 1783 and the event?"

"I don't know. I can only hang my hat on number fourteen, the seventh male and rightful kin. College acquaintance Danny Kuhn, a descendent of Mary Stewart, might have possibly become the final victim if he hadn't moved away to South Carolina. It's all in the timing I suppose."

"Do you think this amusement park is really haunted after everything that has happened and what we experienced during the dig?"

"I guess we'll know that answer shortly. It appears it is time to go inside. After all, this is supposed to be the ultimate haunted experience. At least that's what's printed on my ticket."

T. Allen Winn Published Work
The Detective Trudy Wagner series (Road Rage and North of the Border)
Dark Thirty (Dale Thomas Jackson battles the bullies)
The Perfect Spook House (paranormal thriller)
The Caregiver's Son, Outside the Window Looking In (memoir)

Available on Amazon or where books are sold on line
Pelican Book Store, Sunset Beach, N.C.
Clock Tower Books, Georgetown, S.C.
Grapefull Sisters Vineyard, Tabor City, N.C.

T. Allen Winn on Facebook
T. Allen Winn Blog @ http://originalwhomper.blogspot.com/
TALLENWINN@mail.com

SHORTS

"GHOST WALTZ"

By Joy Summerlin-Glunt

They said the sounds of violins playing The Viennese Waltz lingered in the Whispering Trees around the old mansion even after the celebrations were done.

"Geoffrey, I want you to build the new governor's mansion, subject to the legislature's appropriation of funds, of course," the Governor said, leaning back in his leather and mahogany chair.

"I'd be honored, sir," the architect said, "but first I must complete the house I am building for my dear wife MaryAllis. "I promised her, sir…and this is a promise I must keep."

Three years later, the legislature approved the building of the new governor's mansion. By then, MaryAllis Wright sat on the front porch of her 3 story mansion, inhaling the fragrance of yellow Roses, Sunflowers and purple Wisteria. She sat in a white wicker rocking chair, eyes closed, thinking of names for their first child, and being thankful for her beautiful home.

There was not another mansion around Raleigh like the mansion she called Whispering Trees. Geoffrey Wright designed it for her himself.

From the first time they saw it inhabitants of Raleigh swore that the Victorian mansion had a personality of its own. They said that the house fairly sang out with laughter and merriment when times were good. Sometimes there were the sounds of violins playing waltzes, and the tinkling of silver bells.

"Maryallis McAllister McDermott was imported," the townsfolk said…"imported from Scotland." When Geoffrey told folks that Whispering Trees was a labor of love for MaryAllis, they knew it was so. MaryAllis heard and just smiled.

No one in Raleigh had ever seen such lovely flame-red hair as MaryAllis wore floating about her face and shoulders…naturally curly hair, the envy of women who had to roll theirs up on papers or little spools. Three sons and a daughter that survived had her flame red hair, but the other boy Geoffrey III, the one who looked the most like his father, had brown hair, wore spectacles, and wasn't a bit out-going like his Mother. He left home one summer day and was not heard from again. Neither Geoffrey nor Maryallis spoke of him. The pain was too great. It was rumored that he had been sent to Scotland with one of the relatives to study music. Others simply started rumors that he went to sea.

Then one day audible sobbing could be heard above the whispering, and some folks said the house creaked and groaned aloud with the agony of Geoffrey and MaryAllis after three of their 8 children died of Pneumonia one dark, cold winter when icicles hung like daggers from the porch roof.

Geoffrey had surely built Whispering Trees for MaryAllis but it was their only surviving child Little MaryAllis, who married William Jessup who inherited the mansion Whispering Trees.

MaryAllis Jessup, great granddaughter of the Wrights and their only surviving child
inherited Whispering Trees just as she inherited MaryAllis' name and her flame-red hair.

For a long time Whispering Trees stood silent and empty. No one knew for sure why the Jessups disappeared, why no one had heard from them since that fateful Christmas Eve. Their car still sat in the Carriage House. Remains of a Christmas dinner stayed until eaten by mice and insects. The piano sat in the parlor, still spread with old holly and dried garlands of pine boughs.

The dried Christmas tree laden with decorations made by the children's own hands still sat in the corner in front of the bookcase next to the fireplace where the mantel still hung with red flannel stockings.

With the Jessups' disappearance too had gone the laughter, the music of violins, and the dancing of waltzes, and the tinkling of the silver bells. The only sounds left were the whisperings of the Pine and Oak trees, the mourning doves at dusk, and crickets and cicadas after the sun went down.

The authorities were baffled, having exhausted their search for the family. The Jessups had not left by train, and no one had seen strangers in the area.

The old mansion sagged now under its years while mice built nests in the attic. Weeds grew high and Ivy and orange-flowered Trumpet vines circled the chimneys. Once lush yellow roses grew spindly and wild. Purple Wisteria snaked around most of the trees, while luring bees to their sweetness in the summer.

One bleak winter morning when icicles hung off the house's eaves, Arthur Marclift arrived. He was rotund and grimy and looked like a man who had been on the street too long. He had a greasy stubbled beard…and a mission…to find Mamie Frame who he knew lived at Whispering Trees. He wondered whether Mamie Frame had forgotten that hateful daughter of hers. Norma. When he could see short, raven-haired Norma Frame in his mind, sometimes she was just mean old Norma Frame, and sometimes when he saw her in his mind's eye she was glowing, red-eyed, growling, drooling spit….and calling him names that pierced his very skin.

Arthur Marclift knew where Norma was now…but he was the only one who knew.

Arthur made friends with old Silas the Caretaker of Whispering Trees and his plump wife Mamie, telling them he was happy to meet them, thanking them for staying on and taking some care of the place. He convinced them too that he was the new owner of Whispering Trees and wanted them to stay, same as always.

"Old coot," Marclift muttered under his breath. "You never should have trusted Mamie Frame who had a daughter who cut people to pieces with her words and destroyed their careers."

If the tycoon developers with their briefcases made Silas more than a little worried, Arthur Marclift scared the hell out of him…but he kept silent, because he was old now and Whispering Trees had been his home for almost as long as he could remember. And hadn't Marclift asked them to stay on, look out for things, do what they had been doing all these years, live in the carriage house apartment at Whispering Trees, keep up the Mausoleum--even though no one had been entombed there since the Wright children died.

Marclift also told Silas to spruce up the grounds and make the old mansion livable again so he could rent it to somebody or maybe even sell it for a good price, never telling him that he had sold it already…to a young lawyer Adam Aaron, a young man fresh out of that law school in Chapel Hill, a young man getting married soon, a young man with a beautiful fiancé named Liana Summerfeld, a school teacher…. with beautiful red hair…and a rich grandma named Diana Earhardt who had given them the money to buy the old mansion.

Because he and Mamie loved the place, Silas agreed. They would ask the new tenants if they could stay on and help out…be the new caretakers of Whispering Trees.

Arthur Marclift, saying he'd be back, left on a beat up old green Plymouth with Mississippi license Plates. This had been the first time, Silas and Mamie had ever met Arthur Marclift but they might have been surprised to know the number of times Arthur Marclift had visited Whispering Trees. They might have been terrified to know that when the Jessups disappeared Arthur had been close enough to place a grimy hand on their shoulders…or worse. If they had known he was there, they might have run screaming from Whispering Trees, never to return.

But Arthur was there, and he'd be back. And the new tenants would be there as soon as the lavish wedding on the beach at Debordieu in Pawley's Island was finalized. They'd be on their way to Whispering Trees….and they were everything Arthur Marclift was not.

Adam Aaron had invited Arthur to the wedding but already Arthur was feeling things that made him uneasy. After all he had met Liana Summerfeld. Adam Aaron was a lucky man. Arthur found it hard to stop thinking about Liana's glossy red hair and beautiful eyes. She didn't look anything like Norma, and she hadn't been anything but nice to him that day they signed the papers to buy the mansion…..and that pretty red hair…but she had something Arthur had never had and would never have since his wife had ended her life…someone loved Liana Summerfeld. No one would ever love Arthur Marclift again.

Twice Arthur almost turned around and went back to Raleigh, once in Myrtle Beach and again in Murrell's Inlet, but he stopped for gas and a burger in Litchfield and kept driving. The AC had long since died in the old Plymouth and his neck itched with dirt and sweat in the dingy white shirt collar. His suit had not been worn since he worked in the university, and had never been cleaned. He soothed himself with the thought that the wedding would be worth it…there would be food and lots of it at the reception in the Great Hall. But Arthur Marclift had not counted on what happened next.

The wedding was a grand one with lots of huge white flowers and white tents, and chairs covered in white damask and even a long white trail of carpet for the bride and groom to walk on toward the minister. The I do's said, the bridal bouquet thrown to an eager young bridesmaid in pink, birdseed thrown in all directions, the entourage made its way to the Reception Hall, the 5 tiered wedding cake, the dance by the bride and groom, and the dancing by the relatives with each other.

And then it happened…the waltz…the same one that played that Christmas Eve, the same one that was playing when he found his wife… and suddenly everyone was dancing…and the waltz played on and on and on. The bridal couple was smiling, dancing, kissing, swinging and swaying, whirling around the huge Oaken dance floor, gazing into each other's eyes, letting the whole world know how happy they were and how much they loved each other.

Arthur could barely control his rage as he watched the happy, loving couple embrace.

Diana Earhardt, Liana's svelte blonde grandmother, watched as Arthur Marclift changed from an unkempt guest to a furious one before her eyes, a Jekyl and Hyde in the Summerfeld-Aaron Wedding Reception.

"May I help you, Mr. Marclift?" she asked. "You don't like the music? Would you care for something to eat or drink?"

"No." he said, exiting the hall faster than his legs usually moved, muttering. "Old rich biddy…more money than God….loves, no, worships that pretty waltzing girl with the red hair."

Puzzled, Diana eased from the hall, watched Arthur heading for his car and thought to herself…Dear God in Heaven, I have met the "bogeyman."

Arthur snatched open the drivers -side door of the old green Plymouth and fell inside. He pounded the steering wheel until his stubby fingers bled before he gripped it so hard his knuckles threatened to break through his skin.

Arthur started the car…he was hungry…there had been enough food in that Reception Hall for five armies, but he had not taken a single bite. He had almost lost it…again.

At the Sea Horse corner store he bought some cheddar cheese crackers and a grape soda, wolfed them down, and began the long drive back to Whispering Trees… totally fixated on Liana Summerfeld Aaron, beautiful, flame-haired bride of Attorney Adam Aaron. He would win Liana Summerfeld Aaron to himself—at Whispering Trees…in spite of the mind shattering waltz still playing in his head. "Mine," he said aloud.

An icy shiver snaked down Liana's spine, and in the midst of the happiest day of her life, she suddenly felt uneasy. Adam held her closer.

And the orchestra kept playing…. And the guests kept waltzing… The Palmetto Palms rustled in the salty night air, and baby loggerheads wriggled toward the ocean in the dark.

(This story "Ghost Waltz" is excerpted from my copyrighted novel GHOST WALTZ.)
Joy Summerlin-Glunt (aka Arielle A. Aaron)
I REMEMBER SINGING-A Boy Survives the Holocaust (biography) Amazon & *glunt.joy@gmail.com*
IN THE PRESENCE OF BUTTERFLIES (History of the 1998 Butterfly Project & How to Teach about the Holocaust)-Amazon & *glunt.joy@gmail.com*
THE UNFROGGETTABLE FIONA FAYETTA FROGGEE (Humor for Women) Amazon & *glunt.joy@gmail.com*
A LITTLE BOOK FOR MY ALL GROWN-UP-NOW SONS -- *glunt.joy@gmail.com*
***Website:* inthepresenceofbutterflies.com** FACEBOOK: Arielle A. Aaron
Facebook Group: REMEMBER THE CHILDREN, SURVIVORS, RESCUERS & LIBERATORS
TWITTER: Arielletweets
Non-profit Website: http://www. permanentbutterflymemorialmonument.com

POPCORN MADNESS
By James H. Lucas

I tried to warn you. I posted it on my blog, inserted the warnings into my articles and even went on television to tell you of what was coming, but, as usual, my words (eloquent though they were) fell on deaf ears.

And now I'm here, in this tiny cell writing on unlined paper in blue crayon (they tell me blue is a calming color, but I don't feel calm) trying one last time to convince the world that I'm not crazy.
Yes, I know that writing a manifesto in crayon is not the best way to convince others of your sanity.

I was once like you.

Well, not exactly like you, I had better taste in movies than you, for you see, I was a film critic. It was my duty to praise the films that truly utilized the cinematic medium to its fullest and to condemn the ones that looked as if they were created solely as a receptacle for fart jokes.

Not that you cared. No one listens to film critics. I have seen people approach the art critic, hat in hand (metaphorically, no one wears hats anymore) and ask for their learned opinion on the latest exhibition or the newest painter on the scene and the critic would respond with intelligence, wit and with just the right amount of adoration or scorn. The person would thank the critic for sharing their wisdom and in the same breath turn to me and say, "I liked that movie. You don't know what you're talking about!"

I don't know what I'm talking about.

I have a doctorate in Film Studies from NYU. I've written six books on the subject of cinema and cinema history and have provided commentary tracks for several titles available on Blu-Ray from The

Criterion Collection.

But, I don't know what I'm talking about.

I digress.

Let me start at the beginning.

It was twelve years ago when it started. I was sitting in a critics screening of a new comedy called *Freshman Uprising*. It was awful. Gratuitous nudity, jokes telegraphed a mile away, bad acting, every manner of bodily fluid slung about the screen with wild abandon and one-dimensional characters that had been ripped off from far better films.

I shared my appraisal of this pile of rotten cinematic dung.

Of course it made a ton of money. Number one at the box office for three straight weeks.

I was used to this by now. A poorly conceived and executed comedy or action movie or "slasher" horror film comes out, I pan it and it makes more money than I will ever see in my life. Such is the way of things when you're a film critic. You learn to never underestimate the poor choices of filmgoers.

But there was something different about this film. It was days after my half-star review ran that I began to realize what was so different about this particular picture. It was the film's co-star, the wacky, drunken fool who behaved like an ill-bred jackass for ninety-seven minutes.

His name was Ron Shafer.

He was thin, average height, with shaggy hair and a big goofy grin. His character in *Freshman Uprising* quickly became a fan favorite. There was talk of giving him his own spin-off movie.

Ron Shafer.

The man who would doom us all.

Shafer followed this cinematic pimple with more of the same, *Yellow Belly* (about a man who is afraid of everything until a genie makes him fearless), *The Girl of My Wet Dreams* (about a man who falls for a Playboy Playmate and crosses the country to be with her) and *Repeating Kindergarten* (about a man who has to go back to kindergarten because...well, who cares?) bad movie after bad movie after bad movie. No matter how much I trashed these films, whether I took the high road and explained why they were terrible or I took the low road, angrily pointing fingers at Shafer, the directors, the audience or anyone else who created or viewed this nonsense, it didn't matter. People still flocked to see it. Shafer got richer and richer and I was ignored more and more.

This is why I did not have high hopes for his latest monstrosity: *Little Jimmy Gets Big*, a "comedy" about a man who invents a serum causing the male organ to vastly increase in size. I heard about this film while it was still in production and instantly hung my head in shame.

Why do things like this get green-lit while Scorsese has to struggle to find funding? I wondered.

The film started making headlines a few days later, but you probably didn't hear about it, as it wasn't front-page news. *Little Jimmy Gets Big* had three screenwriters, Thomas Yarborough, Ben Heinz and Kevin Littleton. All three died shortly after production began, and all three under unusual circumstances.

Thomas Yarborough was decapitated when he stuck his head in front of an oncoming train. Supposedly, his last words were, "I want to watch the train approach."

Ben Heinz died of asphyxiation when he sat in his car with the engine running and the garage door closed. He had made a phone call a few minutes prior during which he said "I was going to go somewhere, but I forgot where."

Kevin Littleton blew himself to kingdom come when he left the gas on the stove on and went to light up a joint.

Pretty stupid deaths, right?

Well, it only got stranger.

Grant Henderson, the assistant director on *Little Jimmy Gets*

Big was electrocuted when he tried to play videogames in his bathtub.

Alicia DeWitt, associate producer, was mauled by tigers when she tried to give them hugs at the zoo. (Reportedly, her last words were "Kitty!")

Gina Kramer, who worked in hair and makeup, left work saying she felt bloated. She was found later having drunk an entire bottle of Drain-O.

People were dropping like flies and in increasingly stupid ways. But, the show must go on and on it went. The film finished shooting (three more deaths), was edited (two deaths), scored (four deaths), previewed (eight deaths) and released upon the world, a moronic comedy of doom.

The Four Fart Jokes of the Apocalypse.

I was able to get into one of the advance screenings (the studio, wisely, was not screening the film for critics) and found, to my astonishment, that it was even worse than I had imagined.

The film was one hour and forty-eight minutes of puerile, infantile humor, not once did I so much as smile, let alone laugh as I was barraged with bad jokes, poor acting, a script that made no sense, veteran actors whose embarrassment at being in such a picture was palpable and catch-phrases and vulgarity in place of wit.

I left the film with a headache, feeling as though I had spent all day eating junk food and badly needed some vegetables to settle my stomach. I felt greasy and unclean. I went home and put on some classical music and made a cup of tea, settling into my sofa, hoping that I would feel better soon.

Something was troubling me.

I was a film critic, and a result had sat through more than my fair share of bad movies. I had survived *Battlefield Earth, Showgirls, Gigli, Batman and Robin,* the films of Uwe Boll, *Anaconda, Baby Geniuses,* and every movie that ever starred Paris Hilton, but I had never felt like this after any of those. So why was this one affecting me so?

Perhaps it was because when I closed my eyes, I could still see it, as though I had never left the theater. I could hear, in spite of the Beethoven coming from my stereo, Ray Shafer's catchphrase from the film, "Dingle-dangle-dongle!"

"Dingle-dangle-dongle!"

"Dingle-dangle-dongle!"

"Dingle-dangle-dongle!"

As if he was sitting next to me, screeching it into my ears.

I decided to wait until the next day to type up my review. Finishing my tea, I poured myself a glass of white wine and put on *L'Atalante* to remind myself why I became a critic in the first place.

The next day I went into my office at *The Times-Tribune*. Technically, I could work from home, but I enjoyed coming into work, sitting in an office surrounded by the hurly-burly of a real newspaper. It was a dying thing, being replaced by the more evolved and vicious internet, where any yahoo with a blog could do what I do and often did even if they were of the generation that believed that cinema began with *Star Wars*.

On my way to my office, I spotted Trey Urbanik, the sportswriter, reclining in his chair, his feet propped up on his desk, tossing a baseball up in the air and catching it. Trey was one of those people you never saw actually work, and yet his pieces were always on time, accurate and a thrill to read. I myself am not much of a sports fan, but I enjoyed reading Trey's work simply because I enjoy good writing.

"How's it going?" he asked.

I shook my head. My headache still hadn't completely vanished. "Ugh. I saw the new Ron Shafer last night."

"No good, huh?"

"That's putting it mildly."

"Well, what'd you expect?" He shrugged. "I dunno. The boys wanna see it."

The boys were Trey's two sons, Dan and Barry (named after

a football player and a baseball player, I'm told) and it grieved me to think that those two boys were perfect examples of today's youth and their horrible taste in films. More than once I tried to get them to watch a good movie, a Preston Sturges comedy or a John Ford western, but to no avail. They spent most of the time looking straight down at their phones.

"I wouldn't. That movie gave me a headache that I'm still dealing with."

"How many stars?"

"Zero."

"Zero?!? Shoot, what was the last movie you gave zero stars to?"

"*Saving Christmas*," I replied without even having to think about it. The really awful movies stay with you, as do the really great ones, it's the mediocre ones, the romantic comedies starring TV actors trying to break into movies that are released off-season that you forget.

"Well, have fun writing it," he said and went back to his baseball.

I nodded and headed for my office. Normally, Trey was right, I did enjoy tearing apart really bad movies, partially out of revenge for wasting two hours of my life and partially because sometimes it was kind of fun to be nasty. But, this time was different. I didn't want to think about *Little Jimmy Gets Big*, I didn't want to have to replay scenes in my head or double-check the names of those involved on imdb.com, I wanted to stay away from it all together.

As I waited for my computer to boot up, I tried to find the words that described how I felt and I found myself thinking back to when I was young and one of my neighbors had this great big German shepherd named Duke. As massive as that dog was, it seemed like it could make itself totally invisible until you were right next to it, when it would leap from the shadows and begin to bark its cacophonous, terrifying bark. I would take the long way home, going out of my way to avoid that terrible dog.

That was how I felt about *Little Jimmy Gets Big*.
I was afraid of it.

I was at my favorite lunch spot, Beekman's Diner, sipping on a Sprite and trying to not think about the fact that I was only half-way done with my review of *Little Jimmy Gets Big*. I had spent all morning forcing myself to write about the film and it had left me feeling queasy.

What's wrong with me? I wondered. *I'm not being forced to sit in raw sewage and eat rancid meat, I'm writing a film review, something I've been doing for nearly twenty-five years.*

But I couldn't shake it. The thought of going back to the office and thinking about that movie again filled me with nausea and dread.

I had brought along a notebook and was making little notes in it, to distract myself. I had decided that once I finished the review of *Little Jimmy Gets Big*, I was going to treat myself and add another entry into my list of Cinematic Masterpieces, a series of articles I had been writing off and on for the last few years, talking about a truly magnificent film and why people should see it. I never got as much feedback on those as I did my regular reviews, but those that did comment on them were true lovers of cinema. In the meantime, I did a bit of mental doodling, which is what I call it when I make lists simply for the sake of making them. Lists like "Movies with One Word Titles" or "Greatest Silent Film Directors", just something to keep my mind occupied.

I had started such a list in Beekman's Diner that day, waiting on my club sandwich to arrive.

"Ten Greatest Comedies of All Time" I had titled it. ("All Time" being from now until I decide to do this list again.)

1) *Some Like It Hot*
2) *Duck Soup*
3) *City Lights*
4) *To Be Or Not To Be*
5) *Steamboat Bill, Jr*
6) *Being There*

7) *Annie Hall*
8) *Dr. Strangelove*
9) *Mon Oncle*
10) *Little Jimmy G-*

I froze.

I shook my head.

No, no, no, I thought. I meant to write *My Man Godfrey, The Producers, The Thin Man, The Bank Dick* or *Safety Last*, not that movie. Not that horrible, horrible, unfunny movie.

My sandwich arrived and all I did was stare at it for fifteen minutes before finally asking the waitress to wrap it up for me. She glanced at the untouched food.

"Is something wrong?" she asked.

"I'm not feeling well," I replied. It sounded better than the truth. *I've been poisoned by a movie.*

I trudged back to the office and deposited my lunch on the desk where it landed with an unappetizing thud. Remember *Ikiru*?

Of course you don't.

In that film, right after the old man discovers he has inoperable cancer, he leaves the hospital with the weight of his impending doom crushing him. The film is silent as he walks along, defeated.

That's how I felt, as if the world had become silent and I had been defeated.

I forced myself to finish the review, pulling it out of me like it was a tapeworm.

"...putrid..." I wrote.

"...awful..."

"...painful..."

"...the single worst movie-going experience of my life..."

I typed the last period, hit save and promptly vomited into my trashcan. I let out a groan and spit, trying to clear the taste from my mouth.

I switched off my computer and went home.

I didn't leave my home for about three days after that. I locked myself away, reading James Agee, Andre Bazin and Pauline Kael. I watched *Children of Paradise, Citizen Kane, Seven Samurai, La Strada, Goodfellas, The General, The Circus, The Treasure of the Sierra Madre, The Seventh Seal, Singin' in the Rain, Umberto D, Ace in the Hole, Sunrise, Ivan the Terrible* (both parts), *The Last Laugh* and *Metropolis*, anything to distance myself from…it.

Finally, on Monday morning, feeling more like myself again, I ventured out.

My first stop was the Starbucks on the corner, where I got my usual venti mocha frap (no whipped cream, please). I was in a good mood, having spent the long weekend getting reacquainted with some of the true greats of cinema. Contrary to popular belief, most film critics become film critics not because they want to spend their lives trashing bad movies, but because they want to shout from the mountaintops about great movies, whether they are widely recognized classics, forgotten gems, the latest work from a master filmmaker or the burgeoning of a true talent. It's more about praise than scorn, but sadly, to find something worth praising you have to search, whereas to find something worthy of scorn, you merely have to open your eyes.

As soon as I entered the Starbucks, I could tell something was wrong. Customers were at the counter, yelling at the young staff, who stood around like cattle, not sure who these people were or what they wanted. The display case, usually filled with pastries, was nearly empty and what was in there was either burned to a crisp or raw.

"What's going on here?" I asked a man who was storming past me.

"They're a bunch of idiots!" he shouted, shoving the door open. (Well, this isn't *exactly* what he said, but what he said isn't fit to print.)

I went up to the counter. "Um, excuse me?" I asked the young girl with the pony tail who stood there.

"Yeah?" she asked with timidity, as though afraid I was going to attack her or ask her to do something beyond her capabilities.

"Could I get a venti mocha frap with not whipped cream?"

She shook her head. "I don't know what that is."

"It's a mocha Frappacino, a venti, the big one."

She shook her head again, still not understanding.

Glancing at my watch in annoyance, I said, "Can I just have a large coffee?"

"You want a big cup of coffee?" she asked as though repeating a phrase in a foreign language.

"Yes."

She turned, fixed a cup and handed it to me. As soon as I touched it, I knew there was a problem. Removing the lid, I saw that the cup was full of coffee grounds without a single drop of water.

"Uh, miss," I called out to her as she was beginning to move away from me. "This isn't what I wanted."

"It's a big cup of coffee," she said in child-like defiance.

"Is this some kind of joke?" I was getting agitated, my good movie buzz wearing off.

"It's coffee," she insisted.

I threw the cup down and stormed out, half-expecting to run into a production assistant from a hidden-camera prank show to meet me with a waiver to sign.

It wasn't a joke.

It wasn't a prank.

It was just beginning.

At the office, I found Trey standing at the window, looking down. The blinds were raised and there was a large hole in the glass.

"What's going on?" I asked.

"I dropped my ball," he replied.

"Out the window?!?" I exclaimed.

"I was trying to bounce it off the window and it went through it."

"Well, of course it went through it," I said. "What did you think was going to happen?"

He shrugged. "I dunno."

I stepped into his office and looked him up and down. "Are you okay?" I was genuinely concerned for my friend.

"I dunno," he shrugged again.

I slowly nodded. "Okay. Listen, um, I'll be in my office if you need anything. All right?"

He shrugged a third time.

I went to my office, shaking my head in puzzlement over Trey's odd behavior.

I turned my computer on and checked my e-mails. The usual stuff, people writing to argue with me about some film or another, suggestions of films I should add to my Cinematic Masterpieces collection, a couple of invites from universities to come and speak there and the weekend box office report.

Much to my dismay, *Little Jimmy Gets Big* was number one, with midnight shows selling out across the country. Just reading the title again made my stomach do a somersault. I closed the e-mail in disgust and opened up a blank word document and began typing about the latest addition to Cinematic Masterpieces, *Rear Window*.

I typed straight through until lunch, first about *Rear Window* and then *8 ½,* and finally *Unforgiven*. I had worked up quite an appetite, so I decided to go down to Beekman's Diner and get myself a patty melt. I stopped by Trey's office to check on him, only to find him with his head down on his desk, snoring away, a small puddle of drool accumulating before him. I rolled my eyes and headed to lunch.

Beekman's Diner was about the same as the Starbucks that morning: virtually empty and those few who were there didn't look happy. I sat and ordered a cherry Coke and a patty melt plate. The cherry Coke was okay, so I began to relax and do some mental doodling in my notebook; today's topic was "Greatest Biopics."

My burger arrived and a I took a bite, promptly spitting it out.

"What on Earth?" I pulled back the bread (which wasn't toasted, mind you) and found raw meat.
"Waitress!" I summoned her over.

"Yes?" she asked.

"This burger is *raw!*"

She stared at me, waiting for me to continue.

"It's supposed to be cooked!"

"Oh, you wanted it cooked?" she asked, surprised.

"Well, obviously!"

"I didn't know that. Do you want me to go cook it now?"

"Yes," I handed her the plate. She walked off with it.

I took a big drink to rinse the taste of raw meat out of my mouth. I looked down at my list, trying to remember where I had left off when I heard screaming from the back of the diner. I leapt from my seat and ran to see what was wrong. The cook was standing there, his hand bright red and beginning to blister. My hamburger patty was on the grill and beginning to smoke.

"What happened?"

"I tried to turn the burger over and I burned my hand!" the chef was bawling like a child. He sniffled once and reached out with his other hand for the meat.

"No, wait-!"

He screamed again as he placed his bare hand on the hot grill.

"Use the spatula!" I yelled at him.

He looked at me with confusion. "Which one is that?"

It was my turn to be confused. "What?"

More yelling from the dining room caused me to leave the injured cook. Out front a woman was in near hysterics, yelling at the waitress.

"Now what?" I asked.

The woman looked at me, her eyes wide, tears smearing her make-up. "Maybe you know. I want to get a banana milkshake, but she doesn't know if bananas have gluten in them. Do you know?"

"Of course they don't, it's a banana."

"But how do you know?" she whined like a child.

Before I could explain that gluten came from wheat and that there was not wheat in bananas, there was a terrific crash outside. I ran out the front door, not sure what was happening anymore, thinking that over the course of my long weekend, the entire world had gone crazy.

There was a massive collision in the middle of the intersection, at least ten cars were involved, one of which had hit a power line. Two of the drivers were arguing in the middle of the street.

"Red means stop!"

"No, it doesn't!"

"Yeah, it does!"

"Nuh-uh!"

"Yeah-huh!"

"Nuh-uh!"

"Yeah-huh!"

There was a great cracking noise and the hit power line fell, it's wires dancing like angry snakes on the pavement.

"I'll get 'em!" a fat man cheerfully volunteered.

"NO!" I screamed, but it was too late.

The fat man picked up the power lines and froze and who knows how man volts began coursing through his body, his flesh beginning to blacken and peel, the air filled with the acrid stench of burning flesh.

"Oh my God," I gasped.

The man fell over, dead and the street was silent.

What could have possessed that man to grab live wires? How stupid-

"Dingle-dangle-dongle!" a voice called out.

The entire street burst into raucous laughter.

"No," I whispered, shaking my head and slowly backing away. It was too horrid, too terrible to believe.

That movie.

That movie did this.

I opened the door to the diner. The hysterical banana woman stood between the waitress and the injured cook at the window, watching what was happening outside.

"Dingle-dangle-dongle," I said to them.

They laughed, great belly laughs as if what I had said was the funniest thing ever uttered by human beings.

I ran back to the office, Trey's words echoing in my mind.

The boys wanna see it.

I found Trey sitting at his desk, staring at his computer as if it were a truly difficult puzzle. When he saw me, his face brightened.

"Where's the any key?" he asked.

"What?" I was a little out of breath, having run all the way from Beekman's Diner.

"The any key. It says I'm supposed to push the any key. Which one is that?"

"It's…" I paused, still trying to catch my breath. Finally, I stood and said as clearly as I could, "Dingle-dangle-dongle."

Trey laughed, pounding the desk with his fist and my heart broke for my friend.

I went to my office and began scanning the news sites.

Man Sets Self on Fire

Family Drinks Bleach

Tragic Accident at Theme Park

Woman Bleeds to Death After Using Garbage Disposal to Trim Nails

It was spreading.

I published the bad review, but no one listened.

I wrote about the dangers of the movie on my website, but no one listened.

I went on TV and begged people not to see it, trying to explain that *Little Jimmy Gets Big* was responsible for the mass hysteria and wave of accidental deaths, but no one listened.

Desperate, I tried to physically stop people from going into the theater, and that's when I was caught.

Now, sitting here in my cell, my blue crayon down to a little nub, I am writing this in the hopes that maybe, maybe, someone will read it and be spared. But, everyday, my hope dwindles.

Looking out my tiny window, I can see cars wrecked along the street, abandoned, people stumbling about like toddlers, planes colliding in mid-air and falling to the Earth, taking untold numbers with them, all because of a movie.

I cut myself trying to pry the steel cage off the tiny window, in a futile attempt to escape. With my blood, I wrote on the wall: NO ONE LISTENS TO FILM CRITICS.

My meals are coming with less frequency; I think the staff is forgetting to feed us. They've seen the movie, too.

Little Jimmy Gets Big.

It will be on video soon.

I am laughing.

James H. Lucas

On Twitter @Bcnubooks
Titles:
For Children:
  Tacos From Outer Space
  Billy's Tales of Wonder and Horror
For Adults:
  Vampires in Pimptown
  The Widow Wilkins
  Ramblings and Reveries
  An Undead Wedding

Order through amazon.com, through your local bookstore, or by email at <bcnubooks@yahoo.com>

SHORTS

Blame
By David Griffin

It was so long ago. Four years before the 20th century began. I walked past City Hall all the way to the top of the hill to sell newspapers on the day I watched the Genesee Flats burn to ground. If Da (dah) hadn't dragged me out of my lumpy bed that morning, I can tell you for sure I would not have been out there slogging through the ice and snow, trying to keep the old newspaper in the bottom of my boot from jamming up under my toes. Da complained I didn't bring enough money home, that I could sell more papers the farther I trudged up the hill to Oneida Square and its neighborhood of homes and stores. But my feet almost froze on cold mornings and I was so tired. Just picking up my feet to clomp through a foot of new fallen snow some mornings wore me out.

And I'd be late at getting to school at the Assumption Academy. Jesus … Brother Barnabas would give me a slap on the back of my head that'd sting all morning. He loved to kid around , until you did something wrong. Sometimes we could laugh with him, and at other times he was a holy terror. But we all liked him. He was a strong man who kept his word.

It wasn't my fault Da and I were short on money. After Ma died the old man spent more time up on Court Street in the taverns. I'd wait up for him to get home before I slept. Scared, I went to bed about ten at night, but I wouldn't sleep till I heard him stumble up the steps into the kitchen. In the winter, he loaded the stove up with coal for the night and then staggered to bed. I always got up and made sure the door was locked and checked that he closed the damper down on the stove. A few times he left it wide open. I never forgot the night I fell asleep and didn't hear him come in. I woke up coughing. Da was retching in his bed and the house was filled with smoke. In the kitchen the stove had a cherry red ring around it and a chair he'd left too close was smoking as the varnish melted. After that I couldn't sleep at night until I got up and checked everything after he came home and fell in bed. I had dreams of trying to get out of our burning house. I never escaped, blocked by flames at the front door and the back. The fire came toward me and I couldn't bring myself to run headlong through the flames to where the door would have been.

Maybe that's what happened with the Reilly girl across the street. Her old man forgot to close the damper and burned the house down. She was killed in the fire. We were in the nuns' school together that year and I was about seven years old. I saw her playing with a doll on her front porch the afternoon before the fire. Not many hours later a team of horses came charging down the street. I woke up and looked out the window. Lanterns swung on the side of the steam pumper. Men in another wagon jumped to the ground and ran up to the Reilly house. They never got inside. The flames blasted out the doors and windows on the front wall as though Reilly's home was a huge furnace with he doors left open. By morning the place was leveled.

In class the Reilly girl had sat on the opposite side of the room from me. The next day she just wasn't there anymore, and I wouldn't go near her desk over in front of the radiator. When we made a big circle to pray the Angeles at noon, I wouldn't stand near where she used to sit. When Sister Amolia asked me to fetch the dictionary from the stand next to the radiator, I sat still at my desk with my head down and ignored her. When she stood up and came down the aisle to my desk and tried to pull my chin up to look at her, I ran from the room because my eyes were wet. She sent a note home to Da. He swore and threw it in the stove. He didn't like any of the priests or nuns. I watched the note burn on top of the coals and wondered if a person burned up like that in hell.

If Ma hadn't been at work that afternoon, she would've talked to me and then sent a note back to Sister. Ma was a nice lady and I was always proud of her. People said she kept a fine home and she was a great cook. When Ma was alive we weren't broke all the time. Until she passed away two years before, she worked down at the fish pole factory and tied the little eyelets on the rods that held the fishing line. She'd be proud to know I was turning thirteen in two months. She always called me her little man. I didn't mind helping Da and me pay for our rent and food, but if Ma was alive I wouldn't have had to get up at 4:30 in the morning to sell newspapers on the street. And survive the wrath of Brother Barnabas when I was late.

For all his slapping and hitting I liked Brother Barnabas. He was a brave man. I remember the time he took on a gang of a dozen bullies who came to our school yard one afternoon. He waded into the middle of them punching and kicking and throwing the smaller ones in the air. Twice he flipped boys off his shoulders and fought like a bear as the wolf pack tried to devour him. Finally, a few of us timid classmates joined in his defense and together we beat the thugs off. When it was over, Brother Barnabas lay on the ground bleeding and black and blue. And laughing. "We killed the little bastards," he said. That phrase endeared him to us more than anything else he ever said.

Before school began in the morning I ran down to the Herald

and got a bag of newspapers. I signed a slip that promised to pay the next day and walked the whole shebang up Genesee Street, selling the news to whoever would give me a couple of pennies for the paper. I brought home the coins to Da. He counted them out and handed me the money to put in the old teapot on the window sill, ready to go to the man at the Herald the next day. When I leaned over the radiator to reach up on the sill I always thought of the little Reilly girl.

The Tuesday the Flats burned down, I wasn't thinking about fires as I walked up Genesee Street and wished more folks were out to buy my papers. But the few people I saw were all bundled up against the cold. They were in a hurry to get where they were going and wouldn't stop to fish a couple of coins out of their pockets for the newspaper. I began to think of my bed at home, lumpy as it was. How I wished I had been home in bed and never saw the lady on the balcony. When I thought of her I didn't feel so good.

Half way up the hill at City Hall that day I knew I wouldn't sell all my papers so I decided to keep going. Da wouldn't holler at me about the money if I tried. I walked on up to Oneida Square and the Civil War Monument on the west side of the circle. I was tired and my toes hurt, so I sat on the monument's cold stone bench between one of the soldier statues and a lady with hardly any clothes on. Her face looked like Ma's and I reached up and touched her arm. It was as cold and hard as the arm I touched at Mom's funeral when I reached into the casket before Da grabbed me and spun me away.

I was half asleep most days selling papers, but it was so peaceful in the early morning. Not many people were out and there was a low rumble from the factories that ran all night over on the west side, out Whitesboro Street. In the cold winter air a train whistle screeched from far down the valley and I'd hear the soft swish of tire rims when a weary horse pulled a hack through the snow.

I stood up from the stone bench quickly when I smelled smoke in the air. It was a sharp smell, not at all like wood or coal smoke. A bell clanged about a block away and horses neighed and in another minute all hell broke loose as the team of horses and men from the fire department's Engine Company No.1 pounded through the square. The few people crossing the roadway scattered like pigeons and the rear wheels of the pumper wagon slid sideways when the driver hauled the reins sharply to the left and forced the beasts up Genesee Street. Holy Cripes, they were pulling the huge fire engine pumper, a Cole Brothers Steamer. The firemen's wrenches and hammers and spikes clanged against the copper sides of the big steam dome. It sounded like cannibals banging on a big pot as they waited for their dinner. Every dog in the neighborhood chased the two wagons and the steam pumper. A man ran by and shouted "The Flats is on fire!"

I'd be late for school if I chased after the fire engine, but The Genesee Flats was the new seven story apartment house, the tallest building in Utica. Brother Barnabas was always preaching about us growing to be men and we were to act like it. "Take responsibility and help those in need," he said. I wasn't very big for my age, but I wasn't a weakling kid. To be honest, Reilly's fire and their girl crossed my mind. I wasn't sure I wanted to be at a fire, you know? People lose things at a fire … like their homes and … each other. But I really wanted to see that engine build up a head of steam and watch it pump water from the hydrant through the hoses. I read in the paper it could shoot a stream of water out the nozzle a hundred feet.

Mothers in kerchiefs and kids just pulling on their coats stumbled out of the nearby houses and joined a group of young men running up the street to The Flats. I should have gone back down the hill to school, but I didn't. Instead I threw down the rest of my papers and ran like the dickens to catch up with all of them ... the pumper, the men and women and kids and the dogs.

I came up to the Flats at a run. Fireman pulled their hatchets and pike poles from the wagon and then just stood around waiting for orders. In the lantern lights I could barely see them. Their peaked hats and canvas coats were painted with black stuff to keep from getting soaked. It was too dark to see the building very well, but a few lamps shined out of the windows as shadows moved in front of them inside the apartments. The firemen didn't seem to know what to do. There was a fire right in front of them. A few of the men strolled up to the big fancy front door, as if they were about to politely tell the residents their building was on fire. Maybe they wanted to say please just get dressed and meet across the street for morning tea, while someone searches out the cause of the smoke.

Someone yelled, "It's just a smoker, probably rags in the cellar."

I asked a fireman why the ladder wagon was sent when I couldn't see any flames. There was a hose wagon, too.

"Second alarm," he said. The small sprayer rig had been sent an hour before when the night watchman smelled smoke, but no fire was found

"There's a lot of smoke now," I said.

He didn't answer me.

"Where are all the people from the Flats?" I said, looking around and seeing only the firemen and neighbors on their front porches.

"Inside," he said. "I guess they don't think the fire is serious."

Soon the smoke began to roll out from the The Flats to the road. It seeped around us and under the fire wagons . The horses became jittery and snorted. They didn't like smoke and they may have sensed what was coming. Men began to drag ladders toward the building.

"Out here, Millie," a man's voice shouted from somewhere above me. I heard a scream and then wailing, but no one came out the doorways. Voices in the dark seemed to come from up in the trees, cries and yells for help. I got a little rattled. And then lots of people came out of the doors on the front of The Flats and down into the road. They joined neighbors who now began to crowd around the wagons, but still there were voices up above.

About twenty feet in front of me a loud thud shook the ground as a trunk crashed down and split open. It dropped right out of the sky. Clothing spilled out. From the blackness above more shoes and coats and books rained down. A lady's dress floated toward me. It seemed so strange. They were trying to save their belongings.

The morning sky got lighter and I could finally see the front of The Flats towering seven stories above us. Except for all of the balconies, it looked like a castle built with large red stones. At one end of the building, a man dangled on a rope made of sheets and clothing. I laughed. It was funny and it wasn't. I wanted to shout out, "Go back inside. There aren't any flames." Only a smoker, I wanted to tell him, but the steam pump was starting up and he would not have heard me. I told myself only a couch was burning. The firemen probably would haul it out in the snow in a few minutes and everyone would have a good laugh and go back to bed.

I stayed near the firemen, hoping they would ask me to help out. Brother Barnabas would be proud if I told him I carried a hose or one end of a ladder. I was almost a man, after all. Just a few years away.

The men pulled the hoses toward the building without asking my help. I noticed their stern faces and I didn't ask them if they needed me.

The sun rose and more people on the first and second floors began to crawl down from the balconies like insects. They had waited too long and now the smoke was everywhere inside the Flats. They let themselves down on sheets and blankets to the tops of the ladders. On the higher floors people wailed and shouted for help. Firemen began to tie ladders together to make them longer.

I wondered if anyone was looking at me. Why wasn't I helping? It's not a real bad fire. They'll get out. I probably ought to get to school.

People who made it to the ground tried to find their families. A lady grabbed me and asked if I'd seen her brother. She asked a few times and finally I tried to calm her down instead of ignore her.

"It's not real fire, a bad fire," I said. "I'd go in and help people out, but I shouldn't get in the way."

She looked at me, silent.

"But there's no flames." I said, looking at the ground. "It'll be all right.".

The smoke smelled awful, just like at the Reilly girl's house. And there was crackling and snapping and moaning. The moans seemed to come from the family without shoes standing in the road between the ladder and the hose wagon, but I soon discovered the sound came from the trees. They would bend in toward the fire as the shades on the apartment windows blew in and flapped into the rooms. A wind was sucking through the trees into the building. It made a noise worse than banshees.

The moans began to sound more often and my stomach started to turn. I didn't want to watch the people hanging from the windows and balconies any more. I knew I should go home. I needed to get to school. Somebody might get killed and I didn't want to be there. I was just a kid and I couldn't help. I had to get out of there and go back and get the papers I threw on the ground.

A younger man and a very large lady stood on a fourth floor balcony as smoke billowed out behind them from their apartment. She wore a hat like my mother's before she died, God rest her soul as she walks with all the saints in Paradise. The man was helping the woman climb on to the railing to get on a rope of sheets and blankets he must have tied. He coaxed her up on the railing, but she slid back on the balcony. She was so big. I wondered how he would ever get her down. I turned my eyes away.

Two firemen ran up to me and began yelling about fire engines. I thought they wanted to tell me something, but they only happened to stop in front of me. One man wanted to call for more engines. The other said there was no need. He said all they had to do was find the couch or chair someone had dropped a cigar into and all would be well. He ran off and the other man, a tall fellow who reminded me of my Uncle Jack, asked me if I knew how to use the alarm box up the street on the corner. He wanted more engines.

"I guess you just pull it," I said, and he told me how to break the glass and turn the crank.

I wasn't sure I wanted to and he knew it. I wanted to get out of there. The horses were really getting nervous, snorting and stamping. The men didn't seem to know what they were doing and as we stood there an old fellow jumped from a first floor window and shouted out in pain when he hit the ground with a crack. The sound made my teeth hurt, but it wouldn't be the worst I would hear that day. The fireman said to not be afraid. He put his hand on my shoulder.

"Go crank the alarm," he said. "You'll be saving lives, son."

"But it's only a smoker, isn't it?" I said.

He turned and left.

I sat down on the low pipe fence surrounding the building. Firemen were trying to get as many men as possible to lift the new aerial ladder truck over the fence and up near the building so they could rescue those on the upper floors. People called from the balconies. Some looked like they were still trying to figure it all out. Others were just plain scared and shouted for help. Only a few came down on ropes made from blankets and drapes and even pants.

The old man who had jumped from his window and hit the frozen ground was still yelling for help. Smoke was rolling out the window above him along with red hot embers. I could feel the heat then. I should have gone over to help him away from the building. I wanted to, but it was like I was stuck where I sat on the low fence. I yelled at the old man to crawl away, but I guess he couldn't. Smoke began to push out the windows even faster.

A fireman came up the side of the building. He reached out his hand and the old man stuck out his arm. The fireman grabbed the old fellow by the wrist and dragged him across the snow to me. He said nothing and left. The old man was crying in pain. What could I do? I had no bandages or whiskey.

"You'll be all right," I said. "I'll go get you some help."

I stood and left him. Somebody would come along and tend to him. I was going home. I was just a kid. What could I do?

After a few steps, I knew I shouldn't leave. But the smoke from the building was getting thicker and blacker. I didn't feel so good. I knew I should help. Somehow. I didn't know what to do. I leaned up against the high wheel of the hose wagon and I did what only a Catholic or a Hottentot would do. I said a prayer to my mother.

If I went home and told Da about this, he'd say I should have never followed the fire engine. If I went to school and told Brother Barnabas, I knew what he would say. He'd want to know if I helped out with the injured. I couldn't lie to him. I turned and ran up the street to the alarm box. I was so worked up when I got there I couldn't break the glass with the mitten still on my hand. I found a stone and broke the little window and cut my finger. The tiny crank inside didn't want to move. I banged on it with the heel of my hand and tried it again. It twisted and I heard a clunk inside the box.

I walked back toward the apartment house. The sun was up and shining under a bright blue sky. Smoke billowed out the side windows of the Flats and drifted up the street through the green Hemlocks rooted in the snow covered ground. Icicles glistened in the sun on homes across the wide street from The Flats. A perfect late winter day, except for the smoke and the cries for help.

The firemen were busy getting people down ladders from the lower balconies. Higher up, residents finally used blankets and drapes to work their way down as a few brave souls had tried earlier, tying and re-tying their rope, one floor at a time as they dropped from balcony to balcony. Neighbors had come out on their porches and into the road and some stood at the foot of the building, calling up to those still on the balconies to get a move on. But some of the residents stood as still as death on their balconies, fully dressed in their morning clothes, gripping the railings but doing nothing. One man sucked on a cigar as smoke billowed out from the balcony above him.

Unless they climbed down or found a route through the smoke filled hallways, nothing could be done for all these people who were so close I could have talked to them. It was as if I watched them on a sinking ship from a short distance across the water at sea and they couldn't get off and swim me.

If I lived to be 90 years old I'd never forget what happened next. The young trees near the building suddenly bent way over toward the fire. Louder and louder they moaned as a strong wind sucked through them .... and Wooooosh! One huge sheet of flame shot up from the roof of the building and out every window I could see on the seventh floor. At the same time showers of sparks curled out many of the lower windows scattering in the face of the incoming wind. Window shades ripped themselves into postage stamp pieces. I fell backward and plopped down in the snow on my butt.

Holy Mother Mary, I'd never heard or seen anything like it! All the voices on the balconies and down on the ground hushed for a moment. Then a loud groan went up, a sob from the crowd of neighbors and firemen and victims. Embers and pieces of shade and roofing fluttered to the ground as the blow-up wound down and flames began to lick out the windows and balcony doors behind the victims.

A man on one of the balconies collapsed, sinking to his knees but holding on to the railing with gloved hands. A woman jumped from the second floor screaming. I didn't hear her hit the ground. I heard myself mumbling, "oh, no ... oh, no." I fell all the way back flat on the snow and looked up at the sky. I didn't want to see any more of the burning building and the people. I had to get out of there. In a moment I took a deep breath and sat up, my eyes avoiding the scene. Brother Barnabas would think me a coward. Maybe I was. But this was a huge fire. The biggest building most of us had ever seen was now the biggest fire most of us would ever witness. People were going to die and I didn't want to watch it.

But I could not abide telling Brother Barnabas I didn't try to help. After a few more deep breaths, I got up and walked back toward the Flats. More fire wagons began arriving, but they brought nothing that would help rescue those on the upper floors. On the lower floors fireman came on the balconies and began leading people back inside. They were wrapping their heads in towels and shirts. They must have found routes down the stairs, because I saw other firemen lead people out the first floor doors. Maybe I could help.

The big lady wearing the hat like my mother's was on the string of sheets high over the stone steps in front of the fancy main door. She was coming down real slow, crying all the way. The sheets ended about ten feet above the steps. The younger man in his shirtsleeves at the upper end of the rope shouted down to her. I ran up the steps to a spot below her and yelled up, "Hold on." I held out my arms.

"Just a little farther, old mother!" I shouted. She was a big woman with bare feet and wrapped in a robe. When the wind whipped around her, I saw far up her white heavy legs and I looked away, embarrassed.

She was down to the third floor balcony when the glass on that apartment's door exploded. Smoke and flames shot out toward her. She cried out and began to cough as the smoke danced around her. She held on for dear life. The man who had helped her over the railing disappeared above her in the smoke.

"C'mon! Slide! I'll catch ya!" I shouted. Over my shoulder I began to yell "Help, Help," hoping a fireman would come to our aid. I didn't know what he would have done except try to convince the lady to let go and slide down to us.

A fireman came out on the balcony next door to the woman

and called to her to swing over to him. Maybe he had a plan to get her down the staircase, I don't know. But she'd never have the strength for it.

"C'mon, *c'mon*. I yelled.

All she had to do was slide down to me and she'd be safe. But her hands must have locked on the rope.

She glanced over at the fireman, and then down at me. She looked sick and tired. Her eyes were red and like about to pop out.

"Over here!" the fireman shouted.

"Down here, lady!" I cried

She looked again at the fireman and then down, shouting to me. I couldn't hear her.

"C'mon!" I yelled. "Let go. Let go and slide."

Maybe it was the hat, but I swear I saw my mother's face in hers. She pulled herself up by her arms as if she was going back up. How such a large woman was able to do that I'll never know. She kicked out her feet with probably the only strength she had left. I thought she was trying to shoot herself over to the fireman. I knew she couldn't make it there.

"NO!" I shouted. "Let go. **Let go**."

She kicked again and she completely let go, falling free of the rope. The kick tumbled her over in the air and she came down head first like a battering ram. She came so fast! She hit the stone steps right next to me. On her head.

What an awful sound. I hear it when I wake in the morning and when I doze off at school. I hear it sometimes when I walk by a factory and the machines are banging out whatever they make.

Honest! I tried, I had my hands up. I thought I was right under her. She hit before I could move sideways to catch her. If she hadn't kicked she would not have missed me. I could have caught her.

I looked up and the fireman was gone. A man and a woman ran up the steps while I stood over the big lady. She didn't make a sound. She didn't move.

The man pulled me away and pushed me down the steps.

"That's enough, little man," he said. "You should have let the fireman help her."

"You could have been killed," said his companion, a lady with a pinched face.

She came so *fast*. I couldn't believe I missed her. The next day the Herald said she landed on her shoulder, not her head. Well, I've never before heard either break. But I have to tell you. If you ever hear a head bust open, you'll be sure to know it. It sounds like nothing else in the whole world.

I didn't go to school that day. I took my leftover papers back to the Herald and then I went to sit in Chancellor Park all day. A policeman asked me what school I attended and why I wasn't there. When I told him I was waiting for my father, he left, walking in the direction of the Academy. Late in the afternoon I looked up and saw a figure in black at a distance walking over Bleecker Street. The afternoon sun was quickly dropping and so was the temperature. Brother Barnabas walked briskly along between the old piles of snow with nothing more than a scarf around his neck to augment the cassock he always wore in the classroom.

The burly Irishman sat down on the bench next to me. He shook his head back and forth when I told him my story. I told him everything.

"I should not have gone," I said when I finished.

"Well, you did," he said, "and it's done."

"I can't get that sound out of my head."

"Stop trying," he said. "It'll leave when it wants to."

I wiped my nose with the back of my hand.

"But in fact, you should have come to school instead of going to the fire, Billy," he said.

"I wanted to see the pumper work," I said lamely.

"And then you should have come away and right back down the hill."

"I wanted to help," I said. "I was afraid to … to say I hadn't."

Brother Barnabas looked directly at me and said nothing for a moment.

A cold wind began to blow as the sun dipped below the horizon.

In agony, I finally said, "I should have let the fireman help her."

"But maybe you were right," he said, "she could not have made it over to him."

"But if I'd come back to school …"

"Then it would not have been your fault," he said. "No matter what happened to her, because you would not have been there."

I didn't say anything, just shook my head yes.

"Oh, is that it?" he said. "If you don't show up, it's not your fault. If you never offer to help or take responsibility, then it can never be your fault. How convenient. Is that what you think, Billy?"

"I don't know …"

"OK, Bill, let's get this out. She's dead. You made a stupid mistake and thought you could catch a 300 pound cow dropping down on you from the top of a building. Any idiot would have figured the odds differently and let the lady take her chances with the fireman. But not you. You knew better, right?"

Now I became angry. "I was only trying to help. I did the best I could!"

"You did?" said Brother Barnabas?

"Yes, goddammit," I all but shouted. "I didn't think she'd come so fast. I thought I'd bump her and break her fall when she got to me. I ... I don't know what I thought. But she would have never, never made it up on to the balcony with the fireman."

"Then you see ... you figured the odds, you made a decision and you acted."

"I killed her," I said.

"No, Billy. No, you didn't. The fire killed her."

"I was square below her," I said. "I don't know how I missed her."

"Maybe she missed you," he said.

Three weeks later I dreamed of the lady who fell next to me on the stone steps. We walked together to the firehouse across from St. John's church. She pointed to a side door with a sign over it saying "Firemen Only." I hesitated and then went inside and climbed the stairs to where the firemen slept. At the end of the room the fireman from the balcony sat on a bed. He glanced at me and motioned to the sliding pole. I stepped out over the hole in the floor and got on the pole they used at night to quickly get down to the wagons and horses. I was sliding fast when I looked down to see the little Reilly girl directly below me. I would have slammed into her and hurt her badly, maybe killed her. With a great lunge, I kicked my legs with all my might and threw myself to the side, letting go of the pole. The kick tumbled me over in the air and I came down head first like a battering ram. And missed her. In the dream my head hit the floor and made that awful sound. I haven't heard it since. I didn't save the big lady's life. I still wonder if she saved mine.

David Griffin

Of interest:
The March 3, 1896 tragic fire at the Genesee Flats really happened in Utica, NY. The above story is a fanciful and fictional work based on two historical characters who were not portrayed exactly as they were in life. I don't know William Foley's age and could not verify that Mrs. David B. Hughes, age 70, was a large woman. Three other people succumbed in the fire, a man in the shoe business and a mother and teenage daughter who were related to the Seymours, an old family in Utica. The Genesee flats was almost immediately replaced by the Olbiston Apartments, a building of the same architecture and finish but only 5 stories high in deference to the limits of fire equipment in the saving of lives in that era. The Olbiston was built with the higher safety standards then recommended at the end of the 1890's. It has withstood the test of time and a few fires, however, and remains open to this day providing apartments for rent.

©**copyright 2013, David Griffin**
The Windswept Press
Murrells Inlet, SC www.windsweptrpess.com

Gathering of Warriors
By Bill Hancock

Charlie Canfield, CC to family and friends, has received an induction notice. He will soon report for service, in the Army during the Korean War, in late 1952. Before leaving for service, CC and his parents, Margaret and Robert Canfield, have traveled to Cape Cod. They are there for a family gathering with Robert's brothers Jack, Mike and Cody and his twelve minutes older twin sister Amy and her husband Stanly Bardwell.

A sense of recent history infuses the air, as this family of warriors with a lineage of service back to the Revolution, gather in Amy's living room, to discuss CC's near term future.

Six months after Pearl Harbor, Robert Canfield receives a captain's commission with Army Intelligence. He serves his first year at the War Department in Washington D.C. Then Robert moved to General Eisenhower's staff at SHAFE (Supreme Headquarters; Allied Expeditionary Force) in England. During the Battle of the Bulge he was intelligence liaison on loan to McAuliffe at Bastogne.

[It's 0600 hrs. SHAFE BOQ, the phone rings in Major Robert Canfield's room. "Hello, Canfield here."

"Sir, Sergeant Jabonski at the CIC here, you may want to come down here on the double Sir, there's unusual activity all along our front, from the Losheim Gap and Elsenborn Ridge in the north, all the way down to Echternach in the south with a heavy artillery barrage on going in the Ardennes. "

"OK sergeant, I'm on my way."

Fifteen minutes later, Robert calls his superior Colonel Jerry Goshorn. "Sir Canfield here, it looks like Hitler is giving us a look at what, 'Watch on the Rhine' really means, there is heavy heat across a greater than 100 mile front."

"Are there any Panzers Robert?"

"No Panzers reported so far Sir, only infantry and artillery."

"Robert, do you think we are looking at a major offensive?"

"The weather is lousy, so our air cover cannot provide support. The present forecast is heavy snow storms and generally bad weather for at least a week. So if the Germans can overcome the weather and breakout, then they could make a run on Brussels and Antwerp. As a result, we'll have one hell of a mess to deal with.

Just a second Sir, something is coming in from 2nd Infantry. Sir, the 2nd reports Panzers on its front at Elsenborn Ridge."

"OK, Robert put a briefing together on the double. I'll call Tex Lee (Major Ernest R 'Tex' Lee, General Eisenhower's aide throughout World War II) and see if he can get Ike and Bedell (General Walter Bedell Smith, SHAFE Chief of Staff) into a conference room within the hour.

"Yes Sir."

Later in the day, after the briefing, Robert meets with Colonel Goshorn in his office. Robert asks as he walks in, "You wanted to see Jerry?"

"Yes Robert, take a seat. Ike agreed with your assessment and after a long debate and a surprise very ambitious commitment from George Patton, he has ordered a mass movement of troops into the battle. The Red Ball Express has stopped delivering supplies for the present and is only moving reinforcements to the front. The 82nd and 101st Airborne Divisions are moving into the line and Patton is turning the entire 3rd Army 90 degrees to the north to hit the breakout's southern flank."

"Thanks for the input Sir. I'm sure that Ike is doing the right thing. Everything should workout especially with the move that Patton is making. It's just the sort of thing he's great at."

"Well that's not all of it."

"Oh."

"Bedell wants you to detach and go up and join McAuliffe at Bastogne. Ike would like you in the middle of this thing as his intelligence liaison."

"If that's what the boss wants I'll do it. One thing though, I would like to take Sergeant Jabonski with me."

"OK, take him."

"When do we leave?"

"Leave as soon as you're both ready."

"OK, see you when we get back Sir."

"Right on, and good luck Robert."]

Jack Canfield joined the army six months after Robert. Following basic training he went to Officers Candidate School (OCS). After graduating he served as a tank commander under General Patton in Sicily, then as a tank company commander with Patton's Third Army elements that broke through to relieve the siege at Bastogne, an event, he occasionally, likes to remind his brother Robert about.

[Captain Jack Canfield sits in the open turret hatch of his M4 Sherman tank peering into a heavy snow shower, the snow is falling at such a rate that the sky and earth seem to come together in a blinding white haze. His tanks are in the leading battalions' second grouping as a part of Patton's 3rd Army forced march to relieve Bastogne.

Snow has been falling all day accompanied by a strong swirling wind whipping in from the north; it's miserably cold. Jack has empathy for the infantrymen clinging to the slippery cold steel tops of his and other tanks, while many other men, even less fortunate, plod stoically along both sides of the road. He passes some hot coffee, brewed by the gun crew using engine heat, to the infantrymen riding on his tank.

Suddenly, a stationary, dangerously close, tank appears, directly ahead, through the almost blinding snow shower. A soldier stands off to the side of the stopped tank, he's signaling for Jack's tank to stop. Jack immediately gives the stop order and signals for the tanks that are following close behind, to do the same.

Jack's driver applies heavy pressure to the track brakes but momentum and the slippery ground surface combine to extend the tank's slide forward at speed. The tanks momentum reduces slowly until finally the steel behemoth jerks to a stop inches from the stationary tank blocking the road.

Jack recognizes that the hulking soldier off to the side is Skeeter Rodwell, the tank battalion's first sergeant. He call down, "What's up first sergeant?"

With his usual southern drawl Skeeter replies, Sir, there's a Tiger at the curve bout half mile up. It took out two of our leading tanks. It's holding this here column at bay. Our infantry has not been able to get close with rocket launchers cause the Kraut infantry is protecting the Tigers exposed flank. That Tiger is in an almost perfect location, it's sitting next to a steep slope that goes up over 50-feet, right where the road curves. We've tried to hit it by moving in and out of cover to shoot but everything we fire from long range either bounces off or misses the small exposed portion of the Tigers front end. As you know the front end is not really the place to kill a Tiger.

"Yeah, so what can we do?"

"There's a path 100-yards up on the right that leads to a pass. The pass exits on a road behind the Tiger. Only problem, there's Kraut infantry guarding the pass on this side. So plain and simple, battalion CO wants you to take a detail of tanks with infantry, bust through the pass to the road and shoot that Tiger in the arse."

"OK, I don't know how plain and simple it's going to be, are you going to show us the way in sergeant?"

"Yes Sir, I'd relish having a chance to take a shot at that Tiger, he killed some good men and friends of mine."

Four tanks deploy in single file with some infantry riding, while other spread out to protect the flanks. The column moves slowly through the deep fresh snow. As the column approaches the pass an anti-tank rocket strikes Sergeant Rodwell's led tank. Immediately after the hit, two of the infantry soldiers on the back of the tank are able to slide off and the sergeant, with his uniform on fire, jumps out of the hatch. Just as Rodwell reaches the ground and rolls over the tank explodes with a roar and blinding flash. Sergeant Rodwell and the two infantrymen are not seen again, the tank is a shattered flaming hulk.

Jack orders his tank around the inferno. He fires the turret machine gun at the attackers, while the other two tanks and the infantry spread out and engage the enemy. After a brief bitter firefight the pass defenders are suppressed; those still alive surrender and are detailed to some of the infantry for return to the main column. Jack's three remaining tanks go through the pass and gain the road, once there they turn toward the Tiger's position.

German infantry guarding the Tiger's flank spot Jack's tanks as they trace forward, they warn the Tiger's commander that enemy tanks are moving in from the rear. Immediately responding to the threat he tries to swing the turret around to train the Tiger's lethal 88-mm canon on his attackers. Unfortunately the Tiger is positioned to close to the almost perpendicular slope. As the turret starts to swing its backend slams hard into the natural rock wall, thus it is prevented from rotating into firing position.

The jolt from hitting solid rock bounces the Tiger commander's helmeted head into the hatch opening stunning him for a few moments before he realizes the turrets rotation is stymied. Regaining his cognition he orders an engine start in order to back away from the slope and gain enough room to swing the Tigers formidable gun fully around too meet the oncoming threat.

Jack's tanks are racing up the road and the flat field beside it, side-by-side, toward their target. The three tanks get within firing range just as the Tiger starts moving away from the slope. Jack gives his gun crew the order to start firing their 75mm weapon as quickly as they can load and aim. His tank fires first, quickly followed by shots from the other two tanks. Seconds later, three direct hits slam into the Tigers backend quickly followed two additional hits. In seconds the dark green behemoth is enveloped in fire and billowing black smoke, no one escapes that inferno.

Through clenched teeth Jack growls, "That's for Sergeant Rodwell and his friends."]

Mike Canfield joined the Marines and served with the 1st Marine Division during the first two month of action at Guadalcanal, where he was wounded, after which he went for recoup oration in Australia. From there he went on to New Guinea, where he was field commissioned. After New Guinea he went to Peleliu as a company commander, then on to Okinawa. After the war ended he served with the division on occupation duty in North China for six months before returning home.

[Lance corporal Mike Canfield pays no attention to the mosquitoes that are swarming about his head. After almost a month-and-a-half of sporadic savage fighting, daily noontime air raids, followed by nightly 'Tokyo Express' shelling from the sea and the constant oppressive jungle heat, the mosquitoes are a mere nuisance.

He and other members of the 1st Marine Raider Battalion, on this dark moonless night, move, as quietly as possible, through waste deep putrid smelling swamp water toward an attack position at the far end of a suspected Japanese occupied village, that's just ahead. As the Marines close in on the village a guard spots them and fires at the raiders. Bullets buzz through the air as Mike struggles forward to get out of the water. When on the beach he drops down behind a sand pile and returns fire.

After the first shots are fired other Japanese join the firefight, *they fire at the Marines that are moving in from two sides. The Japanese must be greatly surprised by the attack or very bad shots because none of the attacking Marines are hit during this action. After a brief show of defiance the village defenders hastily withdraw and disappear into the jungle.*

The Marines carefully work their way through the village, searching each hut as they go. Mike discovers some maps and other papers in one of the huts, which he gives to Gunnery Sergeant Terry Whitaker. He, in turn, passes the documents up the chain of command to the battalion commander Lieutenant Colonel Edison. Who because of his flaming red hair has earned the nickname 'Red Mike'; the documents and maps indicate that the enemy troops just encountered are the rear guard for a much larger force that is now on its way to attack Henderson Field.

Returning from delivering the documents Gunny Whitaker calls over to Mike, "Hay Canfield, the CO says thanks. Now, go over to that last hut on the right; it's a supply hut. Pick-up as many cans, as you can carry, of the crabmeat and beef our Japanese friends were nice enough to leave for us. And do it on the double because we're about to leave this here garden spot."

Right, gunny will do."

Three days later, Mike and the other Raiders start digging positions along the top and on the face of the grassy knoll that protects Henderson Field's south end. While they are working several different types of naval aircraft fly over and land on the field. Mike looks up as Gunny Whitaker passes and asks, "What's that all about gunny?"

"Word is those planes are from the 'Wasp'. She got hit real bad by torpedoes and is expected to sink."

"Oh."

Evening of the Raider battalions second day working on the knoll, Japan naval guns bombard the knoll positions. Immediately following the bombardment, Japanese ground troops attack the knoll. Marine artillery hammers the attacking troops, but they keep on coming. Mike fires his rifle at anything made visible by the constant 105mm Howitzer round flashes and overhead flares that provide some light through the smoke, shadows and darkness around him. He fires so quickly, at times, that he can feel rifle barrel heat on his cheek.

During daylight on base Marine P39's, P38's and various other land based and sea launched naval aircraft, virtually anything that will fly, strafe the Japanese position, but for two nights they came out of hiding to keep up the pressure. Finally on the third night they force the Marines to abandon their lower knoll positions and move back up to the crest.

During the move to the crest Mike sustains a wound on his left hip. After reaching the crest with much difficulty, he uses items from his personal first-aid-kit to pack and tape the wound, after which he returns to the fight.

Now with the Marines on top of the knoll the Japanese are forced to climb up the slope to get at them. The Marines pour everything they have into the attackers, finally turning them back. During this fight Mike is wounded again in the upper right arm. Now he can't hold his rifle or throw a grenade. Gunnery Sergeant Whitaker sees him lying bloody on the ground, he walks over and comments as he hands Mike a 45 automatic pistol, "What do'ya want to do, live forever?"

Mike fires the automatic with his left hand, when its empty he waits for someone to reload it for him, after that he empties it again...

Next morning, greatly weakened from loss of blood, Mike is carried off 'Bloody Ridge' on a stretcher that is loaded on a jeep for transfer down to the beach. From the beach he, along with other severely wounded Marines, rides out on an LST to a waiting Destroyer that transports them to Australia.

Cody Canfield, the youngest brother, receives a field commission while serving with the 9th Infantry Division. He is a private first class (PFC) upon landing with the divisions 47th Combat Team at Safi, French Morocco, by the time the division has fought its way into southern Tunisia he has been promoted to master sergeant and is a company first sergeant.

After Africa the division lands near Palermo in Sicily, Cody receives a field commission during the fighting there. After Sicily the division goes to Winchester, England for rest, reinforcement and training. The 9th Division lands on Normandy beach on D-day plus-4 and fights in the French hedgerows where Cody is wounded. After breaking out of the hedgerows the division fights across France. Cody is wounded a second time during fighting at the Rhine River beachhead across the Ludendorff Bridge near Remagen, Germany.

[Lieutenant Cody Canfield peers through his field glasses at the next hedgerow, a little over two hundred yards in front of the one he's lying on. Sergeant Ulbrich next to him whispers, "Did you see that flash of light? That must be the forward observer (FO) for the 88mm that's been pounding us."

"Yeah, I saw it. How far back do you think that field gun or tank is Tony?"

"Based on the short time between the sound that it makes when fired and when the incoming round hits I'd guess about a thousand yards.

"Yeah, that's about what I'd say too. OK, I'm going back to talk with the tanker and setup an attack. You stay here and see if you can spot their machine guns positions and anti-tank weapons. I'll also put some people on your flanks, so we can cover the whole field. And be careful to stay under cover, there must be snipers out there somewhere."

"Yes Sir."

Cody slides three feet down the hedgerows backside through tangled undergrowth and roots. Then, crouching low he walks back a hundred yards to the lead tank, of the four that are supporting his platoon.

Tank Platoon leader, Lieutenant Joe Wicker, a lanky Texan, wearing a battered white cowboy hat, Tempe style black boots and a red bandana as part of his uniform, is standing next to the tank smoking a cigarette and blowing smoke rings. As Cody gets closer Joe calls out, "What'd y'all see out front Cody ol-boy?"

Cody grins and replies, "It looks like the Krauts have setup a FO in the next hedgerow, he's controlling the 88mm firing in this area. I don't think he can see your tanks, because if he could we would have known about it by now."

"Do you want to go after that hedgerow?"

"Yes, but first I want to be sure that our flanks are secure. Don't want to get too far out in front of everyone else and then get cut off or attacked from the rear."

"No problem, both flanks are covered, While you were up on the hedgerow, I got radio messages from the tank platoons on our flanks, saying that they have secured the hedgerow positions next to us."

"OK, good, then let's get some engineers over here to blow a hole in the hedgerow big enough for two of your tanks to pass through at the same time."

"Why don't we get a bulldozer tank and plow a hole through?"

"That hole will only allow one tank through at a time and the FO will see the bulldozer coming through. That will give time for that 88mmto zero in on the opening. Then they will beat the hell out of us as we pass through. Plus the bull dozer tends to leave enough of a ridge to force a tanks nose up as it passes over, that exposes the underside and you know how weak the M4's bottom is."

"Yeah, I know. OK, how do you want to stage the attack?"

"We'll have the engineers blow a hole for your tanks to pass through at one end of the hedgerow. That should surprise the FO *long enough for your people to be on top of the next hedgerow before the 88mm can be effective; now they are probably zeroed in near the center expecting a breach at or near there. It will also allow my infantry to quickly hit and clear the near side hedgerow all the way up to the target line."*

"Are you going to put some infantry on my tanks?"

"Yes, five guys per tank with one of them carrying a BAR and you should bring up operators up for your 50-caliber machine guns.

"I'm running low on 50-caliber ammo, we haven't been re-supplied since last week."

"I'll have Sergeant Scarpelli get some for you."

"How can he get it when I can't?"

"Don't ask. I don't"

"OH, OK!"

Two hours later the attack starts when three engineers blow a very large opening at one end of the hedgerow. Wicker's tanks pass through the opening two abreast and then spread out to make a common front of four as they advance toward the next hedgerow.

Cody leads the infantry attack on foot across an open area along the nearside hedgerow arm leading to the target. As he moves forward he sees a German soldier with a rocket launcher. Cody raises his M1 and fires two shots, the soldier is knocked down before he can fire his weapon. Immediately after firing his M1 Cody is struck in his upper right thigh by a machinegun bullet, he falls to the ground.

The attack continues and the forward hedgerow is captured very quickly. Several defenders are captured and the 88mm never fires a shot.]

Stanley Bardwell served with the 1175th Military Police Company guarding an airfield in England prior to D-day. After D-day the MP Company detaches into small groups to perform special investigations and cleanup activities under intelligence direction in France and Belgium as the war progresses toward

Germany; Stanley is chased back in Belgium, narrowly escaping capture or worse during the Battle of the Bulge.

[Sergeant Stanley Bardwell rides his olive drab Government Issue Indian motorcycle under the aqueduct in Neufchateau, Belgium approximately twenty miles southeast of Bastogne. He is there to check on three men from his MP Company who were sent in to check out this seemingly quite little town. Riding along the dirt road leading into the town's center, he can see a Romanesque Gothic style church, with a very high steeple at the far end of the town.

Moving slowly and carefully forward, Stanley spots Paul Costanzo crouched behind a wall, Paul is waving frantically at him and pointing for him to turn left. Stanley realizes what Costanzo wants, he immediately turns sharply and pulls off the road into an ally between two wood frame buildings; then stopping abruptly a short distance inside the opening.

Just as Stanley started the turn into the alley a bullet wised past his ear and ricocheted off the road creating a spray of dirt behind the motorcycle. Now in the safety of the alley he switches off the engine, lowers the kickstand and dismounts. Then he pulls a 45-caliber Thompson submachine gun out of its leather holster mounted on the bike's front wheel yoke. Staying close to the front buildings side wall Stanley moves back toward the alleys entrance and calls to Costanzo across the road, "What's going on here Paul and where are Hawley and Moncrief?"

Costanzo moves low along the wall that is providing him protection and reaching its end replies, "They're in the building behind me. Hawley got shot by a guy he thought was another MP but that guy turned out to be a Nazi dressed in an American uniform. Moncrief and I heard the shots and arrived just as the sniper up in the church tower hit Hawley again, that's the same guy that just took a shot at you. I gave Moncrieff covering fire while he ran out and dragged Hawley into the alley behind me, then he took him into the building."

How is Hawley doing?"

"Not too well, he lost a lot of blood before Moncrief could get him into the alley and stop the bleeding. We wanted to take him back to an aid station but the sniper kept us pinned down while some of his buddies stole our jeep. I heard the jeep's engine start and saw it leave with two guys dressed in G.I. uniforms in it: they must have been buddies of the guy that Hawley killed and that dam sniper."

"OK, let's take care of that sniper, after that we'll rig up something to get Hawley back to an aid station. Call Moncrief out here to give us covering fire to keep that sniper distracted. Meanwhile, you work your way down behind the buildings on your side to that end building near the church. When you get there go inside and up to the second floor. When I'm in position opposite you on this side, I'll signal for you to take a few shots at the sniper. Then while you're drawing his attention I'll feed him some 45-slugs from Mr. Thompson's special."

"OK."

Both men work their way into position and five minutes later Costanzo starts firing sporadically at the tower while taking care not to expose his self for too long a period. The sniper does not return fire immediately; first he checks to be sure there is no danger in exposing himself to take the shot at Costanzo, who he can see but cannot fire at and hit from the position he's in.

Not seeing any apparent danger the sniper moves into position to dispose of this minor annoyance. Leaning slightly out of the steeple he is able to get the crosshairs of his scope sighted upon Costanzo's helmet. Just as he is about to fire Stanley moves out from under cover and fires his Thompson submachine gun.

The 45-caliber bullets work their way up the steeple wall spraying stone and mortar fragments along the path toward the ultimate target. The sniper exclaims, "WOZU IZ DIS!" just before three of the heavy caliber bullets strike and kill him while others fly by and ricochet off the bell making a strange melodic sound as they *strike and spin harmlessly away.]*

CC is very much aware of his family members exploits, he is deeply concerned about his own ability to live up to their high standards should the need be. The process and adventures he experiences reaching that goal play out in the *'M1 Brothers'* the first book of the *'M-1 Brothers Trilogy'*.

Two other main characters are introduced that play major roles in the trilogy. One is Brian Roberts a young black CIA agent with an innate ability to quickly learn and use languages he is exposed to. The third main character is a North Korean master spy with the mission of overthrowing the South Korean Government.

After the tousle experienced by the three main characters in the first book of the trilogy they are back twenty years later in *'Unfinished Business'.*

CC owns a business that has been contracted to work on a major government contract. He is unknowingly very close to the danger that stalks those who are known as the M1 Brothers.

Brian Roberts has taken on the role of a CIA first responder during crises that occur worldwide. He is supported by a Hmong guerrilla team he recruited in Laos during the Viet Nam War. The team and many others call Brian 'Heise De Lang' (Black Wolf) because of his skill as a hunter. Over the last twenty years Brian has had a burning desire to get Bek Man Sue because of what he did in South Korea. So he divides his time between crises response and pursuit of the evil mastermind.

Bek Man Sue goes to great extent to change his identity. Then he enters the United States with two purposes. The first is to hunt down and lay siege on those known as the M1 Brothers, whom he fought on a hill behind the DMZ in South Korea twenty years earlier. His second and primary goal is to carry out a long planned strike at the heartland of the United States.

The third book of the trilogy *'End Game'* begins its story line minutes before the end of the second book.

Bek Man Sue takes on another identity that allows him to travel worldwide for the purpose of organizing and implementing a scheme that will fund terrorism.

During a close encounter with Bek Man Sue, CC is subjected to severe treatment that threatens his ability to live and perform a normal life.

Brian Roberts discovers that a close associate has been a mole. He continues the same missions as before and manages two critical rescue missions.

The books **'M1 Brothers'** and **'Unfinished Business'** by Bill Hancock are available from Amazon. They can also be purchased from me by email at: billh609@sccoast.net
The third book **'End Game'** will be available late 2015 through the above.

SHORTS

KANGAROO MAN

By Gary F. Lucas

"I didn't do it, man, I didn't do it I tell ya!"

I stared down at him and smiled. "If I had a dime bag for every time I've heard that, I could retire pushin' blow."

"It's true. I don't know how else to tell ya." He looked suddenly depressed, resigned.

"Mr. Magoo, you're a loser. You know you're a loser. The small world you exist in, barely, is made up of the likes of you. You enjoy each other's company since you speak the same 'I'm innocent' line. You begin to believe each other. But one slob starts braggin' about their exploits, then another does, then it's old classless reunion time. "

I pushed him foot-to-kneecap. He feigned needing to catch his balance then chirped like a little girl in a playground. "Hey! Leave me alone! Take me in if you want to…I don't really care." A smirk was next, just enough to show a gold crown, that he likely stole off a dead body, along with ragged teeth the combined color of rotting squash and limp spinach. Then he added, "Been there, done that. Then I'm back in the streets."

This time I slapped him. "You have a rap sheet that goes back to pre-juvie. You got away with your little games and moved up to juvie detention. From the beginning you knew how to dress from Goodwill, nod at the judge's punishing words, accept responsibility while lying through your rotting teeth and over and over again walk away with a slap on the wrist. Not this time Maggie Mayhem."

I picked up my sunglasses, through on my tattered sport coat to conceal the concealed and permitted Glock.

"See ya later."

Before the door slammed, he yelled, "I'll be gone before you get back, a-hole. You'll nev—"

Velta was at the keyboard typing something to somebody. I can't type. I am computer-stupid. I have an un-smart phone. I drive a pre-computer chip gas guzzling Lincoln, the size of a respectable boat moored on the inlet.

She saw me stop.

"What?"

"I can't remember giving you something that needed typing up, like an invoice maybe."

"All my work is done, Mikey-Mike. I'm writing to Jim."

Jim was a brother that she obsesses over. He is now deployed on his second tour somewhere in crazy blowing sand country. I'd be the same way, I guess, if my younger brother, protecting and serving in a good-sized city west of here, hadn't been ambushed and killed by meth-heads on a mission. "Just for fun," they told the judge.

"I'm going to have a chat with Sheriff Joe." I pointed a thumb over my shoulder. "If he acts up you know what to do."

She smiled that gleaming Swede smile that reduced all men to very small and unimportant stature. Those who didn't shrivel and decided to take a test-run testosterone crack at her found themselves quickly subdued, slobbering, mumbling incoherently and cold-sweat shivering from her amazing take down skills. The blonde is crazy-like merciless.

Sheriff Joe is the elected head cop in the small town of Aynor, next to the comparatively super-sized town of Conway, an on-the-way to Myrtle Beach, all part of the reasonably sized state of South

Carolina. There are cities like Greenville that for some reason is called the Upstate and for better reason here at the coast, we are called the Low Country. Atlantic ocean low.

Why was I on my way to Aynor? It was here that the last reported small change theft had occurred. And it had been a long while since I'd last seen one of the finest young men in law enforcement I'd had the pleasure to meet at an off-season conference in Murrells Inlet, where I happen to live.

Joe welcomed me with a smile. "You old dog, what you been up to?"

"This and that. You know, just trying to keep the doors open and my one and only employee employed."

"How's Velta? Still as…"

"Yeah, I know. Hard to hang words around all of that. When I can afford it, I take her to Dead Dog Saloon for lunch. The men peel their fingers instead of their shrimp, and the women they're with just tell them where they'll be sleeping that night."

He sat. I sat. Then he said, "I know you well enough to know this isn't a social call. What's up?"

"I've got Kangaroo Man."

He chewed on that for some time, something that if you are from the south knows better than to interrupt. Then he said, probably just thinking out loud, "I guess I'm the last jurisdiction. He's hit Georgetown, Horry and a few other counties since he got out the last time. If you add up the pages and pages of paperwork and stints in prison and appointed defense team salaries and appointed legals to prosecute, plus all the Badges' time…."

"Yeah, there should be a law written that says 'Your sentence this time is for all the crimes past and present.' That would put guys like him away for life, even though, as far as we know, he hasn't raped or killed anyone."

"As far as we know."

I knew without really hearing it that we both were thinking that we wished someone would plant a gun or put him at a homicide scene or pay someone off to witness against his butt.

The sheriff sighed, coming back from his thoughts. "You say you got him. Are you asking if you should bring him here?"

"Eventually."

Joe smiled. "I've heard of your hidey hole. Not a nice place, I'm thinking, unlike those honey holes you've got staked out in the marsh for redfish, trout and flounder."

"That was a good day wasn't it."?

"Good-Good eatin'. Judy's always tellin' me to call you and beg for another trip."

Judy, his wife, always reminds me of my Deb, the love of my life for all those years until breast cancer took her. I shook off the memory.

"Yeah, I...uhh, was thinking of having him as a house guest for awhile, maybe get him to see the errors of his ways, once and for all. Remember McBride?" I asked. "Worked for him. He actually writes letters to me. Thanking me. Maybe it's not the same. He was younger and responded to the 'Come to Jesus' whippin' up he got."

"You'll never let on where your guests reside on your dime, will ya?"

"Not a chance. Matter of fact, just you and Sheriff Michaels knows some of my unorthodox ways. And he's tried to find my hostel-for-hard-timers. He gave up a year or so ago. He puts up with me."

"Well the official line is, 'We have to.'"

I got up to leave. Sometimes you just get the feeling it's time. "Joe, can I call on you when it's time?"

He grinned, knowing the meaning of the question. "You do that, Mikey."

• • • •

I grabbed a bite at a fish camp I remembered on 701. It was well past lunch, but I had a bad habit of not eating on any schedule. Or drinking. The beer washed down most of the flounder and all of the fries. The belch said, "I'm good to go."

Back at the office, Velta was doing some kind of stretching with one leg over her head and the other one out the door and down the hall. She smiled up at me, her head an inch from the floor. There were cracking sounds, moans, but not the good kind, breathless, but not from pleasure. I shook my head. I pointed to the wall that was not a door but was, and she somehow nodded that he was still where I'd left him.

His first words were, "I need to take a leak."

"Hey, thanks for reminding me. I do to." I turned and went back out, past my contortionist, out the door and down the hall to the men's room. I did my thing, washed up, walked the hall, went to a window and watched the tidewater meander through the marsh on its way out the inlet. I snapped my finger and cursed myself for leaving that last piece of my late lunch fish in the car. I went down the stairs to get it, thinking it could be dinner. With a couple more beers of course.

Velta was wrapped in a tight ball in the far corner of the room. I called her name. She didn't respond or move a muscle. I threw the Styrofoam box to my left, cursing again that the extra time to get it and bring it up was a stupid move. I jumped her overturned chair to get to her. I thought she was dead. I was ready to kill myself. I called 911 on my flip phone; Midway Fire & Rescue was dispatched. I thought better at trying to turn her. I was afraid to look at her once gorgeous face, wondering if it still was. There was a pulse, thank God. And there was still the feeling that I let her down, let this happen.

I followed the obligatory and wrongly named meat wagon to Waccamaw Hospital. The head ER nurse knew us both, from my past needs for a ride and for taking a few stitches.

"She's going in for an MRI. Somebody really laid in to her Mikey. Surprised someone got that close."

"So am I." That's all I could think to say. "So am I."

Her eyes were near shut from the swelling. Black and blue, no purple bruises, laced her right arm in particular. What I could see of her neck, shoulder and chest was reddened from her struggles with the attacker. She tried to talk. I noticed the first sign of any blood come from her nose and corner of her mouth. I hoped that she hadn't lost any of those pearly whites. I used simple one finger tick-tocking to mean NO, don't talk! And then the same finger sign that says QUIET when pressed to lips. She dozed off, thankfully. She would hurt, but she would live.

I went to the nearest saloon, this time the Beaver Bar, for something stronger than beer. Leslye Beaver, the proprietress was there.

"Scotch? What's wrong, Mikey?"

"Velta." I surprised myself with the catch in my throat. Leslye wrapped a bear paw around my forearm.

"Oh, God."

I shook her words off, for the moment. "She'll...live. Pretty beat up. Someone...hell, I don't know, got in and got to her."

"Well that just makes no—"

"I know!" I said too loudly.

"Hey, Mikey, just go catch the b-tard, will ya? That's your job now. Have another and get to work. Times-a-wastin'."

It was just like her to cut to the chase. During Bike Week, she never hesitated to brawl with a Harley drunk or smash a bottle over their bride's nasty noggin. And everyone respected her for it.

Getting back to work was more of an immediate task then trying to put the perp away for a long time. Velta was heavy on my mind. Sheriff Michaels, who I hadn't had a chance to visit, was on my mind. Sheriff Joe, well, I felt embarrassed. Disappointed him for sure. He might not even believe me that Kangaroo Man got away. Maybe thinks I offed him to the satisfaction of all involved. Quick justice. Save the system in what, three counties that I know of?

Okay, I was feeling like a bottle of booze would do the trick verses "Have another and get to work" as was suggested. But, I knew if a loser wants to be more of a loser then that's the way to go. And I didn't want to go there.

Go where? That came to mind. Where would he go? Do we even know his hangouts? If we did, would he be stupid enough to visit them?

I huffed while the Lincoln puffed to get me back to the office. Safe haven. Hide your embarrassment for being a lousy P.I. Find a dark corner, listen to the deafening silence of Velta tapping away on the keyboard. Humming that song…I don't even know which. I think I'm supposed to be in-tune with all the sounds and movements and little gestures that lead me to do what the cops don't have time to do. Go figger.

• • • •

Hours passed, morning came, and my cell phone woke me from a bad dream that was too close to the reality of the last 24 hours.

"Mikey Hemmer here," I barely said, having to clear my head and throat and eyes and ears to sound coherent.

"Mikey, They want to keep me here a couple of days."

"Uh..."

"You Okay? You're in the office aren't you? Sleep in your chair?"

"Yeah. Swivel seemed more like I feel, more than toss and turn."

"Okay. Is it all right if I do as they say? More tests upstairs?"

"Of course. Of course. Do what the doctors say."

"Listen," Velta was turning on the mothering voice. I could hear it in just one word. "Suzie-Q isn't doing anything. She's coming in to answer phones and do whatever until I can come back. That okay?"

Suzie-Q—and no, I do not know what her name is—it could very well be Susanne Quacko for all I knew. She was Velta's Goth younger sister. Black fingernails, black eye shadow and brows, black hair, black lipstick, black bracelets (with silver studs), black everything, I think. I didn't let my mind go there.

"Hey, I'm okay. No need to go there."

"Too late. She's on her way."

(Not nice word here)

"She has a key? I may not—"

"She has mine. She stopped here first. Be nice to her."

Okay mother. "Okay, I will."

Velta barked out a list she insisted I write down, including a reminder about a letter to a county commish that needed to go out, an email to a supplier about a vest I had ordered, and three phone calls that Suzie-Q already knew about, having received orders from mother to nag me to return ASAP.

After disconnecting I walked back to my holding cell-of-sorts and looked for clues as to how he had gotten free from what I had been confident were secure restraints. Guess what? Ankle and arm bracelets were neatly coiled on the metal-framed chair I had bolted to the floor. There was also a note. It read, *I told you I didn't do it. But, you know the truth don't you PY (sic) man? You won't catch me again, I garante (sic) it. Know why? I will kill you. I've got a gun and now I will carry it at all times, thanks to you. Why? Because the way you did me, man. Now I'm really ticked at only 1 person. Show up. Let me see you around. Try to catch me. I dare ya. I WILL shoot first.*

As a final insult, it was written on my stationery. He got loose, did a number on Velta, calmly wrote the note, and placed it where he knew I'd see it.

I looked around, held up my restraints looking for clues, kicked the chair and yelped, forgetting that it wasn't going to move, then just left, slamming the door behind me. Why look? Why try to find some kind of lock kit he must have used? In a shoe? Underwear? No, instead, look inside, man, you're the one who didn't look close enough to begin with. And Velta is paying for it.

Suzie-Q, dressed inappropriately for the job accompanied by matching sullen eyes and inappropriate downturned black-painted lips, didn't look surprised to see me as I stormed out of the back room. She just picked up the pink message slips and without looking up, said, "You need to call them."

Before I would, I needed to check in with Sheriff Joe. After pleasantries, I told him about K-man getting loose—at Velta's expense, He, the gentleman that he is, didn't razz me about it. He knew the self-administered kind was doing just fine. Next I called Sheriff Michaels. I used his last name out of some kind of added respect I felt I was required. I didn't want to spend much time on the phone with him, and his short harrumphs and uh-huhs said he didn't relish the idea either.

"So you're-a goin' to keep after him? I don't have man-time to dog ya, so I'm hopin' that's not why you're fillin' me in."

I assured him it was just a courtesy call to say, Had him, lost him but after him again.

Two five minute conversations later with pink sheet people led to one possible job for me and one cop who wanted to get out of the boys-in-blue world and wanted a job. The last call back was to a breathy gal who finally got around to telling me why she had called, which was to solicit donations to one of the hundreds of Support Your Local orgs. Velta, I knew, thought the latter was from one of whom she calls, "My bimbos." No such luck. And I don't hang with bimbos.

Kangaroo Man left a trail of havoc as though he knew the end was near. He was facing ten plus for sure, if battery and assault weren't added to the charges. And, of course, murder.

The latest was a Stop-&-Go in North Myrtle Beach. That was after a quickie heist in Georgetown. Somewhere in the next few days I had to stop him, or possibly one of the blue-bubble-tops would get lucky and come up on him, maybe even during a lousy traffic stop. The BOLO for his silver-something aged Pontiac—I think Sunbird—was plastered around the Strand like the old days on telephone poles and in store windows, like we were hunting a lost dog. If I didn't catch him soon, he'd become a cult figure with a million hits on Twitter. I could just picture his scrawny butt whooping it up as he drove through certain neighborhoods. They would never squeal on him and he knew it.

The break did come when he made a near fatal mistake. Michael's gave the okay for me to interview the girl from Tennessee in the area for a wedding bash.

"He looked like he hadn't eaten in a year. Or shaved. Or even taken a bath."

Yeah, that sounds like him. "Car?"

She pointed to where a parked car sat, askew to the gas pumps, now getting ready to be towed.

"That thing. He bumped me as I was getting gas, then got out and apologized and all. I thought, okay, no big whoop, hardly a scratch on my Puris. As messy as he was, he seemed harmless. He offered to pay for the gas I was putting in and all. Then he...."

"Took off. In your car. Full of gas."

"Yes." The tears started again. She was a cutie, in the sense that if I had a daughter, I wished I had been there to bash the guy's head in. Still had that feeling, but for my own reasons. "And my purse, phone, clothes, you know."

"Drugs?"

"Why does everybody ask that!"

Palms up. "Whoa. I just want to know if he'll be extra hopped up is all."

"Just some weed. In a baggie in my purse. My purse!"

He'll be smokin' and laughing it up soon, if not already. I went through the Which way did he go, anyone with him, and the dozen other questions that seldom lead to anything useful.

"You refused to go to Grand Strand?"

"I don't even know what that is. But yeah, I guess so. They were nice…the guys in the, you know, ambulance. They said I was lucky."

"I'd say so. About a foot difference between running over the heal of your running shoe and a vital body part that could have been—"

Girl squeals, party pals, and two big sized guys wanting to slay the bad guy and be awarded a night with the bride's best. Oh, to be young again.

She was off, certainly well taken care of even without the long gone weed. I turned to take one last look at the dirty Sunbird. One thing he had an MO for doing was picking off all the Tastykake honey buns he could carry. Wrappers were everywhere. He had used coffee cups from an oft-seen fast food joint to relieve himself in. The odor was evidence enough. But what was crumpled up and hidden under the seat could be my first real break.

I slept for a couple of hours, showered and dressed for the long summer day. I had dreamed of the young girl with the crumpled sneaker in less than an honorable way. Enough said and yes, I scolded myself and swore to not walk around with a Cheshire Cat grin all day.

Suzie-Q was chewing gum—I think—and filing down one of her claws. "No messages."

"Good morning!" I said it loud on purpose.

She shrugged. "Whatever."

"Sleep well?"

"Why are you talking like—"

"Don't you know? Velta said I could pay you by the word."

I sat in my squeaky chair behind by old worn desk and sipped Joe from a cup that read in part, "PRECACION, ESTE CALIENTE!"

I had a client who had paid me to stop this guy, now walking around with a smirk and enjoying his moniker, "Kangaroo Man". I shook my head. I don't fail often, but this was a zinger. No, blooper, wreck, hang up your ego and ID and off-the-rack badge and get a job at Wal-Mart.

I thought about the love letter he wrote to me before he took off. Then what I found under the seat of his car. Something didn't fit. There was something incongruent yet similar.

I laid the two pieces of paper next to each other and read left, than right, than left again to compare.

Dear God. Velta.

I rushed to the hospital only to find her in a wheelchair with a bag of her belongings in her lap.

"Going home," she murmured, almost sad to say it.

"Great!" I gave her a peck on the cheek." All good? Feeling okay to head out?"

She shrugged, in the slightest of ways. "I guess."

I asked the volunteer standing behind Velta to give us a couple of minutes. "Velta, you know something and now I now I know something." I waited.

"I'm kind of tired, Mikey-Mike. I'd like to just go home and rest." She smiled, barely. "They keep you up all night! Blood, samples of this and that, questions, pills, checking my brain waves or whatever. I just want to sleep…."

"Okay. But you can't go home."

"What?"

"You know, Velta."

I called my Georgetown Sheriff's connection, a guy that wears a lot of hats unofficially and doesn't even want me to say his name, even when greeting him on a call like I made. Next, with Velta snug in the deep well-worn leather of my old Lincoln, we pulled up to the Safe House that was, fortunately, unoccupied at the moment. Velta was weak for the first time ever, in my mind. Maybe she just was tired. Or maybe, the damage to her noggin was more serious that I thought.

"Why Mikey-Mike. I don't get the sudden danger."

"Quit playing dumb. You stay here, sleep, watch the tube, sleep some more. No cell, no internet, absolutely do not go wandering around. I will be here later and bring more stuff. Tell me the girl things you need."

She did, and with one more finger pointed warnings she nodded, reclined and was snoring in three minutes. I locked up, took the key and headed back to the office. My little room of horrors needed more inspection. Something I should have done from the start.

I found little clues that supported what I was now sure of. To give myself some credit, I had not been looking for what was now apparent.

Kangaroo Man had an accomplice.

• • • •

The best evidence is never laid out in front of you to just photograph, bag and go. It comes from being curious, suspicious, and doggedly following a trail that may have no end but your instincts say this is what to follow. And only this.

So, two simple pieces of paper with notes about what to do about me, and what to do long term to get away with it all. And two people wrote them.

The one working with K-Man was someone I knew, or thought I knew. She had once been arrested, by me. She looked and talked pretty to her appointed legal-lite lady just out of law school, and between the two of them, one smiling broadly in a short skirt and one bowing her head in apparent shame, the latter got off with 90 days suspended and the threat that next time the book would be thrown at her, and the former got hired by a big law joint because of her legs. So now she had a grudge. And I was more than tired of playing nice-nice and a little more than just surprised at what was planned for me. Why not just mess with me? Have me beat up or something. Kill me? But why?

I knew I'd be pulling a 36 to 48 hour run, starting now. I told Susie-Q to lock up and wait for my call about coming in again. Forget the phone and forget your black nail polish. How Velta and she were related I couldn't figure. That was the least of my "couldn't figure" mind-racings.

I loaded bags of this and that, which Velta asked me to get along with snacks and fruits and other eats she said she'd like to have. She was groggy but seemed to have more color in her cheeks. She said a weak goodbye when I left and made a limp wave sign. I had to trust her to stay put. I was beginning to think she finally understood that she might be in a jam...sorta like me.

It was on my fifth stake out that Kangaroo Man struck. The little Pruis had a few knocks and dings, but it was definitely the one he lifted. With an understated man-in-the-street stroll toward the store he entered and began his walk around.

I saw the gun. Different from the scenes you see on TV, clerks are more than happy to hand over cash and live another day. This one was that easy. Without even looking around, he exited in a slow stride and got in the car sitting where no one would be suspicious, right at the pumps.

My steamroller glided easily to his side of the car and pinned him in without even a crunching sound. It was just enough to see him rock inside and realize he had nowhere to go. The clerk came out with a cell phone in hand.

"Don't call anyone yet." He looked surprised. "I got him, you'll get your money back."

"But—"

"Just call after I leave and say a guy ran off and left his car. Tell them maybe it was stolen. Have them come with a tow, okay?"

After a few move exchanges, with me not giving up more info than I needed to, I loaded K-Man into my car, safely bound and tied to the doorframe.

He looked resigned. And I understood why.

"You're going to serve time now, and a lot of it."

"I know."

"Where's...the gun?"

He looked sideways, out the passenger side window. "I never had one. You know that."

"She has the gun?"

"I guess."

I swatted him. "Tell me more."

"Hey!"

"Hey, hell. I've got the note from under your driver's side seat. Here's your chance for some redemption. Tell me where she is."

He thought he had. He was wrong. And I was more than sad.

• • • •

A day was all it took to do the explaining I had to do before an arrest was made. Kangaroo Man, along with surveillance tapes and eye witnesses knew this was it and gave up without much resistance, except for the usual, 'I didn't do it' but with less bravado.

I got some leeway to finish the whole ordeal before I called for a lockup car. It's good to have friends who trust you.

Susie Q rode along. We were both quiet this time. No shrugs and one-word answers. No questions. As my client from the beginning, she was as sad as I. She wanted to be wrong. Now came the hard part.

We arrived and walked into the house unannounced. Suzie-Q hugged her sister. I sat on a corner of a couch in the small living room and watched it, and the murmuring and wiping away of tears.

When it was over, I asked, "Velta, why?"

"Because I came to hate you Mikey-Mike." She turned to her

sister. "And I hate you now too. You knew all along didn't you?"

"Sorry V. I couldn't let you do this. I saw it in your eyes. You meant to go back to your old ways and do something even worse."

Wow, I'd forgotten that she could speak fluently.

"He beat on our brother!" Velta was on her feet, ready for battle.

Palms up, I countered. "You know how it works, Velta. I never hurt anyone. Just sounded like it maybe."

"But that hole in the ground. The old sewer line. That's just cruel."

"Velta, did you ever see it? No. You know why? It doesn't exist. My threats were enough, sometimes. Not quite enough, others. I've never squeezed anyone down an old sewer pipe. Period. What I told you and others was just to play it up. I thought you knew that."

She gave up on me and turned back to her sister. "You knew how to hurt me just enough, didn't you? But I never saw you come up behind me. I let our brother out and was going to lock up and just leave. You came out of nowhere. You hide behind your Goth get up and hate-the-world attitude and never let on about the training we both received from our father."

"What?" Now I was confused.

Suzie-Q sighed and tried to explain. "We were raised to defend ourselves because our mother had been attacked. Dad insisted that it would never let it happen to us. V took her abilities one way. She was not going down the right road, as dad would often tell her. She didn't care. Before you hired her away every little scheme of hers was worse than the one before. She and the bad seed, our stupid brother with no character like Jim has, were always up to something. People got hurt. I knew about it, most of the time. At least I think I did. I called you because things seemed to be ratcheting up. She was not the person you thought she was.

245

Guns and threats and all were just a little too much. She had to be stopped. They both did. I love her. I even love my low life brother as much as I do Jim. "

Velta wanted to know from me, "When she hired you, didn't you know who you were dealing with?"

"Yeah, your sister. Someone who knew what you had in mind for my sorry a—"

"She's number two in the world!" Velta shook her head and smirked, disgusted with me. "Everybody she fights in the octagon goes home in a daze. She's the top female UFC contender in the world."

No crap, I thought.

Velta turned to her sister. "Q, just stand up for me." She pointed at me. "He has nothing except circumstantial evidence."

"More than that, Velta. I have the gun. K-Man told me where to find it. I have what I thought was your brother's threat to me, but it's in your handwriting on a sheet of my stationery, written to look like his penmanship with the poor spelling and all. You were okay with him being sent up and believed you'd never be caught, even after finding a way to off me. I have the confession from your brother and another note I found with his real handwriting. His 'Notes to self' implicates you clearly. It's all wrapped up and ready for the State's attorney. Attempted murder. Say goodbye, Velta."

• • • •

Two weeks later as I'm about to lock up and head to The Beaver Bar for beer and wings a blonde walks in the door. No, this isn't the start of a dumb blonde joke. Just the opposite in fact.

"Hey, Mikey-Mike. "

The voice was eerily familiar.

"Hey. Help ya?"

She sat in Velta's old chair. Like she knew the place.

"I hear you have a job opening."

I blinked. Twice. "Suzie-Q?"

She waved the question off. "That was my 'In the ring' moniker. Suzanne please."

"And the Goth get up?"

"All part of the act. I stayed in it for longer than I wanted to, but between publicity stuff and weigh-ins and fights, I got to where I liked all the attention."

"Okay. And now?"

"I retired. Don't have to worry about money anymore. And don't have to worry about the wayward siblings." She stared through my wide eyes. "Don't look so shocked. I am V's sister you know."

I exhaled a lot of exclamation and question marks. With a fresh intake of air I asked, "And you came here for a job you don't need?"

She smiled. "A girl's gotta stay busy ya know."

The End

This was written in a not-very-similar way (but the attempt was made) our very own Murrells Inlet resident, the late Mickey Spillane, wrote his great stories. I hope you enjoyed it and that it encourages you in some small way to read for the first time, or read again, his well-crafted stories.

Visit lucastories.com to:
Read about and order autographed novels:
The Appleachians
The Abracadaver
Mayhem & Main
Temp Like Me
And soon to be published, *Preying Hands*

Also find a book of short stories, poetry and musings, titled *EzzzReads*.

For visitors' pleasure, the site also has many short stories to download.

Email: lucastories7@gmail.com
Facebook: Gary F. Lucas

We hope you enjoyed this book. Look for a new edition to come with even more great reading.
You are encouraged to follow us (and "Like" us) on Facebook. Meet the authors, view our book signing and meeting plans, and join us if you'd like to come to a meeting to share your works!

Facebook: Beach Author Network
Our website is always being updated:
www.beachauthornetwork.com
Email us at beachauthors@gmail.com

Made in the USA
Charleston, SC
16 June 2015